Hewes Gordon

Lovers and Thinkers

A Novel

Hewes Gordon

Lovers and Thinkers
A Novel

ISBN/EAN: 9783337001995

Printed in Europe, USA, Canada, Australia, Japan

Cover: Foto ©Andreas Hilbeck / pixelio.de

More available books at **www.hansebooks.com**

LOVERS AND THINKERS.

A Novel.

BY

HEWES GORDON.

"And hail once more to the banner of battle unrolled!
Though many a light shall darken, and many shall weep
For those that are crushed in the clash of jarring claims,
Yet God's just wrath shall be wreaked on a giant liar;
And many a darkness into the light shall leap,
And shine on the sudden making of splendid names,
And noble thought be freer under the sun,
And the heart of a people beat with one desire."

TENNYSON'S MAUD.

NEW YORK:

CARLETON, PUBLISHER, 413 *BROADWAY.*

MDCCCLXV.

R. CRAIGHEAD, PRINTER,

Caxton Building 83 *Centre street.*

LOVERS AND THINKERS.

CHAPTER I.

NEW YORK, our Commercial Metropolis. That is, the centre of activity, wealth, amusement, — of sloth, indigence, misery, — the great symbol of the country's daily life. Boston may be its Athens, the seat of intelligence and culture; this is its Rome, the vast arena of concentrated effort and practical skill. The aim of the average American, but especially of the New-Yorker, is riches, material success. Pick out any one, of a morning, from its thousands rushing down town, and ask him why he thus tears along; his answer, if he shall stop long enough to give it faithfully, will be, " Money, money: what do we live for ?"

Stella Maign was a child of this city, though not of its spirit and circumstances. Her father was, perhaps, one of its " representative men." He was a merchant, doing an extensive and prosperous business, when she, his only daughter, was born. He was a man of the

1 *　　　　　　　　　　　　　　(5)

world, — still more, a man of New York. He was active and enterprising, and believed in precisely the qualities which he himself possessed. All others he undervalued. He had accumulated considerable property, and was called rich. Respecting and applauding business qualifications, these, combined with wealth, made, in his eyes, a man of men, — one to be sought and honored. Thinkers, scholars, men of ideas, held but a corner of his esteem. They were well enough, he thought ; they contributed aliment to the leisure of the rich ; they afforded him amusement : but they were always poor fellows, of little account in the world. Here we have his estimate of the world : he meant Wall street, Broadway, and the fine houses up town, of which his own was one of the best, and in the midst of the best.

Mrs. Maign, his wife, had been, when young, a somewhat aspiring and superior maiden ; but, without decided force of character, she had settled down, soon after her marriage, quite to the level of the circle around her. Now she presided over her husband's mansion as he thought a woman of means and fashion should do. Costly pictures were hung on its walls ; statues dignified the appropriate niches. The parties given in it were among the gayest of the season. And outside, was the lady's carriage, with driver and footman in waiting, whenever she desired to take the air. Mr. and Mrs. Maign scanned their establishment with proud satisfaction. "I have come to think with you, Mr. M.," she said, "that it would be quite impossible for one who really *is anybody*, to do without the like."

This mutual thought very naturally entered into their

plan of education for their daughter, and into their determination regarding her future career. At fourteen years of age, after fitting studies near home, she was sent away to be placed in the well-known seminary of Madam de Villier, at Ironton. Here it was supposed she could receive as thorough and accomplished an education as any young lady of wealth and superior prospects would require. Graduated from such an institution, her father deemed she would be fitted to adorn any man's drawing-room as well as the good Mrs. Maign had herself done, and in exactly the same way.

Stella's conduct, during the three years she was in charge of Madam de Villier, was satisfactory to parents and teachers. She was a keen, appreciative scholar, a healthful, cheerful, dignified person, with whom but little fault of any kind was found. Though spirited, and occasionally wilful if opposed when she regarded herself in the right, she seldom broke over, or evaded, the prescribed limits of restraint, which, at a school like Madame de Villier's, were necessarily rather strict. She was allowed to leave the seminary only once a week, to visit some friend known to her parents, or for shopping, unless, indeed, when in company with forty or fifty others, she took a morning or evening walk for exercise. The latter practice she did not at first wholly enjoy. It seemed very strange scarcely ever to appear in the street except as one of a long double file of young ladies — maiden soldiers of culture.

And the line was not always viewed by spectators as martial and imposing. Now and then an imaginative urchin was evidently reminded by it of a flock of sheep, and would apostrophize it with the bleating cry by which those innocent and pretty creatures seem wont to express their ordinary emotions.

On one occasion, largely in sport, though with much pretended vexation, Stella caught hold of a child who was thus shouting near her, and shook him completely beyond any further display of his wit or wits, — a feat which was a palpable breach of decorum, but which caused much merriment in the street. She looked up and saw the eyes of a handsome, stately youth fixed upon hers, and fairly dancing with mirth. She broke into a ringing laugh, blushed to her temples, and hastened back to her place in the ranks, without looking back. The stripling regarded her admiringly for a moment, and murmuring, " What a dear Amazon to be sure," he too passed on.

The incident was simple enough to have been unremembered and unrecorded. But it appears they were to meet again, and to one of them it was to be rather singularly recalled.

Stella's education was, at the end of the appointed time, called finished. She left Madame de Villier's seminary, one of the most accomplished of its scholars, as well as one of the fairest and most attractive. She had been placed there to study ; and though extraordinary application was not the most prominent of her good qualities, she had attended faithfully to all her allotted tasks.

She had, at this period, a passion for the beautiful, which distinguished her in all matters of taste, and was remarked by every one about her. But it penetrated deeper than their glances, unconsciously, even to herself, underlying her success in particular studies. She did not know, for instance, why she learned French without effort — almost intuitively. It was much more difficult to many of her classmates, who in other branches were her equals. It was the same with music, in which she at last excelled both scholars and teachers. But French is the high-bred language of courtly elegance. In it, if one cannot cry, it is said: "*il n'étoit plus le maître de verser des larmes.*"* It is the mother tongue of formal taste, as Italian is that of harmonious witchery. Music again, as far as it goes — and that certainly is far — is the most beautiful of all vehicles of expression. Roses and the choicest flowers, may in their way and sphere compare with it. What else can?

When Stella returned home to New York, it was — to be married. Yes, that was the goal of her youthful destiny, as her father had settled it. She must be married and located. It must be well done too. This he had figured. It was a most important business transaction, in which he must not fail to do himself credit.

Did he not love his only daughter? Certainly he did. He would have affirmed it as strenuously as any man. Only he supposed that he knew her best interests a great deal better than she did. He did not believe in "overmuch sentiment;" in any "undue weight of love." Taste should have its proper influence, to be sure. But affection had never taken an all-engrossing hold upon him: why should other people go crazy about it?

---

* Madame de Staël's dubious hero "Oswald" (in "Corinne") will be remembered as "no longer the master of shedding tears."

" Happiness, my dear sir," he was accustomed to say, — " that consists of a proper establishment, and easy, agreeable surroundings. There is nothing in the world like position and plenty. These, I believe, sir, are available when kisses and notions have melted away."

So he reasoned, after the manner of heavy Saxons.

Stella had dreamed of love, — of some one unspeakably dear to her, to whom she could be as dear. What maiden has not? But she had found no one who realized her vision. She had of course seen those whom she preferred to others, — those whom she fancied for the time that she could love, — whom perhaps she fancied that she did love. But they had all quickly waned in brightness, and disappeared from her heart, without leaving any deep traces of their fulness or decline. She began to feel that perhaps she should never meet a man who could call forth such vivid emotions as she had imagined; to whom she could devote her whole nature; on whom she could lavish her whole existence, content with being received and being loved.

Her father, however, had seen one to whom he was quite content that she should be given in marriage, — a Boston gentleman of wealth, station, and forty-five years. During the year previous to her last at Madame de Villier's, she had met him at a fashionable summer resort, where she had gone with her mother and a friend, to spend a portion of her usual vacation.

He was much pleased, from the first, with her appearance, and as he was a friend of her father's, and she had met him a few times at her own home, she did not hesitate to receive such customary attentions as he chose to offer. Neither did she decline to make herself

agreeable to him by any of the accomplishments in her
possession. He liked music, he said ; and she played
for him. At the piano she was conscious of excellence,
though she never displayed her power with the least os-
tentation.

Of all self-love, that which is gratified by gratifying
others, is certainly the most delicate, and the least liable to detection. It can scarcely be unlovely or wrong
in the practice, only in the motive. Perhaps a tinge
of vanity, possibly the slightest touch of coquetry,
mingled, unsuspected by herself, with Stella's endeavors. For say what we will, the desire to please even
those we care little for, is everywhere a temptation to
the amiable.

But the idea of loving Mr. Torson never entered her
mind. She accepted his offerings of French books and
of flowers, very much in the spirit in which he said they
were tendered, — " as partial payments for the pleasure
she gave him by her playing."

But he cared less for the music than he asserted.
He gave her the books and the flowers, because he was
aware that she was fond of them, and because it was
no trouble to him ; just as he would have caressed any
pet that he had begun to desire should follow him. He
had grown attached to Stella, as far as he was capable
of attachment, and had determined to ask her hand of
Mr. Maign. He had been a bachelor up to this time,
but now there was no need of it. He had made money
— enough money — and could have everything it could
buy. What more could any young woman want ?
He, too, reasoned very much like Stella's father, and
supposed himself quite good enough for Stella herself.

But he had the subtilty and tact not to exhibit all he felt. He accepted the assertion, that language is to "conceal thought," as well as to express it. He admired Stella, and wanted her as a finish to his leisure, his house, and equipage. He sometimes felt there was something about her that he could not completely understand. But what of that? He had no misgiving about his being able to conceive and appreciate all that was worth the while.

He knew that she was to remain with Madame de Villier one more year, and that her parents would then be quite willing she should marry, provided the marriage were one of wealth and the proper social position. He thought that his friend, his old business acquaintance, Mr. Maign, would not object to a still nearer intimacy. So, fully assured that he would encounter no opposition from him, he broached the subject, a month or two afterward, in a plain, unhesitating, commercial way, saying that, with his friend's consent, he should like to pay his addresses to Stella, and subsequently, with the consent of the young lady, he should like to marry her. He added that he had a couple of hundred thousand dollars, could take good care of a wife, and that he thought Stella excellently well fitted to take charge of his mansion on B—— street, which he had no doubt she would consider one of the best.

This conversation, this manner, was precisely after Mr. Maign's own heart. Nothing could have suited him better. He scratched his head, pulled the ends of his side-whiskers, and said:

"Ah, yes, certainly, my boy; I see no objection; I think we may call it as good as settled. Stella would be very silly to hesitate, very unreasonable to refuse you; and it seems to me, she is a pretty sensible girl. My old friend too! No, she can't be so foolish as to deny us: we could never allow it; could we? It would put my mind quite at ease to see her well established, and with you. Besides, girls sometimes get strange freaks into their heads; it is best to put them on the right track early. If permitted to go any way, she might fancy some poor devil who could do nothing but paint a picture or write a song. That would bring me to the grave-digger at once. I will speak to Stella, myself; and you may rest perfectly content. And come to our house as often as your time warrants. Make it your home. You and I understand each other perfectly. Mrs. Maign will be glad to know you better."

Mr. Jabed Z. Torson had reason to be satisfied with this conversation. His friend's reply was about as he had expected. It was, if anything, more flattering and unreserved. He felt certain of possessing Stella Maign without half trying. He saw that her own father would be an energetic suitor in his behalf, and would end by dropping her into his arms. This was all the better. It would save a long, perhaps a difficult wooing, which might be romantic and engaging to some, but was without charm for him. The end to be attained was herself; the easiest and speediest way to it, he regarded as the most desirable.

When the winter holidays came, Stella went home for a week, and her father spoke to her, as he had said he should do, in reference to Mr. Torson.

"Stella," he began, "Mr. Torson, whom you met

2

at Saratoga last summer, has long been a friend of mine; he wishes to become my son; in short, he wants you for his wife. Treat him well; you will like him. He is one of the smartest fellows in Boston. He is a solid. He is worth a quarter of a million, and has made it himself. He is a self-made man. In ten years he will double his fortune. He can take the very best care of you, and place you in a circle you are fitted for. Stella, it is a good thing. You have always placed some confidence in my judgment. Don't belie yourself now; don't stand in your own light, in this most important instance. I told him you were a sensible girl, who knew a man from a humming-bird. I am sure you will prove that I was right."

Stella was somewhat surprised at her father's directness, and his disposal, as it could not but seem, of her person and affections. She saw at once that he was determined upon the match; that with him it was already a decree. But she was not wholly unprepared for the information he gave her. Hints in her mother's letters had signified that Mr. Torson had been " very much taken " with her, and would probably find occasion to visit New York and her father's house, oftener than he had previously done. But she did not love him: how could she, why should she love him? She had regarded him as a substantial, complaisant gentleman, silver-gray, rather high-fed, quite as strict in manners as in morals, of sound business qualifications, and a handsome fortune. She had seen him occasionally, since she could first distinguish one person from another. For the past three years he had been abroad much of the time, regulating and closing up some commercial transactions in England and France. Meanwhile she had sprung up from girlhood to womanhood; and now it was plain that he desired to add her to his list of valuables.

"But, father," she said, "it would appear very strange for me to marry him. It appears very strange that he wants me. Pardon me, but if I had been accustomed to respect him a little more, I should think of him as an uncle, — your brother, and scarcely a younger one. I have often heard you speak of his ability and industry. I ought, certainly, to respect his good qualities. But have I not heard even you touch depreciatingly upon some of his frailties? Have I not, for example, heard you speak of him, with a slight shrug of the shoulders, as 'a little wild,' in his younger days? It is unnecessary to hide from you that others have alluded to him in the same manner. He has been courteous and respectful to me; I have found no fault with his deportment. But, my dear father, now that I know his intentions, I can't help a slight shrinking from him."

"Well, well, Stella," responded Mr. Maign, "that will do. 'Frailties!' — 'a little wild,' indeed! One would think you were a Beecher, and had gone to preaching infidelity over in Brooklyn. What do you suppose you know about the world as it is? ✦ Have you learned from a few books, and two or three languages, that men are mixed of sanctity, sprinkled with cologne, and set on their feet so as never to slip and get the least soiled? Do you imagine, child, that I have lived over fifty years without knowing a thing or two? Is there anybody that can have your interest nearer at heart than I? Can anybody manage it better? I have considered all your objections. Torson isn't Saint John, nor Adam before the fall; but he is a sensible, sober man, who has attended to his affairs and got rich. Any spirited woman in the country would be glad to catch him. He moves in the most respectable society, and nobody but a British peer could carry you higher. He hasn't done anything so very bad, either. Old men shrug their shoulders over young ones, and, at fifty, over themselves at twenty-five. Torson had a few wild oats to sow. Now they are all disposed of, and done with. He is established and sure, — much more so than any youngster I could trust you to. If he had been married, twenty years ago, perhaps you would have heard no pretty stories about him. As it is, all the stories are old ones, and, like the scars of an old soldier, they have brought experience with them. He will treat you better than any boy, believe me. Ask your mother if I'm not right."

"I know already," replied Stella, "from what she has hinted and looked, what she will say. I do not mean to be capricious or undutiful. Certainly I have no want of confidence in my parents. I will try to look upon Mr. Torson as you do. Perhaps by the time my term at school is finished, I can view him more favorably. I am to be there six months yet; then I will try to do as you think best."

Stella shut herself up in her room, and wept. The reality, then, had come. She must try to love Mr. Torson. Or could she marry him without loving him? — without at least respecting him? She felt as though she would throw herself on his pride and generosity,

and flatly beg him not to persist in his suit. But no.
He wanted her. He was cool, unenthusiastic, and not
used to being thwarted. He would think her disinclination for him a mere freak, which he could easily
overcome. Her father, too, would so declare it. And
might it not be so? she asked herself. He had endeavored to please her. He would probably be kind to
her; and, at any rate, all the pleasures to be procured
by affluence and society would be at her command.
He had travelled, and in particulars and details, could
make himself interesting. He would soon go to Europe again, her father had told her, and she should go
with him, — thus fulfilling a dream of her youth which
had so often transported her to the scenes of the old
world. Love? — well, would she ever really love any
one as she had fancied? Would she ever see any one to
love thus? She could only answer that her ideal had
not appeared. But if he should appear, what then?
God alone could tell. It seemed to her that her father
did not appreciate her nature, — that he could not understand the depths of her feeling; but only judged of
her as of others about her, whom she felt to be more
selfish and frivolous. But had he not experienced all
that had agitated her? Perhaps so, and that all had
passed away as her illusions would vanish. Oh, yes!
he must know best. Yet she trembled, as though fate
itself thrilled her with a denial of the thought. There
was a clogging, painful sensation in her chest, as if an
opinion, gross and monstrous, had become a material
substance, and lodged there.

She went to the window, and threw back the cur-

2*

tains. The day had been murky and dismal. But as
she stood there, a flood of sunshine poured out of the
heavens, and filled the horizon. It lasted but a moment; then all was again gray and sombre.

Stella had scarcely a tinge of superstition in her
mind. But her eye was quick to note all phases of
nature that appeared applicable to persons and condi-
tions of feeling. She paid no attention to them as
signs or warnings ; but they intensified her emotions.

" Foolish child that I am ! " she exclaimed, " yet
what if I should sometime stand for an instant in the
sunlight of an absorbing fondness, then be thrust back
again into the remorseless, abiding gloom ! "

When New-year's had passed, Stella returned to
school. She was more sad and thoughtful than formerly, but confided her feelings to no one, and uttered
no complaints. She had grown dreamy, and seemed
constantly debating within herself, some question that
she could not decide. Still, her conduct was not such
as to cause remark. Her recitations were as promptly
and faithfully rendered as ever. Only when she sat at
the piano, and there threw out her soul in strains which
seemed to sob, and beg, and bewail ; to rave, to pray,
to doubt and tremble, — only then was it plain to those
to whom music was a living tongue, that there was a
weight upon her soul, a terror within her heart.

As the term drew to a close, she prepared to leave
the school, and proceed home to fulfil her father's
behest. Her heart had succumbed to his will.

" Yes," she said, " I must do as Fate and he together demand."

Sad and tearful, but loaded with compliments and prizes, Stella bade adieu to Madame de Villier, and in a few hours was once again in her father's mansion. Two months from that day she was married, and became Mrs. J. Z. Torson. Forgive her: she was not yet eighteen.

CHAPTER II.

MR. AND MRS. TORSON, after making an American tour of about a month's duration, during which they visited some of the most notable places in the country, repaired to their residence in Boston, where they remained a few days, and then sailed for England.

Stella had not loved her husband when he was her lover, nor had she since learned to love him more. But she had determined to be a reasonable and faithful wife. This was all he could ask, she thought; for he had known her feelings when he took her.

She had anticipated much pleasure from her visit to the old world. To look upon the parent countries of her own fair land, had been, as we have seen, one of the constant longings of her youth. But she connected their distinguished places, their time-worn edifices, their charming natural scenes, with momentous epochs full of aspiration and endeavor, and with majestic men or noble women who had made them hallowed. Apart from these, palaces, parks, or ruined piles of granite, had no more interest for her than other grand or beautiful objects, which she could see without the fatigue and exposure of travel. They were pleasant enough,

(20)

even to the eye alone; but she demanded that, in
viewing them, the eye should reflect upon the soul, en-
lightment and elevation.

Her husband was wholly different. He could give
her the square feet of St. Paul's, and catalogue its dec-
orations; he could point out the statues and relics of
kings, or queens, or lords, and gaze on them with
reverence, whether the dead had, when living, done
aught but eat, drink, and misgovern, or whether their
presence and action had been a lever and a blessing to
the race. He could designate castles, altars, monu-
ments, telling when they were built, their height, and
bulk, and material. Then he supposed he had told all
that was to be said. He delighted in meeting and
associating with the nobility, and could remember the
day or hour when he conversed with Lord Bigburgh,
or was at the palace of the Earl of Sundryland. For
the sake of their society, he would cater to their tastes,
their desires or excesses. To him, they were the distinguished men of the realm.

But Stella cared nothing for them, or for their society
and attentions. A few of their number she would have
delighted to honor for their large public capacity and
worth, which she had read of, and well understood.
But she felt that she would not consume the time of
these great and busy men, even if the opportunity were
offered her. She venerated real power and nobleness
so highly, that the famed possessors of these qualities
were like distant and almost sacred beings to her. But
titled mediocrity, still more, titled vulgarity, however
lofty they appeared to others, she looked upon partly
with indifference, partly with pity.

She could not, at this time, fully understand her own nature — why she lived in the world, or what she most desired in it. She was, however, a persistent, though unconscious realist, searching below customs and conventionalities, for their meaning and essence, and through the multiplied ambitions, endeavors, and performances of men, to the underlying spirit and end.

Her husband's mind dwelt wholly amid surfaces — the commonplace affairs and spectacles of the world — and could no more comprehend hers, than Bonaparte, with all his boasted knowledge of ordinary persons — Frenchmen and others — could comprehend a patriot or saint. Mr. Jabed Torson thought, too, that all which he could not appreciate in his young wife, was sentimental and girlish ; — that her enthusiasms were weaknesses with which no man like him should be soft enough to sympathize.

She plainly read this opinion in his words and actions, and felt, for her part, that, like most others, he was merely one side of a man : — that his mind was stationary and executive, without the perception of enlargement and progression ; that he had practical talent, but no spiritual insight. To him, she was " an idealist," — a word which he used without knowing its meaning, except that it signified something for which his own nature had no correlative, and consequently something which must be dreamy, exaggerative, and futile. But to her, *he* was no mystery. She could define and classify him, placing him where he belonged ; because she possessed the properties of his nature — the practical, the definite — and with them also, even at this time, the perception of higher properties by which those were included.

But he was her husband; and she must love, honor, and obey him, as she had promised to do by becoming his bride. Indeed, she had no inclination to disregard the obligations of a faithful wife; though at times, when enraptured by some mighty work of nature or of art, she longed, with a full heart, for a companion to whom the scene would not be one of mere cubic magnitude and regularity, or solely of material wealth and grandeur.

Stella remained in England about six weeks, when, Mr. Torson's business being at an end, they crossed "the Channel," and were in France. Stella had not seen in Britain all that she had desired and expected to see; but she was quite willing to leave it, and now looked forward with equal willingness to the time when she should quit France and return to Boston. In a foreign land, the one nearest her person far from her heart, in spite of her efforts to love him as a duty — he having little real sympathy with her in the objects which most interested her, and sometimes deprecating her loftiest qualities, of which he had no adequate conception — she had become weary of the very objects from which she anticipated deriving the most pleasure. Her stay in France was brief and unsatisfactory; and, in another month, it was a relief to be again in New York, at her father's house. There she was to remain a few days, before proceeding to Boston.

"Well, Stella," inquired Mr. Maign, soon after her arrival, "didn't I do a pretty good thing for you, after all?"

"I fear not," she replied. "I shall have much to forgive you. But we cannot improve the matter now.

1 shall try to do my duty, and shall do my best to be content."

Mr. Torson could not help observing that, although Stella was kind and gentle to him, it was from a sense of right, not from love. He could not fail to see that, sometimes, when she could not impose her wonted restraint upon herself, she appeared to regard him as only her conventional lord, but as her real and natural inferior. This irritated him almost beyond endurance. Only a thoughtful and noble man, as we have often heard, can bear the self-consciousness of superiority in a woman.

In society he was proud of Stella, and not without cause. As soon as she became fairly settled in her new home, she had paid more attention than ever to her music, as by it she expressed to herself all her joys, her regrets, and sorrows. And when, in social circles, she sat at the piano, she was at once the queen of a charmed and almost breathless group of listeners. Her rather tall and perfectly symmetrical figure; her fine shoulders; her delicate features, not strictly of the feminine Grecian mould, but rather suggestive of the intuitive, thoughtful, Grecian spirit as a whole; her long, heavy hair, dressed low at the sides, with no ornament save its own large glossy twist at the back, — seemed to reanimate, with but little change, the simplicity and power of antique classic beauty. Her appearance itself was an instantaneous assertion of the delight which her first touch of the keys would certainly afford. Others were often asked to play out of compliment, or to fill up the time; she, never except for the pure gratification to be derived from the music itself. Her perform-

ance was always unaffected and genuine, — never for
the sake of performance, — never with any attempt at
display of execution. Every note was palpable, perfect, and in its place. But all endeavor, all labor, was
subordinate to the end — deliciousness of sound — harmony — and still deeper, the expression of emotions,
and even powers of nature, by this entrancing utterance
of the boundless. Children would gather round her,
delighted with some gay waltz or polka — the ear alone
tickled with time and tune; young men and maidens
would name some piece which, as she played it, would
utter in melody, perhaps unconsciously to themselves,
their own vague ideas and dreamy longings. Then, if
she struck up the air of a powerful song, or some deep,
threatening march, through which she was now and
then secretly wont to throw off her combative and disagreeable emotions, — a sensitive person could scarcely
listen without clenched hands and the fire of conflict in
his eye. To be sure, most of the sturdy, moneyed
friends and acquaintances of Mr. Torson were not
people who, with Novalis, *thought* to music, delving to
find its inmost spirit. But they could easily perceive
its outward fascination, and thus compliment Stella
with earnest looks and words of unfeigned admiration.

Yes, Jabed Torson was proud of his wife on such
occasions, and pleased with the praises bestowed on one
of his possessions. It would have been the same,
though no doubt in a somewhat less degree, had the
encomiums been lavished upon his carriage or country
residence. He knew that Stella played remarkably
well. He could even enjoy the music himself, to a
limited extent. But he regarded the wondrous gift as

3

merely an expert and graceful accomplishment, which
his position and his money encouraged and sustained.
Stella continued to cherish it, because she loved it.
Her piano was now one of her chief comforts, — a partial solace for many regrets and wearisome reflections.

Mr. Torson had, in his house, what would be termed
a handsome library. It contained a fair proportion of
the miscellaneous works of the time. As a book became fashionable, or was talked of, he bought it, sometimes looking into it, but much oftener placing it on a
shelf where others could see it, and know that it belonged to his collection. Old books, which the ages
had venerated — which there was high authority for
possessing, if not reading — were better represented
there than any others: they gave repute to the whole
assemblage. The poets had their allotted space, but
were seldom so much as glanced at by the owner of the
volumes. Modern thinkers, too, had their position on
the shelves, but small place in Mr. Torson's mind.
The *Journal of Commerce,* a paper published in New
York, was, in general, his daily literature.

But for Stella, this library became every day a richer
treasure. She was not disposed to be a book-worm, —
to hunt amidst the dust of the ages for words, and
maxims, and innumerable facts. She was not disposed
to convert herself into an encyclopædia. So many historical incidents and actions seemed to proceed from
some one impulse, or foible, or desire, that she regarded
it frivolous and mechanical to catalogue a thousand
symbols of the same thing. She sought rather for the
cause, the explanation, and end of the desire or emotion itself, out of which the multiplicity of facts pro-

ceeded. Her soul asked questions which ordinary minds that she met in her parlors, and stronger, but not deeper minds, such as she commonly heard from the pulpit or rostrum, could not answer. Partly on this account, partly to lure her thoughts from immediate distasteful surroundings, she spent many hours in her husband's library, while he was on State street or at the Revere House, as his business or his leisure dictated.

As Stella had intimated in conversation with her father, Mr. Torson had not always in his younger days been strict in morals, though discreet and guarded in manners. We know that such men, when advanced in life, especially if they have young wives, are the most exacting and suspicious of husbands.

As Mr. Torson knew that Stella had only kindness, not love for him, he had occasionally asked himself if any one else enjoyed, or had ever engaged her affection. But her unexceptionable deportment in society, and her coveted seclusion at home, gave him no chance for a response injurious to her. One peculiarity offended him, as he watched her in the social circle. When occasionally some young thinker, uninterested in the ordinary topics of the street and the drawing-room, would speak to her of an interior meaning to some strain of music, or to some painting or statue, or would allude to certain men whose names were largely under the ban of popular odium, but who had, as she knew, devoted their time, their lives and fortunes, to elevating public sentiment, and particularly to lifting their countrymen up to the principle of universal freedom, — her eye kindled with an admiring enthusiasm, she lost all restraint, and speaking from the depths of her soul, her face beamed upon her companion with sympathetic generosity and fervor.

"What a fool she is," muttered her husband, when he saw her thus; "I believe she could love a painter or scribbler, while she would make nothing of snubbing a governor! How many grandiloquent words she has, too, for those miserable devils, the fanatics, who have wellnigh brought the country to disruption and ruin! Bah! she makes me sick of her!"

But he never discovered anything else in her conduct, to afflict him with sickness of head or heart.

Mr. Torson and Stella lived thus together, "very pleasantly," as people said, — "she having everything that heart could wish, and he proud of so beautiful and accomplished a wife."

But on the fourth anniversary of their marriage, he was suddenly and severely attacked with a malady which seemed at first much like bilious colic (unpleasant even to speak of), but which settled into a fever, and finally affected his brain. His physician declared that he could not live.

The day preceding the first attack, he had attended a large dinner at the Revere House, given in honor of a distinguished Southern politician, who had many times threatened the dissolution of the Union and the cessation of Southern trade, unless slavery, the paramount interest of his section, should be more effectually established and supported. Boston merchants and lawyers — conservative men of wealth, influence, and standing — had met him on this occasion, to toast his sentiments, and to show him that no one of conse-

quence in the city, possessed the smallest particle of
unfriendliness for him, or held any weak, fanatical
opinions regarding the chivalrous South.

Mr. Torson was a forward and delighted participant
in these festivities. He was eager to eat with, drink
with, smoke with, and in every way felicitate, the great
and distinguished guest. He showed much capacity
for solids and fluids, and was profuse and voluble in his
attentions. But alas! his geniality was too sumptuous
for his health! He passed one troubled, confused night,
then grew dangerously ill, and in five days the banquet
of life had itself closed. Jabed Z. Torson was dead.

Stella had faithfully attended him during these five
days, and had bestowed upon his distress every allevia-
tion that kindness and duty could suggest. She had
even wished, as she saw him lying helpless before her,
that Heaven had given her a commoner nature, and
that she could have sympathized with her husband,
and loved him. But she had done what she could,
and now, at twenty-two years of age, she was a widow.

3*

CHAPTER III.

"SO Torson is dead. Very sudden, isn't it? What a magnificent fortune he must have left his wife! I've heard he was worth half a million."

Such were the remarks which Mr. Loudun Braigh addressed to Simeon Ecrit, Esq., Mr. Torson's attorney, the morning after Mr. T.'s death.

"Not so much," replied the attorney. "'Twill do no harm to speak of it now, and to you. 'Tis a good deal under half a million; but then, 'tis a clean three hundred and fifty thousand. But Torson was a man of sense; he was rather particular about putting even that modest sum completely into the hands of his wife. He had his wits about him, and she, you know, is touched with some slight peculiarities. Besides, her father's money went by the board in '57, a year after her marriage; and of late, he and Torson haven't been such good friends as formerly. I suspect Jabed desired that the old man shouldn't have too much benefit from anything the daughter could control. Anyhow, there are certain pretty little provisions and restrictions in the will. But she can be comfortable enough if she pleases, notwithstanding."

The fact was, as Mr. Ecrit continued to explain, that

Mr. Torson had devised to Stella, as long as she should remain unmarried, any sum not exceeding ten thousand dollars annually, that she might choose to expend for her own support and convenience.

He premised that he wished her to live like a lady, as his wife always had done. But he had noticed traits of her character which he had been reluctantly obliged to condemn. He thought her imaginative far more than practical; and not likely to use his fortune, if placed entirely at her disposal, in a manner that, if living, would merit his approbation. He had observed, too, that she admired, not only works of art, together with poetry and literature generally, but that her nature inclined her also to the producers of these things; and as they were seldom competent, either to appreciate money or to take proper care of a wife, he had determined that, if he could prevent it, neither his wife nor his fortune should fall to the lot of any individual of their class.

Moreover, Stella, unlike himself, had a tendency to particular fanaticisms. He had no doubt that a designing man, by an appeal to her sympathies, could persuade her to give thousands of dollars to the cause even of abolition itself, which had always received his frequent and hearty curse. He had resolved that his money should float in no such channel.

Considering all these matters, he had concluded to make her an annual provision of the ten thousand dollars, or any smaller amount which she might wish to draw for the actual expenses of living,—for conducting her household, travelling, etc.

He had provided that the remainder of the income

should be employed for the accumulation of the principal.

No part of Stella's income was to be drawn by her, except for the actual purposes specified; and in no one year was she to expend in charity, more than three hundred dollars, — a sum which he thought sufficient for any lady of sane mind to dispose of in that way.

His house was to be retained as a part of the estate; and he made a moderate yearly allowance for improvements and changes upon the place, and repairs of equipage. This residence was designed for the occupancy of his widow.

But if she should marry, or should disregard any of the specifications of his will, she should be at once deprived of her income, and all benefit arising from his property, except one third. the value of the residence, furniture, etc. — her lawful claim on his only real estate.

In such case, the entire residue of the property was to go to one Clara Summers, a niece, whom he had seen but once, but who was supposed to be resident somewhere at the South; unless, indeed, she had died there, in which event the estate was to be devoted to the diffusion of arguments and facts opposed to the "disseminations of the American Anti-Slavery Society," and to the lamentable tendency to "rationalism, transcendentalism, and other forms of infidelity," which he stated that he had observed were fast gaining ground throughout New England.

But in case his wife should do nothing, during her life, to deprive herself of the advantages of his will, at her death the fortune was still to go to Clara Summers, if living, and if not, to be divided among the heirs of one of his distant relatives, who was himself very wealthy.

Thus Stella was left the serf of a considerable fortune. She was surrounded by every material comfort and luxury that her tastes could crave, but was debarred from opening her heart to love, or her conscience and generosity to their natural action and satisfaction. On the other hand, if she sought to free herself from her bondage — disregarding the will and spurning its aid — it would immediately be turned against objects and ideas which she regarded as the most sacred and beneficent then agitating the mind and heart of the world. For Clara Summers, evidently a Southern woman, would doubtless use the property in Southern fashion, investing perhaps the whole of it in slaves. Or if she were dead, the matter would be yet worse, — the money being hurled directly against the mental and moral revolutions of New England, which, instead of anarchical and infidel in their tendency, as Mr. Torson had considered them, Stella deemed grand, and highly important to the progress of the human race.

She felt as if bound hand and foot; which had of course been intended by her husband. His interest in political questions had been keen, and his negative attachment to certain religious forms had been conspicuous; but not sufficient to secure his deliberate intention to award them his whole property. His will was unmistakably designed to be a chain for Stella, which, with her ideas and convictions, would irresistibly fetter her to a course of life prescribed by his wishes.

CHAPTER IV.

MR. JABED Z. TORSON died in September, 1860. Stella appeared at the funeral in deep mourning, which she continued to wear during that month and the one following, and then exchanged for less heavy and dismal, but still plain dark colors.

Her independence of thought had for several years led her to interrogate fashions and customs of all kinds.

"These sombre weeds," she said to herself, "are the natural expression of our emotions when we are obliged to resign a friend to the dead. We are sad within; how can we be gay without? If we loved and respected the one who is with us no more, we receive a melancholy solace, as well as food for our self-respect, in bearing with us a constant suggestion of his former presence, and of the void now caused by his absence. How could we be worthy of the departed if we should not constantly think of him? should not constantly surround ourselves with objects impelling us so to think? Thus the custom inevitably sprung from human sentiments, and when not carried to a hollow mockery or a formal excess, it is appropriate and beautiful. Other sentiments, however, which are less admirable, often mingle in it. Material minds generally

(34)

associate death with fearful gloom and ungainly terror. They have painted him as a bony skeleton on a spectral horse. These follies sometimes enter into their mourning robes, which are then typical of mysterious blackness. Faith is not beneath them, and nothing bright can be seen beyond the solid earth. Could we behold the spirits of those who have passed away from us, being ourselves able to rise above our own selfish sorrow at the separation, I suppose we should follow them to the tomb with roses on our brows, rejoicing that, if noble and beautiful of soul, they had gone to a sphere of increased and increasing enjoyment, and if gross and sensual here, they had now become freed from the temptations and downwardness of a bulky body, and by being severed from it, could have scope for the reception of higher powers and satisfactions than it had been possible for them even to imagine, much less to know."

Stella could not feel that her husband's condition had been changed for a worse, by his death; nor could she mourn him for her own sake, like one who had been loved by him, had been understood and trusted. But she deemed it proper to respect the usual customs of the society around her, and to act as nearly as she could, in accordance with what she thought would be his own wishes.

Her most immediate reason for such compliance, was, perhaps, that she would not tolerate in herself the smallest vengeful impulse toward Mr. Torson, on account of the narrowness of his will. As he had exhibited meanness, she must beware of entertaining hatred. She must not condescend in anger, to even an appearance of insult.

Mr. Torson's mansion was closed to music and festivities: there was silence in the unopened shutters, and
an air of solemnity in the faces of even the domestics.
So it remained several months; and there, a placid
young woman with mild voice and tender eye, seemed
to lament, though with sufficient moderation, the de-
cease of a worthy husband.

Indeed, Stella felt that, even if he were not greatly
missed, there was sufficient cause for quiet consideration,
if not for mourning, in the strangely-fettered circumstances in which she had been placed, and in the mistaken endeavors of those who, when she was scarcely
more than a child, had thrust her forward to such an
untoward destiny.

But she did not complain of her lot with peevish in-
anition. She settled into it serenely, with the determination to consider, carefully and leisurely, what she
could best do for her own happiness and that of others.

As Mr. Ecrit observed in his colloquy with Mr.
Braigh, her father had lost his property. He had been
obliged to sell even his house, — the house of her infancy and childhood. It was through no fault of his.
He was an energetic and able merchant, as it was his
ambition to be. But he had become involved in large
transactions with parties whose credit was unlimited,
and whose resources were supposed to be almost un-
bounded. Then came the " panic " of '57. Every
merchant began to distrust his neighbor. The alarm
increased. The best paper, thrown on Wall street,
could not be converted into money without an enormous
sacrifice, if at all. But he had resolved, as he said, to
" go through." His notes, which, in the height of the

calamity, amounted to fifty thousand dollars a week,
" must and should every one be paid." At first he
sacrificed thousands of dollars in real-estate and the best
fabrics, rather than "suspend." Then came a large
loss through fire and the insolvency of several insurance
companies which had been presumed to be perfectly
sound. At last the notes of some Eastern manufac-
turers, whose paper, as everybody had declared, was
" A No. 1 " — the best, or as good as any in America
— proved almost valueless — not worth fifteen cents on
the dollar. Mr. Maign held a large amount of this
paper, and when it was protested, he could no longer
meet his own notes. Still, perhaps, he might have
weathered the storm, and come out with a little canvas
flying, — a few thousands left, — but as previously he
had been over-confident and self-reliant, now he was
wholly dispirited. He became emaciated and sleepless,
and it was even feared that he would be insane. He
allowed his property to pass into other hands for settle-
ment, and soon it was reported on 'change that Rufus
Maign was " completely wound up."

He was now a poor man, unable to commence business anew in his own name. But, his depression gone,
his knowledge of trade made him a valuable assistant to
others, and he could still live comfortably. Yet this
was a steep and long descent for so proud a man. Besides, he had lived in affluence twenty-five years, becoming so fully accustomed to wealth, with its many
attendant.luxuries, that the loss of his mansion or his
carriage was like the amputation of a limb. He could
not resign himself to such a fate. He had no ambition
but a commercial one, and no simple, inexpensive tastes,

4

by the gratification of which he could pleasurably occupy his mind.

Stella pitied him with all her heart. Moreover, as he had imperiously insisted on her marriage, and as the older she had grown, the more her heart had been estranged from his, she was fearful that, in not wholly respecting his characteristics, she might also be prone to overlook a daughter's duty toward a parent now unfortunate and fast growing aged. Here was a point upon which she was extremely sensitive; and she determined to soothe his declining years by every comfort that she could possibly offer him.

Thanks either to an oversight of Mr. Torson, or else to a mitigating disinclination on his part to prevent her from making *any* congenial or conscientious use of her income, he had indirectly left one way open in the will, for her to aid her parents. He had not specified whom she should have in her house, what company she should receive, or how much she should pay any person or persons for managing her household, if she should choose to put it in charge of others than herself.

In fact, the will paid her one very flattering compliment. It explicitly forbade the bringing of an action against her for breaking it, provided that when any question might arise on the subject, she should first solemnly affirm that she had neither avoided nor infringed any of its provisions.

Mr. Torson asserted, in this connection, that whatever might be his wife's faults and singularities which he wished to correct, he had never known her to deviate, in a single instance, from what she regarded the exact truth; and he firmly believed she would forego

all the benefits of his fortune rather than tell a downright lie.

Mr. Ecrit, when drawing up the document, had inclined to sneer at this clause, intimating that it would
counteract all the others. But Mr. Torson told him
that he knew what he was about, and needed no dicta-
tion; that the will began by affirming him to be in
sound mind, which he felt himself to be. Moreover,
he begged the attorney to bear in mind that it was *his*
will they were preparing, not that gentleman's own.
Mr. Ecrit thereupon proceeded without further com-
ment, and the testament was completed.

Stella gladly owned that, in this one instance, her
husband had done her justice. It filled her with surprise. She could with difficulty understand how he
could so implicitly trust a conscience which he could
still so meanly restrain. But she was thankful that he
had comprehended her even sufficiently to rely thus
upon one virtue, — her sincerity.

"It is true," said she, "that ' we can see only that
which we ourselves are.' He, too, possessed a sort of
coarse, common honesty, and could accredit me with
unbending truthfulness. He meant well in other
things, I doubt not, as far as he could see; but his
higher perceptions were dwarfed and bounded. Sorrow I *must* feel for him; unkindness, why should I
cherish?"

When Stella perceived that she could yet aid her
parents, or indeed any one else whom a young woman
of rectitude could include in her household, she wrote
to her father, stating that as his daughter, fully appre-
ciating his pride and his former independent position,

she blushed to make him a proposition which she was about to offer, though still she felt it proper, and even necessary to her own happiness, to do so.

" You know, my dear father," she continued, " that I am young, and, as you used to say, rather ' *enthusi-musy.*' Especially during the last year or two, I have given myself up to being musical when not literary, and a blue-stocking when away from my piano.

" I intend to remain, at present, where I am ; yet I don't want the trouble of superintending affairs in the house.

" You know how I am situated, — money enough, a fine house, equipage, servants, comforts, luxuries, all around me, and I their prisoner, — a poor little chippy in a golden cage.

" I can't lend you ten or twenty thousand dollars, as I should like to do, and which, with your business capacity, you could treble in a few years. But I can do *something* for you, nevertheless, while I can relieve myself of many annoying cares.

" Now if you and mother will come to Boston, and take charge of your little girl's house for her, as she dares not give or lend, she will *pay* you three thousand dollars the first year, or more if you desire it. Then you can do some sort of business, and be with business men, just as well on our Washington or State street, as on your Broadway or Wall street. Why not ?

" My carriage, too, shall always be at your disposal, and you can ride as often as you like. Now it is idle and almost useless. As for myself, I scarcely ever ride ; as when I go into the street, I need a walk ; and, like most of our ladies, I get too little air and exercise at that. Once in awhile I ride out to Cambridge or Mount Auburn. But you can have the carriage six days in the week, and with my company for one or two rides, you can have it the whole seven.

" Mother may arrange everything in the house to suit herself, except the library and a small room next it, which I am going to turn into a kind of retired musical sanctum. These two apartments will be consecrated to my own tastes and habits, — to order or disorder, silence or sound. All the rest may be as nice and as much like old times as you please.

" Tell mother how much I need her, and do come as soon as you can.

" Lovingly,

" STELLA."

Mr. Maign was deeply affected by this letter. Like so many daily occurrences in the world, it caused him both pleasure and sadness. It seemed, at first thought, a terrible event, for that haughty merchant, whose mustache was now gray, to become a dependant upon his daughter. Yet such a fate promised him the indulgence of all his former habitudes, with even the means of gradually mending his fortune. He was touched, too, by the manner in which Stella made him her offer, — by the feeling of need which she expressed for having him and her mother near her, and her delicacy in volunteering to give up to them the arrangement of almost her whole house, that they might feel at home in it.

" The dear child ! " he exclaimed, " she would do this too ; — she who was always so particular herself,

4 *

and from childhood had the best taste imaginable! Well, she is as singular as ever. I never did know exactly what to make of her ways. But she is the best girl in the world: I'm sure of it. Besides, she shrunk so from the marriage! Yes, we will go and live with her; and perhaps I shall learn something in my old age; who knows?"

Accordingly, Mr. and Mrs. Maign went to Boston, where they were soon settled in the Torson mansion.

The old gentleman made arrangements to close up some few debts that still hung over him, and to engage again in business. As he became accustomed to State street, he forgot to pine for Wall street, and as Stella converted her stately house into his home, he could even recall the Fifth Avenue without a shrug of the shoulders or a sigh.

CHAPTER V.

SEVERAL months passed quietly away, during which Stella remained with her parents in their new home. Much of the time she was secluded in the two rooms she had set apart for herself, and every one in the house became accustomed to her habits of solitude.

But a few days before the beginning of April, in the spring following her husband's death, she prepared to leave Boston for a brief visit to Ironton, where she had spent three years of her girlhood with Madame de Villier.

While at school she had formed several pleasant attachments; but Cora Clandon, a girl of about her own age, had been her favorite and most intimate friend.

Cora Clandon, like Stella, was the daughter of an enterprising merchant. But he was older than Mr. Maign, and had retired from business with a large property. His wife was dead, and Cora was his only daughter. He had one son who was in the army, and was most of the time absent from home.

Cora was a pleasant, handsome person, not much like Stella, but very fond of her. Her nature was lighter and gayer than her friend's, but she was very brilliant,

(43)

good-hearted, and agreeable. She was constantly striving to please Stella, while at school, almost every day bringing her delicacies from home, and making her little presents. She regarded her, in fact, with an affection only less ardent than she would have felt for a lover. When they had parted, she had made Stella promise to visit her sometime, and had written to her occasionally, ever since. Stella's marriage, and the four years or more which had now elapsed, made no difference with Cora. She had visited her friend in Boston, and was still determined that the promise should be fulfilled.

Stella thought that a slight change would be beneficial to her health and spirits, while it would be very pleasant to revisit the scenes of her school-days, at the same time gratifying Cora. The season was forward, the weather already sunny and genial. She sent Cora a few lines to tell of her approach, and the day after the letter was received, she herself arrived at Ironton.

Not long afterward, as she sat chatting with Cora, a young gentleman called. Cora introduced him as Mr. Merlow, and when she addressed him, she familiarly called him Charley. He was a person rather above the medium height, of slender proportions, quick and somewhat angular motions, having keen, but frank, expressive eyes, and short curling brown hair. When he spoke, there was noticeable in some of his words the trifling difference between the New England and the New York pronunciation, and Stella at once located him as a Massachusetts boy who had spent more or less of his time a little west of that State.

"It will be a fine evening for those exercises," said

he to Cora, after they had conversed some minutes on general topics, and he had addressed a few pleasant remarks to Stella. "I suppose there is nothing to prevent your going with me."

Then he looked suddenly up, first at Stella, and from her to Cora, as though he had spoken carelessly, and was annoyed at it.

"I must disappoint you, Charley," replied Cora, "unless my friend would like to go too; and I think she had better not: she has been in the cars all the morning, and will be tired to-night.

"We were speaking, Stella," she continued, "of the closing exercises of a literary society that Mr. Merlow is interested in. The members close the season, this evening, with 'efforts of overflowing eloquence, effusions of inspiriting poetry, and accordant examples of impassioned song,' as one of our newspapers has it: all of which means, I presume, that they are to have a pleasant affair.

"Now I don't care about it at all," she added, smiling, "except that this young man invited me to attend with him, and hear a poem read by a friend of his, whom he calls superior, profound, and many other nice adjectives. The friend evidently has no taste; for he has been invited several times by Mr. Merlow, to come here with him and call on me, — which the youth has never done. But not wanting to break Mr. Merlow's heart over a small matter, I accepted his invitation, and we were to hear the poem to-night. Now there's the whole story; and the point of it is, that I shall be delighted, not to go with you, Charley, but to stay at home with you, Stella."

Charley Merlow's dark eyes leaped and capered at this sally.

"Good!" he exclaimed, "but I hereby invite and implore your friend, Mrs. Torson, to accompany us. Who knows but she may herself prefer hearing the poem, to the enjoyment of your charming though solitary attention?"

Thus appealed to, Stella said that she should be much pleased to go; that she could not, in fact, be persuaded to withstand the temptation of such an entertainment.

Her decision settled the matter, and at the appointed hour they started for the hall in which the exercises were to be held.

On the way, Charley Merlow talked incessantly about his friend, Earnest Acton. The subject of his poem was to be, "Chivalry."

"It is a minor effort," said he, "what Earnest himself calls a little affair, — something he has almost extemporized. I haven't seen it; but I am sure of one thing — he never writes a line that is not thoughtful, at least. He has had a more than ordinary inward experience, and never thinks or speaks from mere authority. His mind has much less than the customary respect for names, and perhaps much more than the customary veneration for men whom he regards as the exponents of truth. It grasps individuals, standards and customs, not accepting them because they are such, but demanding on what final and absolute grounds they rest. Comparatively few think and act from such a stand-point."

Stella was much interested in these observations.

She was aware that friendship easily praises the objects which attract it ; but this criticism touched her own experience, and a part of it seemed as though it might have been said of herself. She felt that she already liked Mr. Merlow, and was prepared to look with favor on his friend.

As for Cora, she bantered, and laughed at her escort, the whole way, telling him that he repeated Mr. Acton's ideas constantly, and was " a second little Bozzy, with by no means a second Dr. Johnson."

CHAPTER VI.

AS soon as Earnest Acton appeared on the rostrum, Stella remembered having somewhere seen his face. But her attention immediately recurred to his poem, which was as follows :

> " In ages old, but when those lands were young
>   Which gave the fathers of our fathers birth ;
> When Europe, strong of arm and fierce of tongue,
>   Had newly broken from the sombre girth

> " Of tangled forests which encompassed her ;
>   When men almost as savage as the beast,
> Had bristled out from wilds of oak and fir,
>   ·Slaying the Roman Empire for a feast ;

> " And by their strife to root all culture up,
>   Had shaken off a portion of their own
> Huge shagginess — had learned to taste the cup
>   Of that refinement first despised alone ;

> " In those old times which wear the name of 'good,'
>   When worldly honor shone but from the sword ;
> When all of labor save the trade in blood —
>   The battle's reeking barter — was ignored ;

> " When kingship's pride was to dethrone a king ;
>   A noble's, to subject nobility ;

And strength and will to slay a foe, the thing
    Most sought, and felt the greatest need to be ;

" When freedom was by chance of birth controlled,
    And man as man, in vain the boon might crave ;
When he who sowed and reaped, or bought and sold,
    Or delved the arts, was everywhere a slave ;

" In ' good old times ' like these — for such they were —
    When rudeness was the background of the scene,
And in the front, with warriors circling her,
    Arrayed most loosely, Anarchy sat queen : —

" One figure gleamed with bright attractive mien,
    Though belted like the rest, and wrapped in steel ;
For sense of duty, like its armor's sheen,
    Cased it in length of light, from head to heel.

" Its helm thrown up, there glistened on its brow,
    Like diamond flash, the glow of piety ; —
Not soft, but sharp ; — and men began to bow,
    And said with awe and fervor : ' Chivalry ! '

" The figure passed : it traversed many a land,
    And grew in grandeur as it fared along ;
And sometimes, lance in rest, leisure in hand,
    Attuned its spirit, thus perchance, to song : —

" ' There is wrong in the world, and the strength of the flesh,
With skill like the spider, hath woven a mesh
Where the wings of the harmless, the limbs of the fair,
Are tortured and torn by the monster that's there.

" ' The castle of stone, though its lord mounts a crest
That looms as with honor, is often a nest
Whence the robber swoops down, a mere hawk on his prey,
And returns with the booty his beck reft away.

5

" ' The trader is spoiled of his wares on the road,
    And they crush down the poor as ye tread on a toad;
    The highways are swarming, as bees from the hive,
    With bandits whose sting scarcely leaves you alive.

" ' The pilgrim who journeys to tire out his sin, —
    Holy man, doing penance for that which hath been; —
    Aye, even the priest, though the people revere,
    Must mix with his mission the bitter of fear.

" ' And we know — what a shame! — that the Mussulman horde
    Rear the impious mosque near the grave of our Lord; —
    That the infidel Turk has encompassed the shrine
    Where once lay incarnate, the Ruler Divine!

" ' Yes, there's wrong in the world, and who shall protect,
    Where the plague-spots of harm the defenceless infect,
    Or where God's holy Church must to Mahomet bend,
    If the arm of the knight is not raised to defend?

" ' So I wend through the world, and my home is my steed;
    My shelter is serving the weak in their need;
    For though storms swell above me, or carnage sweep round,
    Where I rest on good deeds, there my safety is found.

" ' My lance is a pillar that props up the saints;
    And my sword, a support when the wayfarer faints;
    My axe is a fate unbelievers confess;
    And my shield an asylum for those in distress.

" ' My course bears me East or it hurries me West,
    Where a grief can be soothed, or a crime be redressed; ·
    God guards and rewards me, the good give me fame,
    And the bad do me honor by cursing my name.'

" So sang that ancient rider, Chivalry,
    And was refreshed while chanting martial deeds,
  In stormy days of hate and bigotry,
    Of rapines, legends, signs, and counted beads.

" Then sturdy Talbot, honest in his thought,
    Had said that God, were He a man-at-arms,
Would be a pillager : — as Talbot fought
    For spoils, he deemed that God must feel their charms.

" Then cried La Hire, who always bent the knee
    And prayed before he fought: ' O God! be near,
And do for me, this day, what I for Thee
    Would do, if I were God, Thou wert La Hire!'

" Old stormy days, harsh men, fantastic dreams, —
    They lie as ashes in their stately urn,
The solemn past ; and only flitting gleams,
    The ghosts of what they were, we now discern.

" But Chivalry, the generous, the grand, —
    Has that impassioned figure lost its fire
And chilled to ashes too ? — its flaming brand
    Sunk quenched in selfishness and Mammon's mire ?

" Or has it leaped the centuries, and found
    Its chosen foothold, as some lips assert,
Beneath those fervid skies, on Southern ground —
    The 'sacred soil,' unlike all other dirt ?

" High-blooded Chivalry ! — has it disdained
    The world that works, and trades in common ware,
To roam where Barbarism, enervate-brained,
    Struts peddling men and maids by piece or pair ?

" 'Tis there, methinks, though sadly masked and bent,
    And bowed in sackcloth of self-sacrifice ;
But there, if there at all, its arm is lent
    To stay oppression, help the crushed to rise.

" Its symbol never was the curling lash,
    Nor ever was its boast the cringing back :
For God and man was lit its sabre's flash —
    A sunbeam e'en when blood imbrued its track.

" And when no more was seen that mail-clad form,
　As it had lived its time in such stern guise,
Its spirit lingered still to cheer and warm,
　And lead each lofty, hallowed enterprise.

" The castle was not now the robber's den ;
　His corselet shielded not the shark of gain :
A savage little imp had come to men,
　To batter walls and cut them to the grain.

" They called him ' Gunpowder.'　He crashed at sight,
　Straight through the bandit's thickest iron hide ;
Where he appeared the vulture-flock took flight,
　And despots in his presence grew sore-eyed.

" The Christians, too, such Christians as they were,
　No longer rumbled East, to belch God's wrath
At those who held the holy sepulchre,
　And speed each Moslem soul to endless scath.

" Two millions of their bodies strewed the way
　To Palestine ! two hundred years they fought !
Still God permitted Mahomet his sway ;
　Had they not done all mortals could or ought ?

" Stout Christian hearts ! — there was a deeper sense
　In their religion than their eyes could see :
The tomb of Jesus was its own defence,
　And he had died for all humanity !

" But when what seemed a duty to perform,
　Filled their horizon, and they strove, and bore,
And wrought it — conscience-bound in that war-storm,
　(God bless them !) men or saints could do no more.

" And when, the storm at end, they sank away,
　Their glory arched the broad historic sky,
As though 'twere Iris, veiled in light and spray,
　There smiling at their deeds through tears on high.

" Then Chivalry threw off its mail and helm,
 And taking on itself a plainer suit,
It gladly entered a more modern realm,
 Where newer thought was bearing richer fruit.

" Had it once slain the Mussulman, to wrench
 Him from his miry faith ? Now through the one
Itself so long had held it cut a trench,
 That standing pools of life might freely run.

" It spoke from Luther's lips, when firmly braced
 On conscience, he defied authority ;
When true to truth, all other powers he faced,
 And said : ' Here must I stand, God helping me ! '

" It spurred Columbus to his weary task
 Of groping for a hidden continent : —
To age through manhood doomed in vain to ask,
 That he might bless the world, the world's consent.

" ' He dreams a golden dream,' the schoolman said ;
 ' Yes,' cried the priest, ' a dream of unbelief ! '
While urchins, pointing, pitied his poor head,
 Who was that misty epoch's mental chief.

" But like true errant knight, his gaze was set
 On God above and distant lady's smile ;
Till her, at last, our mother-land, he met,
 In person of the blooming Indian isle.

" Thus rolled the orb of ·progress to the West,
 And Chivalry, whose soul had wandered through
The olden world with each exalted breast,
 From many a port took passage for the new.

" But cavaliers, who claimed its pristine shape,
 Oft lost its meaning by repressing man ;
While sad as if all heaven were hung with crape,
 It sojourned with the gloomy Puritan. .

5 *

" 'Twas far from noble then to giddy eyes ;
   To them solemnity but veiled deceit.
Yet 'neath that veil, though choked with needless sighs,
   Duty to God and freedom found retreat.

" When later still, the youthful continent
   High prizes for heroic feats had won,
What choicest flowers of chivalry were blent
   In one bright wreath — the life of Washington !

" The boy who, erring, would not tell a lie ;
   The chief who conquered but would not be crowned ;
Enriched by slaves, the man who would not die
   Until their broken fetters touched the ground !

" Great soul exhaled, and childless borne away !
   Yet Father to America the fair ! —
Oh ! would that she would imitate to-day
   Her sire's last blessed act, his kindest care !

" ' God give her speed ! ' I heard that voice exclaim
   Which filled the medieval ear with song —
The voice of Chivalry — and then there came
   These parting accents, as it throbbed along : —

" ' Still there's wrong in the world, though the features of crime
   Have softened their red with the changes of time,
   Since housed in the glitter of ponderous steel
   I crushed the iniquities nothing could heal.

" ' The plundering chief is a handful of dust ;
   His armor is food for the hunger of rust ;
   For the hawk of the castle, the buzzard his shade,
   Is filching the poor by extortions of trade.

" ' And there breaks on my ear the fetter's dull clank,
   As I heard it whilom in the realms of the Frank ;
   But harsher, and sadder, and worse it must be,
   Where nature established the home of the free.

"' No hermit-led armies now surge to the East,
Though the cross has won strength, and the crescent decreased;
From the creed of the Christian the edge of the sword,
Has been ground by the cultured to sharpness of word.

"' But an idol has often been reared in the fold,
For the chosen to worship — the Dollar of Gold!
While the spirit of faith has been bundled in form,
Until smothered itself, it was lifeless to warm.

"' So I've leaped to the saddle for truth and the right,
And levelled their lance with a sacred delight, —
Dismounting old errors and checking the new,
While freeing the many from bonds of the few.

"' The foolish have laughed, and the heartless have sneered,
Not knowing me now as I freshly appeared;
They have shot at me arrows empoisoned with blame,
By the venom distilled from some odious name.

"' Then saddened when wounded, not turned from my way,
I have fought the hard fight, gaining ground with each day;
But I hoped that this Nation would need not again,
The blow from my hand that would leave the blood-stain.

"' I trusted that mind, not the battle-axe broad,
Would hew roughest hatreds to kindly accord;
Yet a monster seems raising his head for a stroke
That will drench it in crimson 'mid thunder and smoke.

"' If oppression must die by the gash it would make,
Once again to the clangor of arms I must wake:
For the virtue heroic now leading the van,
Is fealty to God by freedom to man !' "

CHAPTER VII

"WELL, what do you think of my friend? and what about the poem?" inquired Charley Merlow, of the two ladies, after the exercises of the evening had concluded.

"Yes," replied Cora, "I supposed you would ask that, the first thing. Know, then, that the poem was tolerable for a young man, — just passable — nothing more. There wasn't a thing to laugh at from the beginning to the end of it, — not a single right down spicy line, unless the one about the 'sacred soil, unlike all other dirt;' and that was bitter.

"It was a fling at the South, and our Southern brethren," she added, looking up mischievously at Stella.

Charley Merlow laughed.

"Very well, Miss Lively," he said; "now we have your weighty opinion, which I know you will hold at least five minutes; but, Mrs. Torson, may I ask for yours?"

He had seen from the expression of her face, that his new acquaintance had listened to Earnest with close attention and keen sympathy. Her eye had kindled with his, and had softened as his voice was modulated to the

(56)

key of some tender or beneficent sentiment. It was evident that she had been deeply interested. But thus far Charley knew nothing about her, except that she was a young widow from Boston, rich, and accustomed, as he understood, to " the best society." He was very naturally surprised, therefore, at this deliberate response which she gave to his question :

" I was not disappointed, Mr. Merlow, in your friend's poem. I will not speak like our sprightly Cora here ; but quite as I feel. The poem seems to me a brief history of Chivalry, a criticism on it, and an impersonation, in the two songs, of its real spirit in ancient and modern times. The distinction between the heroism of the soldier and that of the self-sacrificing thinker, is clearly drawn, perhaps, while I fancy that your friend's preference for the latter is more decided than he has portrayed it. His allusions to pseudo Chivalry, which vaunts itself as real, because six and a half centuries after *Richard Cœur de Lion*, it still surrounds itself with the worst faults and barbarisms of his epoch, is, as Cora asserts, *bitter*. I think nothing on that point can be too bitter, if spoken from the indignation of justice, not from anger. The closing lines of the poem, viewed from the highest possible stand-point, are not the wisest that could be. They are local and temporary, their application being to immediate time and place. I have sometimes thought that the highest art should always close its efforts by lifting us out of locality into what Plato has called ' that one sole science which embraces all : ' — into insights of the infinity of absolute wisdom, love, beauty. There the mind always finally loses itself ; there is the natural climax, the natural peroration of all its perceptions and endeavors. But one can hardly compress the ordinary and actual, then time and space, into a few stanzas which he is called upon to make interesting to a thousand different listeners.

" Chivalry," she continued, " in its early and usual sense, was, as the poem paints it, the much-needed application of warfare, in a rude age, to justice, magnanimity, love, mercy. And as, in the minds of the many, a special glory has always hovered about the pursuit of arms, the era when the brilliant knight was lawgiver, protector, lover, friend, has always lingered long both in memory and imagination. But Chivalry itself — its spirit, its essence — can of course pertain as much to an age of commerce, as to an epoch of tournaments and courts of love. It is with us in the world; it has always been so. I think one of its most signal examples, in the medieval, physical sense, was before us not long since at Harper's Ferry. For the most exalted spiritual instance known, we must look back through eighteen centuries, to Mount Calvary and the Cross."

As Stella spoke thus, she had given herself wholly up to the impressions presented to her mind, and for the moment had nearly forgotten where she was, or with whom she was conversing. It is true that her first words were uttered partly with a special design. She had been really charmed with Earnest, and she wished to know him. It seemed as though he might be a friend with whom her inmost soul could commune. So she had intended that her criticisms should not appear to Charley Merlow as altogether commonplace, and that he should repeat them to his friend. This inten-

tion had soon been overpowered by the thoughts which
pressed upon her, and she had spoken even more ideally
and enthusiastically than she anticipated.

"Upon my soul!" cried Cora, "how completely
you sermonize! Did you ever preach, over there in
Boston, where everybody does such strange things? I
shall have to look after you, my dear; you never were
quite like any one else. But in these parts there is a
great deal of decorum. The ladies think highly of
Saint Paul: they don't speechify much, unless, indeed,
about the clothes and the frailties of their neighbors.
There now, your 'sprightly Cora,' as you call her, has
delivered *her* little address; here is the moral of it."
And as they entered the hall of her father's house, she
put her arms about Stella and kissed her.

Charley Merlow said but little. He appeared to
have been stunned into a sort of deferential silence,
which pleased Cora amazingly. She kept looking at
him in a way which signified, "How now, Charley?
Perhaps somebody else has a friend too!"

He soon took leave of the ladies, and made straight
for Earnest.

"Great guns, my boy! great guns!" he exclaimed,
as soon as he saw the latter; "I've a peach for you to
peel now — blooming, ripe, and rosy — a desperately
charming widow, just — well, I should say just twenty-
three. I took her with Cora, to-night, to hear your
poem, and asked her opinion of it. Straightway she
threw bonnet and strings clean over the moon in her
criticism, — went up out of sight, with high art, Plato,
philosophy, Richard the lion-hearted, Jerusalem, and
John Brown. You shall go with me to see her, to-

morrow night; and if you don't talk the lights out of her, I'll disinherit you from every penny-weight of my affection.   Now don't say no: she's Aspasia, Lucretia (the Mott), Cleopatra, Mary Queen of Scots, and Mother Ann Lee."

Charley finally sobered down to an explanation of his meaning, and repeated Stella's remarks as nearly as he could recall them.

"Now there's no need of your reading and writing, twenty-five hours to-morrow," he persisted; "you *shall* go to Cora's with me in the evening."

Earnest said that he should certainly like to meet so charming a person as Charley had described, and that, if he still insisted, after sleeping off his "afflatus," they would visit her and Cora on the coming evening.

But the call was intercepted by a somewhat singular and unpleasant occurrence.

CHAPTER VIII.

THE next day, while Stella and Cora were in the street together, they were accosted by an unusually bright, pretty child, who asked something from Stella in charity. The little one's feet were bare, and she appeared to be clad in but two garments — a tattered dress, and a small, miserable shawl, pinned about her head and shoulders. But her features were delicate, her eyes were soft and truthful. She seemed to possess the germs of intelligence and refinement, which even a tolerable fate might develop into beauty and goodness.

Stella's soul always shrank from extreme poverty, which so generally forces upon its victims an existence scarcely more than animal. But the sight of a pretty little girl, thrown on the street, with its vices, to beg, caused her the saddest pang that she ever felt for the poor. She longed to raise every such child above a need so wretched. But she could not help all, and she could not refuse to help any, without feeling that perhaps she had added an impulsion to the ultimate career of " one more unfortunate " — society's worst sorrow and disgrace. She gave the child now before her a few

6   (61)

bits of coin, asked where she lived, and said that she would perhaps go to see her some time during the day.

"That child, at any rate," said she to Cora, "ought to have one decent change of clothing, and a few kind words to touch her with hope. She shall have them. I will do so much for her, if I cannot do more."

Accordingly she procured a small bundle of such articles as were required, and immediately after tea, she and Cora started to find the house where the child lived.

It was fast growing dark; but they expected to be back again in half an hour. There were a few dubious clouds to be seen, and Stella took with her a small iron-framed umbrella.

Just east of Ironton, and on which, in fact, the city is partly built, is a range of steep, high grounds, which the Irontonians call "the Hill." Somewhat less than half-way up this hill, a street called High street, runs north and south, opposite the central and upper portions of the city. One section of the street was at this time but little more than a road, except that a double stone-wall, built against the upper division of the hill, for purposes of drainage and for security against landslides, made a good foot-path as well as carriage-way.

It was near this portion of High street, that Stella and Cora went in search of the little girl. It was some time before they could find her, and when their errand was done, it had grown pretty dark. They thought nothing about it, however, but stepped briskly along, intending to come down into the city by a different cross-street. They soon came to the stone-wall; but as the road was hard and free from dust, they continued on that.

From the foot-path or sidewalk above them, which was often, in summer, the resort of promenaders, one could look down the hill, seeing the portion of it below, then the streets and houses, and extending the view, could have a fine prospect beyond the city, north, south, and west. From the east side of the road, where Stella and Cora were now walking, all this could be seen except the lower portion of the hill itself.

As they reached the most deserted part of the street, yet were within a hundred and fifty yards of some small tenant houses, they were met by a coarse, hard-featured young man, who, as he came near them, glanced quickly about him, then attempted to snatch Cora's watch-chain, and tear the watch from her pocket. Her shawl had blown aside, leaving the chain partly exposed, and the thief's quick eye had detected it.

But Cora's motions were almost as quick as his glance. She instinctively sprang aside just enough to avoid his clutch, at the same time shouting with surprise and terror. She placed her hands firmly over her watch, but trembled, and begged that she might not be molested.

"Give it up, right away!" said the man, "or I'll kill you!"

"I think not!" sharply responded a voice, which this time astonished all parties; and as the words were spoken, the blow of a fist, from a person running, sounded from the face and teeth of the ruffian. It knocked him away from Cora, but though he stumbled and staggered, he did not quite fall. He was a desperate as well as cool fellow, and on recovering his balance — finding that his new antagonist was unarmed and breathing heavily, as though exhausted — he drew a short club from under his coat, and struck the man with it, partly upon his head, partly upon his arm, which was raised to protect the head.

"He will kill Mr. Acton," cried Cora. "Murder! murder!"

Stella, too, screamed, and in her exasperation she struck the robber full across the face with her umbrella, and broke it so that it held together only by the silk covering.

Half a minute had passed since he attempted to snatch the chain. Earnest Acton — for it was he who had interfered — was on the ground, nearly senseless.

But still another person was now seen approaching the group. He came running toward them, with an uneven, bandy-legged gait, shouting, swearing, and brandishing a huge knotted stick.

"Wait till I git forninst ye, ye divl!" he exclaimed, with a savage Irish accent. "Ye'll be in the middle uv Hill afore iver ye'll murther agin!"

But the "divl," as he was called, would not wait. He saw that now he was fairly foiled, and the best he could do for himself was to hurry away, which he did with all the celerity his legs could command. In another instant he was out of reach, and very soon out of sight.

"Oh! it's Jerry Kay, it's Jerry Kay!" cried Cora, as the Irishman came up to them. "Jerry, it's I — Cora Clandon; you came just in time; we were frightened almost to death! Come and help Mr. Acton!"

"Oh! the grace uv God now! and is it yersilf, Miss

Clandon?" responded Jerry. "And what wud that thafe uv the wurld be doin' wid ye? Luk at the way now he's kilt Misther Acthon — the nischest young man in the city, that's allays had a good wurd for me and the ould ooman! If it wasn't the damn bad pair uv ligs I have on me, I'd uv been up to the schoundhrel and shlivered the brain out uv 'im!"

And here, poor old Jerry Kay burst into tears of sorrow and wrath.

"Misther Acthon, and are ye much hurted now?" sobbed he. "Shure ye wouldn't be goin' to die for the sthroke of a blaggard!"

But Earnest had received an ugly blow near the top of his head, which had stunned him for the time, and left a gash from which the blood was flowing copiously. In a short time, however, with the assistance of Jerry, he was able to rise. Supported by him on one side, and by Stella on the other, he walked slowly to Jerry's house, which was near by. There a bandage was extemporized by the "ould ooman" and the young ladies, the blood was washed from his face, and at Jerry's urgent solicitation, he took a "small smather uv whiskey."

"Now, Jerry," said he, "if you can get me a carriage, I will ride home. Miss Clandon, if I may, I will ask you and your friend to accompany me. The carriage can leave me at my door, then carry you straight to yours."

This proposal was at once accepted; for Ernest was pale and weak, and would be liable to faint at any moment on his way home.

"Mike," said Jerry, to a boy about fourteen years

6 *

old, who had betaken himself to a corner, out of the way, — "Mike, git yersilf sthraight dooun till the daypo, and bring up a carriage — a nische one d'ye mind ; and luk now, if iver ye got a lickin' in yer life, think of the one ye'll git now, if ye'r long gone."

Admonished by this very palpable suggestion, Mike soon returned with a carriage.

"Say now, Misther Acthon," said Jerry, after Earnest and the ladies had entered it, "may I go dooun to luk at ye to-morry ? Shure I'm thinkin' ye wudn't objict."

"Object! my good old friend?" replied Earnest, "of course not. Why should I? Come down by all means, if you should feel like it; I shall be especially glad to see you."

"Ahah, now! luk a' that!" still continued Jerry. "But I'm remembrin' ye niver were too proud — way up intirely over a poor man. Good luck t'ye, Misther Acthon; God 'lmighty bless yersilf an' the darlint ladies. Dthriver, kape yer eyes roound aboout ye ; for ye've got the most gintlemanly load uv the sexes that iver yer mares was forninst."

Saying this, Jerry bowed and scraped a still further adieu, while the carriage rolled away.

The next morning *The Ironton Daily Pitchfork and Raker*, contained the following account of the event.

"A DARING ATTEMPT AT ROBBERY AND MURDER. *A sad Catastrophe.* — Last evening, just at dusk, as Miss Cora Clandon, a worthy and estimable young lady of our city, the daughter of Richard Clandon, Esq., was walking along High street, in company with a lady friend, whose name we have not learned, they were suddenly attacked by a ruffian, supposed to be the notorious Himmer Gilspe, who demanded her watch and chain, threatening violence in case of refusal.

" With rare presence of mind, Miss Clandon immediately placed her hands over her watch, which is said to be a very valuable article, and importuned the scoundrel to desist.

" At this moment, Earnest Acton, Esq., who was taking an evening walk, approached High street by the steep, unfrequented acclivity between Crag and Bowdry, having selected that mode of ascending the hill, as affording him the most vigorous exercise. Of course he could not be seen, even when near the top of the acclivity, by persons on the upper side of High street. The intended robber deemed himself perfectly secure in his depredations, when suddenly he was knocked down by a blow from Mr. Acton. But the young gentleman was unarmed, and was, besides, much fatigued by his exertions in climbing the hill. The ruffian, seeing this, drew a 'billy' and a knife, striking and stabbing him on the head and neck.

" Meanwhile our old friend, Jerry Kay, well known about Bugsley Corners and the Grumby Market, hearing the disturbance and cries of 'murder!' hastened to the scene, bearing in hand his inevitable 'purty little cane,' as he terms it, which many who have noticed it, will remember as a knotted 'shillaly' about the size of a heavy flail. At his appearance the thief ran.

" If the precious villian should be detected, he will probably be found considerably bruised, as apart from the punishment inflicted by Mr. Acton, Miss Clandon's

friend — who by no means contented herself with faint-
ing — broke an iron-framed umbrella, as we are informed, three times across his face, while he was mal-
treating that gentleman.   Our principal informant
(Jerry Kay himself) says he is sure 'she painted a
very nate picture of Purgatory about both eyes of 'im.'
It is quite probable that but for her coolness and per-
tinacious courage, Mr. Acton might have fared much
worse than he did.   As it is, he was in a critical condition when we last heard from him.

" Every effort should be put forth to find the detestable
villain who was the cause of this sorrowful calamity,
and to bring him to condign punishment.   Our present
police-force is not, we think, exactly what it should be,
and not, as we stated before the last election, what it
would be, if in the hands of the party we have the
honor to represent.   But we give due notice that the
least negligence or carelessness in looking after this
matter, will not be lightly criticised by the *Pitchfork
and Raker.*"

CHAPTER IX.

THE main points of this account, as we have seen, were true. Earnest Acton, however, at ten o'clock the next morning, was sitting up in an easy chair, and was pretty comfortable for one who had been so severely handled the previous night. He was reading *The Pitchfork and Raker*, rather enjoying the article in reference to the " daring attempt at robbery," etc., and smiling at the remembrance of Jerry Kay, when the latter called, desiring to see him.

" Is he sittin' up and dthressht did ye say now ?" asked Jerry of the girl who went to the door. " And I dramed the doctor had 'im kilt ! Thanks to God ! Shure I'm thinkin' ye may show me up to 'im ; but go an ax 'imsilf. Till 'im its Jerry Kay."

Jerry was of course invited in.

A few minutes afterward, Stella and Cora called.

They said they did not expect to see Mr. Acton, but had heard conflicting rumors regarding him, and wishing to learn in the most direct manner how he really was, they had stopped to inquire.

Earnest heard their voices from the room in which he sat talking with Jerry, and said, so that they heard him :

" Request the ladies to walk in, if they have time and the wish to do so."

" You will find here," he continued, with a smile, as he met them, " both the vanquished opponent and the conquering hero ; for our friend, Jerry, has come in to see me."

Their attention thus directed to Jerry, he arose, and suddenly dropping the upper half of his body to a line nearly parallel with the floor, he made an exceedingly angular but very deferential bow.

" Good morning t'yes, ladies," said he. " I hope yes are both will after the runcontry uv th' avenin'. Misther Acthon, I'm thinkin', is gittin' on fine, only he's a little pale, like a sisther uv marcy. He'll be hardy agin in a couple uv days."

" And how is yer arm ? " he inquired of Stella. " Wasn't it some pursuadin' welts ye gave the thafe wid yer umbril ! He'll think a wake was hild on his face, if he looks in acre a glass this mornin'."

Stella was slightly annoyed at this compliment to a sort of prowess which she was far from priding herself upon ; but smiling, she answered Jerry that her arm was still in good condition, though she trusted that she should never be obliged to use it again in the manner he alluded to.

" I trust not, indeed," said Earnest, who had noticed her momentary annoyance ; " although now that we have all escaped with so little injury, I shall scarcely regret, in one sense, having given you the trouble. Had I been armed, as sometimes I am in the evening, perhaps I should have shot the man dead on the spot. By doing so, I should have saved your

womanly delicacy a few twinges of vexation ; — for it
instinctively shrinks from striking a person ; — but I
should have had something it may be to disturb *me*
during my life. For the old Scandinavian fierceness of
the race shoots through our blood at such a sight as
suddenly appeared before me last evening, and is liable,
for the time, to deprive us of all considerateness. Yet
I always feel that if, by any misfortune, I should kill
even the worst man on earth, the act would cloud my
calmer moments with sadness. The laws might justify
it, but I fancy I should constantly see the dead with
pity and anguish."

"And I, the divl a bit!" roared Jerry Kay.
"Why, man! if ye'd a shot the thafe, all yer sins wud
been forgiven ye for that! I wudn't mind crackin' the
head uv 'im more nor a louse. Didn't Miss Clandon
till me he said he wud be wiolent wid her if she didn't
give up the watch? Shure the baste hadn't a soul in
'im at all at all : he was the manest scut intirely that
iver unbuttoned a lip to threaten a lady."

Jerry had settled the point to his own satisfaction,
and no one contradicted him.

The young ladies soon arose to go. After Cora had
invited Earnest to call on her and Mrs. Torson, as soon
as he should be able to appear again in the street, she
turned to Jerry.

"My good old friend," said she, "let me give you
this ; " and she tried to put a gold eagle into his hand.

"Don't think I mean to *pay* you for your kindness,
by any such bit of money : you were worth more to us
than our gold can be worth to you ; but you, and your
wife, and the boy all busied yourselves for us ; so we

want you to get a few little things to recall the occasion, and to remind you how much we think of you."

At first Jerry withdrew his hand. He looked at Cora, then at the piece of gold.

" Well, God bliss ye, Miss Clandon," he finally exclaimed, " I know ye've got plinty more uv um, an' I'm thankful to God for it. Ye raelly want to give it me now, I know. Yis, I'll take it.

" It's purty hard," he added, with a very extended smile, " for a poor divl to shut his fisht agin a thing like that. Shure, Misther Acton, I know ye'll till me the thruth: 'Tisn't ungintlemanly for me to be takin' the gould-pace, is it ? "

Earnest had viewed the scene, not without interest and emotion. Cora's hesitation; her delicacy in impressing upon this poor Irishman, to whom ten dollars was certainly a temptation, that she was not paying him for services, but rather conferring a favor on herself in doing him a kindness; his reluctance to receive compensation for what he had been so glad to do; his innate perception of her feelings and the right of the matter: — all this was very touching to Earnest. When Jerry looked up to him and made the final appeal to his judgment, there was a bright, pleasant gleam on his face, there was also moisture in his eye.

" Take it, Jerry," said he; " you would hurt Miss Clandon's feelings far more by refusing it, than you would please yourself by accepting it."

" Well, now, I thought jusht that," returned Jerry; " for that wud be the way wid yersilf."

" Ladies, if ye'll hould on, the half of a minit, I'll

till ye a story about Misther Acthon when he was a little boy, so, up to me hip.

" He was fishin' dooun beyont there, at the dock, in a yawl that was tied to a schooner. He got a bite, and began to pul up. It came tufer and tufer; and when the thing got nare till the top of the wather, it was an ael nare the lingth uv one uv yersilves, so it was. That ael was the divl. He was nigh till pulin' Misther Acthon out of the yawl. I was goin' by jusht thin, and a nagur. Me and the nagur tuk oursilves dooun into the yawl lively. Afther a while the three of us had the ael in; and he was more nor the lingth uv the breadth uv the yawl. He was like the schooner's cable. Well, well, wasn't Misther Acthon tickled. thin? He hadn't got a cint of money wid im; so what does he do but give the nagur the fish-line, — a moighty nische fish-line it was too. Me, he takes along wid 'im up to his fadther's house, and afther measurin' the ael roound aboout and ivery way, he turns the coddy over to me. I has a wathery mouth for aels, and this feller made a slammin' dinner for me, and the ould ooman, and Mike, and siveral uv the naburs."

" Not a very commendable business transaction on my part; was it, ladies? " said Earnest, as the laughter subsided, which had arisen from Jerry's method of telling the story, and still more from his gestures.

" Perhaps it was so, after all, in the highest sense of all such transactions," replied Stella; and she looked at him with both of her deep, pure eyes so full of frank kindness and sympathy, that he felt the glance penetrate and warm his blood, while that beautiful face, in one of its loveliest moods, was impressed upon his soul.

". Yes," he responded, looking, in his turn, with that peculiar smile of mingled sadness, earnestness, and gentleness, which is so often the reflection of a deep, sensitive nature;—"yes, you are right; I have not received the last instalment in the matter, I find, until now; but that alone should compensate me a thousand times."

This was said in so honest a manner, as if every word were weighed and completely felt; with so little the appearance of any mere compliment of gallantry; and with so rapid a change of subject, as though Earnest's delicate acuteness predicted some slight pleasing embarrassment on her part, at the turn he gave to her remark;—that, although a gentle tinge, like a ray of the sunset, consciously glowed on Stella's cheek, her heart found no fault; she was pleased, and still further charmed.

"Now, Jerry," said Earnest, after the ladies had left them, "I am going to take a glass of light wine which the doctor prescribed for this hour. If you were not an old man, always accustomed to your 'wee drop,' I should hesitate to ask you to drink. I am rather particular about it. But as it is, you must take a glass of wine with me, or, if you prefer it, a glass of brandy. There is some brandy in the house, made from the vineyard of a gentleman of this country — a friend of mine. It is very nice. Would you rather have some of that?"

"Thank yer honor," replied Jerry, "I *will* take a small, healthy snifther uv that, if ye plase; but I'm no grate joondge uv th'article. If ye shud put the bist glass uv brandy forninst me, and the worst, maybe I cudn't till ye the differ between um, but I cud dthrink both."

Jerry took his "small, healthy snifther," which by no means restrained his loquacity. He sat quiet for a moment, then broke out thus:

"I say, Misther Acthon, that's a very nische lady with the dark dhress — the Miss Thorson, I blave ye called her. What a swate eye she has; it almost milts out uv her hed intirely on ye. Shure I'm thinkin' she has a punchang for you, as the Miss de Gusty says aboout the roses she picks in the gardin."

"A what?" asked Earnest.

"A punchang, shure," persisted Jerry; — "a takin' to a thing — a likin' of it."

"Oh! yes, I understand! — a *penchant,*" laughed Earnest.

"Well, I don't know about any special *penchant* that Mrs. Torson may have for me; but I suspect she is a noble, kind-hearted, intelligent young lady, and such a person almost always finds something to like in everybody. Don't you think so?"

"Indade I do, thin," Jerry answered; "and they ain't proud nather: they allays spakes to a poor man. There's the Gineral — Gineral Bull; he allays siz, 'Jerry, how ar ye,' when he mates me; and he's one of the grate min intirely — boss of all the sogers roound aboout. But there's more uv um nor doesn't spake nor luk at me. But they's the cods — the small fish wid very disfragrant airs. The min wid the high stations, like the Gineral, and the min wid the brains in um — like yersilf, Misther Acthon, savin' yer modesty — thim's the min that don't go by me."

Thus Jerry rattled away for several minutes, till bethinking himself that perhaps Earnest had been sitting

up too long, and was becoming too much fatigued, he
snatched up his hat and stick, and saying that it would
be too bad to kill Mr. Acton with himself after saving
him from a thief, the strange old man hurried away
into the street.

CHAPTER X.

"IT seems to me, our dear young widow has been struck by something. What is her dream all about?"

Such were the words which Cora addressed to Stella, after their interview with Earnest Acton, and when they had proceeded some distance toward Cora's home, while Stella had remained silent and pensive.

"I was thinking," Stella answered, "how very dissimilar are different people, and yet how nearly alike at heart are all of us who are well disposed, and who trust ourselves to our own natures."

"Yes," suggested Cora, with a little chuckle, "and how much nicer, how much more sensitive and elegant some young men are, whom one meets occasionally, than most others whom one sees every day."

"Perhaps so, if you will, my dear Cora," was Stella's reply; "but we must not form such preferences too hastily."

"Oh, no! certainly not," said Cora; "and especially if we are from Athens the Hub; if we are scholarly and profound; if we are staid, dignified, queenly, and have arrived at the venerable age of twenty-three. But if we should happen to be myself now — a pleasant

7*

body only twenty-two, who dearly loves her friend, but who doesn't think a great deal, and whose mouth opens easily to chatter or to kiss, — why, then we should declare that we can't help entertaining preferences rather nimbly and speedily; we should own right up, for instance, that we liked Charley Merlow amazingly, and were inclined just now to take a friend of his into our heart, but generously forebore doing so, because we thought the friend himself would like a dear friend of ours much better than he would like us."

"Child of twenty-two," retorted Stella, with mock gravity, "do you settle fates too, with as much celerity as you form preferences? What have I to do with your Charley's friend? How do you know that we have seen anything in special to admire in each other?"

"How do I know? Why, bless you, I feel it. The heart has big eyes sometimes, even when the head isn't so very spacious. When Charley Merlow and I were setting our caps for each other, didn't he use to look at me in the very way I saw you look at Mr. Acton, and the very way, moreover, in which Mr. Acton returned the look? Of course he did. I suppose Charley and I didn't fully know what we were doing at first; but we found out, after awhile."

If Cora had thoroughly understood Stella, and the position in which she had been placed by Mr. Torson's will, she would not have talked to her as she was now doing, partly in earnest, partly in jest, and partly to afford herself the pleasure of referring to Charley Merlow. But Stella had said as little as possible concerning her husband. All that Cora knew about him, was that Stella had married him reluctantly, that afterward they had lived together kindly, though not with perfect congeniality, and that now Stella had discarded her mourning, as also the frequent mention of his name. She had heard the will spoken of as a strange one; but had not learned the particulars of it.

At first Stella could return badinage for badinage; but as she continued listening to her friend's playful, bantering, confiding words, feeling that Cora's heart was happy in its love and trust of one who seemed worthy of its overflowing affection; that her own heart, which throbbed with such vehement, impassioned, exalted emotions, had found no rest for its yearnings; that now it could scarcely dare hope for such rest in any event; — now, too, that she had seen one who, as she acknowledged to herself, caused the suggestion that her youthful vision of love might be a possibility in the world: — poor Stella, with all this in her soul, how could she suppress the single crystal drop that melted through those long, dark lashes, suffusing with still deeper tenderness and beauty the look of affection and sympathy which beamed from her eye upon her joyous companion.

Cora noticed it, and her playful smile was immediately an exile. A troubled cloud of sadness and regret spread itself over her face, and not a trace of lightness was left. But they were near her father's house, and she did not speak again until they had reached her own room, where they went to dispose of their street apparel. She hastily threw off her own, then, going to Stella, untied her bonnet-strings, drew off her mantle, and putting an arm about her friend's waist, hastened into the little parlor adjoining, where, seating herself in front of the cheery grate, she pulled the young widow down into her lap.

"What have I done to you, my dear Stella?" she inquired, now just ready to weep. "I am so full of nonsense that I am always wounding the feelings of somebody. But I did not mean anything by what I said. I should think you would have known the harmless sound of my rattle-box, especially when I am so fond of you. I know you are not frivolous and giddy, but very thoughtful and good. Was I foolish enough to attribute to you, even in a joke, any injustice to memories of the past? What was it, my darling friend?"

"Why, nothing, Cora, child, — nothing, at any rate, worth wet eyes; so don't let me see tears between your laughing lids, even if one foolish drop did fall from my own. I have but few memories of the past to trouble me in the way you were thinking of. I was only touched by your happiness, and was comparing, perhaps selfishly, the fulness of your heart with the void in my own, though Heaven knows I would not take a single joy from your life, if by doing so I could wreathe mine with constant delights. But you are frank and honest, my Cora; you are sympathizing; you can be reticent too, if you know I wish it. I will tell you a story of my past three or four years, which you are not wholly acquainted with. I trust the good angels will not let me be unjust in the very manner you were fearful that I shrank from being; for I shall speak to you of my husband, — a man whom I remember with kindness only, not with love, not even with complete respect."

Then she told Cora of her marriage; of her reluctance to it at the beginning; of the wide difference between Mr. Torson's nature and tastes and her own; of her struggles, as a conscientious woman, to love him, which only ended in driving their souls still farther apart; and last, she gave the particulars of the will. But she told nothing of her husband's rudest vices, — for there were some such to be locked forever in her own breast; she palliated some of his harshest evident faults, and appeared to tremble lest any revengeful sentiment should enter into her statement.

" You see, Cora," she said, in conclusion, " that Mr. Torson did not mean to be a very vicious man. I don't know but many a better girl than I would have been content in my position. He wished to leave me, too, with every material comfort, and his will was largely generous in that respect. But my integrity was almost the only one of my qualities he would trust. It was impossible for him to understand me. Those of my virtues that I knew to be the highest before God and man, he regarded as visionary weaknesses — even wicked absurdities. I could look through his mind and comprehend his motives, because I stood above both, — having experienced, as it were, his characteristics, in my commonest and lowest moods; while he could not know what his nature had never reached. He was honest, in the ordinary business sense; he was lavish, not to say liberal, of mere physical surroundings, — wanting me to have everything that conventionality required; but he had, and could have, no conception of the demands of an aspiring soul. He was of the earth and was earthy, — a common man, who had accumulated a third of a million of dollars, and in that, con-

sidered the great aim of life accomplished.   He was no
worse than a thousand others I saw every day, — my
heart has always acknowledged it; — and for him, as
for all such, it has never had — at least for more than
an occasional moment — any feeling harsher than pity.

"Well, I have told you of my husband.   You know
something about my own views, and what I conceive
to be my duties.   You see the position in which I am
placed — virtually forbidden to love ; — my heart pitted
against my conscience, with a third of a million for the
wager.   If love should win, I shall not only be poor,
which, perhaps, I could bear well enough, but the
money will be used to crucify conscience and duty
themselves.   I have never loved ; but God knows how
dearly I could love.   You have sometimes attributed
superiority of intellect to me.   Others have been kind
enough to do so.   Some have called me mental and
frigid.   It is true, that my heart, yearning for deep,
full, responsive throbs, baffled by the living, has turned
to the dead.   I could not be the bride of a beloved,
for I found no one whose nobleness forced me to adoration.   So I gave myself up to the lovers and poets
of all ages and all climes.   Their sentences and songs
wooed my spirit — pressed themselves to my inmost
life.   They knew me.   Our souls sympathized in truth,
in justice, in beauty.   Thus was a vacant place in my
heart partly tenanted, while thus it could not, of course,
be wholly filled.

"You spoke of Mr. Acton.   I was not troubled by
that.   As I have talked with you so freely now, why
should I hesitate to tell you, as far as I know, the
impression I have received from him ?   I don't love

him, certainly. How could I so soon? I don't believe in ' love at first sight.' A person's first glance, a
single word, a tone of voice, may strike vividly and
pleasurably upon some related chord of our nature, and
oblige memory to reproduce it a hundred times. We
want to see the glance, to hear the word again. If
other properties correspond to this, and the whole nature
inclines to us, we love. My heart would never risk the
mention of love for one I had seen but two or three
times. We all have some good phases; we all have so
many bad ones!

" Yet I will own that Mr. Acton has revived visions
of mine that had almost faded away; that I began to
see vanish with considerable resignation. Here is a
young man who suggests to me, by his presence, that
the earth could perhaps afford me the happiness of
pouring out my whole soul into another. But by the
time I have seen him again, it may quite easily be,
that through some one of his words or actions, the veil
will fall once more over my eyes, the dreams still be lifeless. And perhaps I ought to tremble if it were not so."

" I don't think you ought to do anything of the
kind," cried Cora, who had listened to her friend, first
with glances of sorrowing sympathy; then with
flushes of indignation and scorn, as she gave the particulars of Mr. Torson's will; and then with patient
silence while she drew her inferences of a general nature.

" It was monstrous to fetter you so! How can you
speak with a sort of kind, reasoning indifference of so
mean a man? I would have soaped the stairs to break
his neck! No, I wouldn't, either; but I would love

somebody, if I could, with all my heart, now he had taken himself decently out of the way. You needn't smile : I would, anyhow ! How ridiculous it was of the conceited old dollar-grab, to say that no other sort of man than himself amounted to anything, or would be able to take care of you ! That's all he knew — the old stomach ! I'm glad you didn't love him any more than you did. But you shall love Mr. Acton now, if you like, or anybody but my Charley. Let the money go to the dogs. More can be got. I shall have plenty, I suppose, and you can have some of that. And if your ideas are right, God will take care of *them.* How is a big pile of pennies going to outweigh Providence ? "

Cora stopped to breathe, and laughed at her own questions and statements. Stella could not help joining her.

" True, my dear Miss Impetuous," she said, when Cora was ready to listen : " No amount of money, no mountain even, of present wrong, should at all trouble our serene faith in the ultimate right. But that is scarcely the question. Would it be possible, in any case, for *me* to do as much by yielding to love, toward performing the duties I regard highest in life, as a large fortune, hurled directly upon them, could do against them ? "

" Well," responded Cora, " I don't know : but I think God intended we should enjoy such a dear blessing as love."

" Certainly, Cora ; He intends we should enjoy every dear blessing ; He made us to enjoy ; but He made us to do our duty first and foremost ; for that, in the end, is always the sweetest, the loftiest enjoyment."

"Yes, I suppose so;" still insisted Cora: "but a body would think that in a case like this, you would be the last to be hampered and imposed upon. You value money so lightly; it passes through your hands so easily, and, as I have often thought, with a kind of contemptuous indifference. You know everything best, my dear Stella; but let me ask you a question on your own ground. I've heard you speak with enthusiasm of certain men in this country, for instance, as the leaders of great reforms. Now my good papa, and Captain Bub, my brother, don't think much of these men. But you do, and Charley Merlow does. But take one of these notables — say Mr. Curtis. Do you think that any sum of money, used by common or bad men against the truths he utters in his beautiful way, could be at all the measure of his influence?"

"Surely not, my sweet little Meno," answered Stella; "but what then?"

"Not Meno, if you please," said Cora, with much pretended dignity; "for I read somewhere, the other day, that he was the man that Socrates twisted out of his sandals so neatly that he couldn't tell the meaning of the very things he had talked about a hundred times. Let me cure you of the illusion that I am any other than Socrates himself. You acknowledge, then, that no sum of money could measure the influence of a great man?"

"Yes, Socrates," laughed Stella, "you are going right at it in your ancient method, I find."

"Well, now," continued Cora, "haven't I heard

8

you say that one of your friends, whom you regard as among the greatest minds of the time, has often acknowledged that more than half of his power and perseverance came from the heroic sympathy and encouragement lavished on him by his wife? You know I have heard you say it. Now, finally, you could love only a superior man, and you know well enough that nobody in creation could hold such a man up to his task of greatness and goodness, better than yourself. So, unless you would cut a man's influence in two, and spoil it wholly, by declaring that your half in it were worth less than some fellow's money-bag, I'm sure my argument ''has laid you out,' as the boys say, ' flat and clean.' "

" Precisely, my Cora," was Stella's response; " I fancied I knew the end you were approaching, and have frequently thought of it myself. But I should be obliged to have a great deal of confidence in my own worth before I should dare avail myself of your inferences.

" However, now that we have finished arguing, can you tell me anything more than I have already learned about the young man who was the cause of the argument? What do you know of your Charley's friend? I shall be with you several weeks, and shall meet him. I shall be enticed to his acquaintance, for the study of a marked human soul that has come to me differently from others, if for nothing else. I am interested in him, and feel curious concerning his history. What has Charley Merlow told you about him? "

Cora felt, and was determined to feel, that Stella, in case her great, noble soul should flame into passion, would not be called upon to sacrifice its fondness, as she seemed to contemplate. Something of this prepossession might have colored the account she gave of Earnest; for she spoke of him ardently and sincerely, though partly still with the capricious pleasantry in which she delighted.

CHAPTER XI

"ALMOST all I know about him," she began, "Charley has told me; but Charley, as you have observed, is very fond of him, and talks about him a great deal. They have known each other ever since they were children. The way they became acquainted was odd, and a bit romantic; but ask Charley to tell you that part of the story himself. You won't have to ask him but once. He would spend the day, any time, in conversing with you about Earnest. They used to live in the same town, somewhere in Massachusetts, — I forget the name of it. Earnest came here when he was a little boy, ten or eleven years old, and afterwards Charley came on and stayed awhile with him, attending the same school. Charley is rather older than Earnest, though he looks younger. Earnest's face is so quiet and meditative; — I suppose that is the reason. He has entirely changed, Charley says, since he was about fifteen. Before that, he used to be full of activity and sport, — not what you would call a downright bad boy, but always ready to run, frolic, be saucy, or fight. Isn't it a shame that little boys all *will* fight? They're not half so nice as little girls. My brother, Captain Bub, used to worry the

(88)

life out of me. He would have had a bloody nose
every day, if papa hadn't talked to him, and whipped
him, and shamed him constantly. He went into the
army, at last, as it was. But he has sobered down into
a very pleasant relation.

" Charley and Earnest were not a great deal together, for the few years before they became young
men. But they used to correspond ; and at last Charley came to Ironton, and went into business. I have
known him a year, and he has started several times to
bring Earnest here ; but something has occurred to
prevent, on each occasion. So we have known each
other well enough, have bowed as we met in the street,
yet we had hardly spoken a dozen words to each other,
until that scapegrace tried to steal my watch."

" Well," inquired Stella, " what has Earnest been
doing, all his life ? That, you know, is one of the first
questions we all ask about each other. What profession, or business, has he been engaged in ? "

" He hasn't any profession," replied Cora ; " and
now, I believe, he isn't in any business. A little while
ago, he was with Mr. Wether, a produce merchant, —
as a salesman and accountant, I suppose. But he had
a good deal of leisure, which he occupied by reading
and hard study. Charley says he understands business
very well, but has little taste for it. Besides, some of
the most customary transactions connected with it, appear to him so hard and selfish as to be almost dishonest. He says that, particularly in speculative seasons,
when he has stood and regulated the price of a product
more by one's need than by its real value, — stretching
the market a little, if possible, — squeezing out the last

8 *

cent, — he has felt that, although pleasing his employer
and showing the smartness of a salesman, he was pretty
nearly picking a pocket; only he was doing it lawfully,
and more dexterously than the coarse blackleg.   When,
too, he has seen Mr. Wether selling a cargo of grain
or salt; worming the price up to the highest notch;
declaring he would not sell so low to any other man,
and, in his excitement, meaning it, although he would
say the same thing to the next comer; — declaring,
protesting, whining even in the voice of an old woman,
all for ten or twenty extra dollars, on perhaps five
thousand; — then the clerk has pitied the employer,
who had grown rich while his face had grown narrow
and pinched, and while his soul had been crammed
into his purse.

   " When Charley told me this, I said I didn't think
his friend had cause to feel so; — that it was necessary
for people to have money, and, as they couldn't do
without it, they must try their best to get it.   Charley
said yes, and told me Earnest saw the fact as plainly
as anybody; that he liked business men, and often
declared that the very excess of the accumulative spirit,
which he deprecated for himself, was the means of
developing vast material resources; — levelling moun-
tains, filling up swamps, making corn grow, and comforts increase.   'You mustn't think,' he continued,
' that Earnest despises any class of men, or sort of
vocation.   He says that men are dependent on each
other throughout, and are brothers in spite of themselves; that he should be without a coat and a breakfast, if it were not for some enterprising tailor or
butcher among his friends.'

" Then Charley went on to tell me a lot of stuff about its being right for men to do what they think right, until they can take higher views and so higher grounds of action ; and about its being right, in that sense, for men to do things that Earnest could not do. He told me that I mustn't judge such a person by common rules ; for he was rather a representative of the future, when men would be better, than a mere dweller in the present time. Perhaps I didn't quite understand all these nice distinctions. At any rate, I'm not going to risk getting into the dusk myself, by trying to bring them to the light for you."

" But in spite of himself and his ideas, Mr. Acton did, it seems, sell produce for Mr. Wether, and keep accounts for him," said Stella.

" Yes," answered Cora ; " but he never liked it, Charley says, even at first, when a mere boy ; though he always had the reputation of attending to it conscientiously and well. But, according to his friend and my oracle, he wasn't made for success in that direction. He was too thoughtful, scrupulous, and independent.

" You remember the passage in ' Corinne,' that we used to read at school :

" ' Les hommes frivoles sont très-capables de devenir habiles dans la direction de leur propres intérêts ; car, dans tout ce qui s'appelle la science politique de la vie privée, comme de la ,vie publique, on réussit encore plus souvent par les qualités qu'on n'a pas, que par celles qu'on possède. Absence d'enthousiasme, absence d'opinion, absence de sensibilité, un peu d'esprit combiné avec ce trésor négatif, et la vie sociale proprement dite, c'est-à-dire la fortune et le rang, s'acquièrent ou se maintiennent assez bien.'

" Now I missed my lesson once, on this same choice
bit of French, and I've never seen any truth or beauty
in it since ; but I remember it only too well.   Charley
quoted it in reference to his friend ; and I could antici-
pate him at every word, — not allowing him to air his
scholarship singly, you perceive.   He declared that
nothing could be better applicable to Earnest ; and that
every syllable of it was true.   He said that he met,
every day, a score of his friends, who had grown rich
far more from qualities which they had not, than from
those which they had ; that ' absence of enthusiasm, absence of opinion, absence of sensibility, a little smartness ' — say a little more than the mere average — not
only ' acquire and maintain fortune and rank, but are
always the absolute and necessary foundation of fashionable power and respectability.

" ' For,' said he, ' superiority is inevitably trying to
improve conventionality, while mediocrity struts satisfied
with it, and is active and important in presenting and
insisting upon its forms.'

" That is the way Charley sermonizes to me.   But,
you see, he knows a thing or two, as well as Earnest.

" In his opinion, his friend has, of course, just the
reverse of the dear Madame de Staël's requisites for
fashionable success.   He has enthusiasm, opinion, sensibility, and almost no ' smartness,' in the sense, at least,
of that calculative sharpness which thrives itself by the
suppression and injury of others.

" You have seen plainly enough that he has some
strange ideas.   In fact, his ideas about religion, politics,
and everything are strange.   But I believe, in my heart,
he is a good fellow, or Charley wouldn't think so much

of him.   Besides, my dear Stella, I can't help thinking
he is a great deal like you.   You and he would make a
right nice match, — the most harmonious pair in existence.   I'm sure you are bound to like each other.

"Don't interrupt me now : I'm going to tell you
something more about him.

"While with Mr. Wether, he grew from a boy to a
man.   His mind formed, and on many subjects he
differed from his employer.   I know Mr. Wether.   He
is a kind-hearted, quick-tempered man, well-meaning
and honest, but old-fashioned, narrow-minded, and
prejudiced.   Earnest never talked much with him, because he knew that the old gentleman was fixed in his
convictions, and because he thought it wasn't in good
taste to force discussion where it would be of no use.
But Mr. Wether was aggressive in his views, and often
very severe in his comments upon men whom Earnest
regarded as among the greatest and best in the world.
At such times, when directly addressed, he always said
exactly what he thought.   Charley used to ask him
why he didn't smooth the subject over, and let it
drop.

"'Not at all,' he replied ; 'when a person asks me
a question, he shall be answered.   The honesty which
would preserve me from taking money from a man's
till, would never permit me to give him a dishonest
opinion.   If I could do one of these things, I could do
both.'

"It seems to me, he carried the point too far ; but
that was what he said.

"After awhile, Mr. Wether began to look on Earnest as an Abolitionist, then as an Infidel.   The old

gentleman is very religious, — a strong Presbyterian, and a constant reader of the *Observer*.

"By the way, it was over that newspaper that he and Earnest at last fell completely out with each other.

"Mr. Wether began a conversation, and quoted the *Observer* to maintain something or other, when Earnest called that journal itself in question. He said it wasn't always more scrupulous than even the *Herald*. For only a few days before, he had seen a sentence of Theodore Parker's warped and misconstrued by it in the most dishonest and shameful manner. Mr. Wether defied him to prove it. Earnest found the paper, and showed him that it quoted Theodore Parker as saying: ' Since my eighth year, I have had no fear of God,' and then it took the text: ' the fear of the Lord is the beginning of wisdom,' and expatiated on Theodore Parker's infidelity and wickedness.

"' Well, now,' said Earnest, ' hear the whole sentence as it is: — *Since my eighth year I have had no fear of God, only an ever greatening love and trust.* Your paper, Mr. Wether, cut a sentence in two, and pilfered half of it to defame a great man.'

"This was too much for Mr. Wether. He couldn't see anything wrong on the part of his theological weekly, but he was very indignant at Earnest.

"A few weeks afterwards it was whispered; at a meeting of the Ladies' Sewing Society of the reverend Mr. Defogy's church (Mr. Wether is a member of it), that the young ' infidel and abolitionist,' Earnest Acton, had been tolerated quite long enough by his employer, and that, in another month, his place was to be occupied

by a more pious and useful member of society. It was
Deacon Jewer, of their own church. Deacon Jewer was
twenty years older than Earnest, and had himself been
a merchant. But fire and flood had suddenly broken
him down.

"' What can be done for him?' asked one of the
Greeds — his particular friends — and Mrs. Crutch
and Dea. Longswell, at a circle held two or three
weeks before the one that I spoke of.

"' Perhaps Mr. Wether could be persuaded to
change assistants,' suggested another of the Greeds.

"' What a fortunate suggestion,' said Mrs. Crutch;
' and undoubtedly it would be a pious duty to bring
about such a change. I have heard sad reports about
that fellow Acton; and they say he hasn't any reverence for God, or respect for good people. He told
Mrs. Orter, the other day, that I was a woman who
meant well enough, but was a busy-body and a gossip,
and that my superior righteousness was all in my eye.
What a vulgar expression wasn't it? ` and everybody
knows that I never gossip, but only say what comes
into my head, and what is on everybody's tongue. I
think we had better use our exertions for Deacon
Jewer. I know Mrs. Wether, very well: she is an
intimate friend of mine. She is very partial to Mrs.
Jewer too. She has much influence over her husband: some say, in fact, that she wears the ——— Well, I
don't like to use every common phrase that we hear in
the wicked world; but I have often been told that she
manages matters much in her own way.'

" O Stella! I thought I should die laughing, when

Charley told me all this, and imitated the different persons, some of whom I knew very well."

" But how did the affair terminate ? " asked Stella.

" Oh ! " said Cora, the conversations at the Sewing Circles were of course repeated, and it wasn't long before the reports came round to Earnest. He went immediately to Mr. Wether, stated their substance, and asked if it was true. He thought, if so, he ought to have been informed of it as soon as the old ladies from whom he had indirectly heard. Yet he had few doubts on the subject. Mr. Wether coughed a few times, tugged away at the muscles of his throat, and finally said : ' Yes, he had thought it best to make a change.' Earnest found no fault ; and Deacon Jewer soon presented himself.

" Some of Earnest's friends called him foolish, — altogether too docile and easy.

" ' Put the accounts into a fog,' said one or two of them : ' make everything as hard as possible.'

" ' No indeed,' said Earnest ; ' I have not been treated quite after my own heart, as no breath of fault or warning ever came to me. But what of that ? Men must think and act according to their light, Mr. Wether as well as I. I am not docile and easy, but tough and heady. I don't think that a single trader, or a church-full of his goodish friends, can be a feather in my path ; especially if God has given me anything worth doing on his earth. And if not, what matter little circumstances of this kind, one way or the other ? '

" That was an odd view to take, wasn't it, Stella ? It seems to me, Earnest has no appreciation of the

events and interests which make up the life of our
kindly, good and bad, every-day people of the world ;
but looks so intently upon the great that he forgets
there is a common and a little.

" But Charlotte Bronte says something like that, of
one of her characters in ' Jane Eyre,' doesn't she ?

" At any rate, I don't altogether like such people.
Charley suits me much better than Earnest would.
That's fortunate for you, my lady : who knows but *I*
might get him, if I should try ?

" The very indignation he felt over the affair I've
been telling you about, seemed only an indignation of
the head. He disliked it because he thought it ought
to be disliked : scarcely more because he had been its
victim, than as though he hadn't been at all interested
in it. Here's philosophy for you, perhaps, — mental
power, with other ' lofty tumbling,' — but where's the
flesh and blood ?

" No, positively ; I wouldn't have him. I should
find, some fine morning, that the man had dissected
himself, to ascertain or confirm some theory or other.

" Mr. Wether he regards with no unfriendly feeling,
but merely as one more specimen of the *genus homo*, to
be encountered thankfully, considered attentively, then
shelved in his cabinet. The same with Deacon Jewer.
To Earnest, the Deacon, too, is merely pictorial, — regarded as part of a scenic effect ; though he had some
reason to disrelish him before they came directly in
each other's way.

" He laughed with Charley, a while since, and told
him the Deacon would be a far more valuable *employé*
than himself, being sure to save every penny, which he

9

knew how to value above all things; and that his
efforts, indeed, had already been praiseworthy as an
agent for others.

" It appears that, several years ago, a pew in Mr.
Defogy's church fell into the hands of Earnest's father,
for some debt, or through some business transaction,
and was estimated to be worth about a hundred dollars. The old gentleman Acton is quiet and easy;
and believing, as Charley says, less in theology and
more in religion, than Mr. Defogy and his congrega-
tion, he seldom used the pew himself, or was present
by the proxy of any member of his family. So Deacon Jewer, Deacon Longswell, and the other trustees
let the pew and pocketed the proceeds; — 'for the Lord,
of course,' added Earnest; ' for no one ever supposed
they did it for themselves.'

" The paternal Acton, hearing of the disposal of his
pew, made no objection to the result, but disliked the
method. The easy man felt as though there would
have been some propriety in consulting him in the
matter. He was content that they should use the pew
for the occupancy of strangers; he said that he would
give it to the church right out, if he could afford to do
so; for, although Mr. Defogy's preaching wasn't very
high, nor wholly Christian, still his church and his
sermons did much good, by holding up even to their
standard, certain men who wouldn't believe in anything better, and who would doubtless be worse than
they were, if they couldn't believe in these. But he
said he couldn't give the pew absolutely away; and as
the trustees had taken it to themselves to let, he
wished them to have a legitimate title to it, and would

sell it to them for fifty dollars, half its estimated value. The matter was referred to Deacon Jewer, and he offered *fifteen*.

"'Yes!' exclaimed Earnest, 'if I were the Lord, and would own that church, I would certainly displace any such individual as I am myself now conscious of being, for the sake of having Deacon Jewer attend to my affairs. How, then, can I blame Mr. Wether for wanting so valuable a person?'

"It was horrible in him to say so, wasn't it, Stella? Yet Charley persists in telling me that his friend has more real, sensible reverence for God, than Mr. De-fogy's whole assembly have.

"Now, Stella, I've told you almost all I know about the man you're going to break your heart over; and the bell has just been touched for dinner. Let's go down. Pa will wait for us at table."

Thus Cora finished, or rather broke off, her chatty, rambling account of Earnest Acton, and she and Stella, with their arms around each other, went to join Mr. Clandon in his dining-room.

CHAPTER XII.

IN the evening Charley Merlow called. He had just come from Earnest, he said, who was quite as well as when the ladies had seen him in the morning, and would be out in a day or two.

" Then," Charley continued, " I shall bring him here. We were coming last night; but the High-street adventure spoiled our plan. How glad I am, Cora, that neither you nor Mrs. Torson sustained any injury from that rascal Gilspe, or whoever he is."

"And I am quite as much delighted," said Stella, " that your kind friend fared no worse than he did. Cora and I have been speaking of him to-day, and I already know him sufficiently well to appreciate many reasons for your attachment to him."

" As for Earnest," replied Charley, " he takes the matter so complacently, pitying himself so little, that I may as well do the same. He regards the occurrence as one more item of experience ; the thief, as an individual who aided him to know from the fact itself, how indignation rises against villainy, and how pleasant it is to thwart a ruffian ; his pains he watches, to see what effect they have on his moods ; .and if he should be disfigured, I have no doubt he will scrutinize the scars, to ascertain how such things appeal to personal vanity. So you perceive he is occupied and content in his misfortune. But don't think I have for a friend, a man without a heart. He acknowledges the best of the occasion is, that he has made two warm friends, at first sight, by a condensation of events.

"'A man can afford to be knocked down, and carry an inch or so of scars for that,' as he said to me just before I left him.

"'Moreover,' he added, 'these two friends are both very beautiful and noble examples of our dear humanity; and if I am not mistaken, one of them is quite the loftiest woman I have seen for many a day.'

"Now, Cora, if Earnest had said that of you, I should have been jealous; so, Mrs. Torson — I beg your pardon — I ventured to think he referred to you."

Stella could not help smiling, and even blushing, with just perceptible confusion; and Charley felt that she too was "penetrable stuff."

If, on his return from hearing Earnest's poem, he had been slightly surprised and startled by Stella, now he was determined to be completely at his ease. He had not been provoked at her, but piqued with himself, at that time; and he intended to go to the other extreme, being almost saucy, rather than at all disconcerted again, especially in the presence of Cora.

"I have been told by Cora, as well as by yourself," said Stella, taking up the cue of the conversation a short distance back, "that Mr. Acton is what they term 'philosophical,' — considering whatever happens to him, good or bad, as a contribution to his knowledge and advancement. I, too, am a good deal interested in

9*

such views of the world, and as much so in those who entertain them. You told me, the other evening, that your friend had been favored with a somewhat extraordinary inward experience. Cora has detailed for me, some of the facts of his external life. You have known him from childhood. May I ask you to tell me, by and by, or whenever you please, something more about him? We shall meet, now and then, I presume, while I am in your city. I always like to know my friends, when I can, before actually coming in contact with them. It gives one the advantage, perhaps, of a speedier intimacy, and is certainly very pleasant. You will not, I am sure, be surprised at my request, or look upon it as causing you too much trouble, when it refers to one you have commended so highly, and spoken of with so much interest."

Charley Merlow was appeased and happy in an instant. Stella's kind smile; her frankness and simplicity; her freedom from any intention of being imposing, — her care not to make stricken subjects, but happy companions, — which he could not but perceive, in spite of his own accidental moment of confusion; and still more, her acknowledged interest in his chosen friend: — drew Charley directly into the circle of her sympathies, making him heartily ashamed of the suggestion of pertness in her presence. *She* was so far above it, that *he* must not sink to its level.

He said that the most important portions of Earnest's experience, — his revolutions and successions of thought and feeling, — he should prefer to have his friend state for himself.

"I have travelled so often," said he, " or at least

attempted to travel in the orbit of Earnest's mind, that I might possibly draw a tolerable picture of it. But I incline to dread the task. Few things, however, would be more agreeable to me, than to recount all that I can do justice to. He has been my friend almost from infancy. If some facts of his childish and youthful days, with what he thinks of them, would be interesting to you, nothing would suit me better than to begin the recital of them as soon as you like. I have no doubt he will tell you the rest himself. He likes very much to talk in that strain, as he deems his perceptions and emotions, his convulsions, his 'regenerations,' as he terms them, largely expressive and confirmatory of the present epoch in the world's history. It will be easy enough to draw him out. When shall I commence my part? — Now?"

"Bless me! no, not yet!" exclaimed Cora; "I have been discoursing all day myself; and now you'll discourse all night. But don't be frightened: I won't stop you but a minute, just to place myself in position where I can be easy, and enjoy my share of the exhibition.".

So saying, she sat down on the tête-à-tête, and, taking Charley's hand, put his arm around her waist.

"Now the other hand and arm you may have for gestures, my good fellow," she said, with a shrewd smile; "but this set, please bear in mind, is reserved for me, these fine evenings. Be perfectly quiet now, perfectly unabashed. If a couple of young people think a good deal of each other, and my dear, deep, wonderful Stella can't comprehend it, what's the use of all her Plato and the other mighties? But it won't trouble her, I assure

you.   I couldn't help telling her I thought you a very
sweet young man.   Now see that you act like one, and
go straight on with your sermon."

What could Charley Merlow do, but smile, in his
turn, take up the small caressive hand which rested
partly on his knee, kiss it, and proceed?   For he was
a sensible person of twenty-six.

CHAPTER XIII.

"WHEN I first saw Earnest," Charley began, "he was only four years old. His home was just out of the village of Laurel, twenty miles from Boston. I was a year older than he. My father had recently moved from another part of New England, and had settled with his family in that village. He started from our house, one pleasant summer evening, an hour before dark, to take a walk. I asked, as usual, to go too. He seldom refused me. I trotted along at his side, and he walked out of the village, on the road to Boston. We passed the house of Alger Acton — Earnest's father — and having proceeded a short distance beyond it, were returning, when we saw coming down the road toward us, a high-spirited white horse, of Arabian mould, drawing a light single carriage, in which were two children. They were very young, the smallest being scarcely more than an infant. The other seemed a year or two older. He sat up straight and important, holding the reins. The horse quickened his trot, and approached us faster and faster. My father felt assured that something was wrong. He scanned the horse quickly, then the children, and as they came up, he stepped in front of the horse, spoke to him, and stopped him.

" ' My young friends,' he asked, ' where are you going with this large fiery horse ? '

" ' Just to take a little ride, sir,' replied the oldest child.

" ' What is your name,' continued my father.

" ' Earnest Acton, sir; I live in the first house back there.'

" ' Well, how old are you, my bright young horseman ? '

" ' I'm four years old, sir, and my cousin Doty Tetson here, is two and a half.'

" My good father was sure he had made no mistake in stopping this precocious party.

" We heard, now, another voice on the road, and, in an instant, a middle-aged, blue-eyed man, with a look of vexation, humor, and gratitude commingled on his face, was added to the group. He glanced at the children, at the horse, then at my father.

" ' I thank you, sir,' he said, ' for taking the responsibility to check the pleasures of these hopefuls. The eldest is my son; the other is my nephew. They were in a fair way to be killed in a very few minutes. The least flourish of the whip over that horse, would have been their destruction. I allow no one to drive him but myself.'

" The affair was explained to us. Mr. Acton had returned, a few minutes before, from a drive to a neighboring village. He had left the horse fastened near his barn, and had entered the house. The little boys were together near by. When he had disappeared, Earnest had proposed to Doty that they should take a ride. Earnest said he could drive, of course he could.

He helped Doty into the carriage, unhitched the horse, and climbed in himself. The horse, without much guidance, turned the vehicle round, and started off on the turnpike, toward Boston.

" But my father had interfered with this proceeding.

" Earnest was directed to get out of the carriage, and walk home. Mr. Acton permitted Doty to ride back to the house with him. But Earnest was in disgrace. He started along the road with his head down.

" In the mean time, however, I had made a hero of him. Such a little fellow, driving that big horse, in so much danger, yet perfectly confident, was surely worth knowing. I must make him my friend.

" Well, said I, going up to him, you brought the horse along pretty well, as far as you came, anyhow.

" My opinion seemed partly to dispel his shame. We walked together, chatting, until we reached his father's house ; then my father and I proceeded home. But Earnest and I knew each other ; we had come to a good understanding, and were to be friends.

" But the particulars of our attachment, during the next ten years, the actions of my friend, a mere child, though no doubt interesting to ourselves, at the time, could hardly be entertaining to others.

" When he was ten years old, his father moved, with the family, here to Ironton. Earnest was thus torn away from me, and for four years I saw him only twice. But on parting, we promised to remain friends forever. We frequently wrote to each other. When he had grown to be a fine fellow of fourteen, I visited him, and we attended the same school for a year. During the year, several little incidents which the school-boys regarded exciting, occurred in Earnest's life, and were impressed upon my memory. Do you think it would be worth while to recount them?"

"Yes," said Stella, "let us have them."

"Yes," echoed Cora, with a wink at Stella, "if I *must* listen, I like to hear about people before they grow to be so big and stupid, that when you continue their history, no one can believe or understand it."

Charley proceeded.

"Our instructor was Mr. Tome.

"'Earnest Acton,' said he, one day as the boys came in from recess, — 'Earnest Acton, come here. What did you kick Henry Logbun for, from one end of the yard to the other, as I saw you do just now?'

"'I kicked him a few times, sir, to show him what I thought of tell-tales; but I didn't hurt him much.'

"Such was the question that Mr. Tome asked, and such the answer he received.

"Earnest was called up before his teacher, and Henry Logbun was told to stand at his side.

"Logbun was older than Earnest, and was taller and stouter. He was a dull, heavy boy, remiss in his studies, and clumsy in play. He had acted the part of an informer against Doty Tetson, Earnest's cousin — the little fellow that was riding with him on the day our acquaintance began. They had lived together ever since, and were like brothers.

"Doty was a favorite. He was now twelve years old. He was loved by Earnest, loved by all others. He was crammed so full of fun that no amount of repression could quite hold it. If he laughed aloud, or if his chubby mouth took to whistling, it was as

nearly a matter of spontaneous combustion as could
possibly occur, where the tempering waters of free-will
were supposed to be bottled with the qualities which
caused the explosion.

"Doty Tetson whistled. Mr. Tome knew well
enough it was Doty, and no one else; but he turned
round, with severe dignity, desiring to know who had
made that noise.

"The many blank faces which met his inquiry, the
many surprised, wandering eyes, turned every way but
the right one, assured him unmistakably, that his
scholars had all been wholly devoted to their books, at
just that important juncture, and couldn't possibly give
him satisfactory information.

"Earnest sat directly behind Doty; but when Mr.
Tome spoke, he was very busy with his lesson, or appeared to be so. The expression of his face, if any inference could be drawn from it, showed that the whole
affair, the whistling and the investigation of it, was a
matter entirely beneath his smallest attention.

"Mr. Tome passed him by without a word. He
knew that if directly questioned, Earnest would not lie;
he would flatly refuse to answer, taking the conse-
quences. This would be a point of honor with him.

"Besides, Mr. Tome didn't really desire to be told
that Doty Tetson was a culprit who, as a matter of example at least, deserved the rod. In his heart he
didn't want to punish the little fellow. But his school
must be kept quiet and orderly. It wouldn't do to ignore a case of plain, round, palpable whistling. So
he repeated his question.

"'Who made that noise?'

10

"If no one had answered it, this time, he would have soundly rapped some bench near his hand, then, holding up the ruler, would have reminded the boys of what would be the fate of him who should again transgress.

"This was one of his methods of government that his brightest scholars had long since discovered, and made application of.

"But dull Henry Logbun had not. Trembling, and at the same time grinning, he whined out:

"'It was Doty Tetson, sir.'

"'Doty Tetson, was it?' replied Mr. Tome. 'Well, Logbun, sit up in your seat! stop your laughing immediately! I will have nothing of the kind.' And down went the ruler across Logbun's fat shoulders.

"He screamed, then whimpered for a moment, and as soon as Mr. Tome turned away, made a face at him.

"Earnest saw it, and a word from him would have insured Henry another and a heartier admonition of the rod. He said nothing, however, but, as Doty Tetson followed Mr. Tome out on the floor, in front of the benches, there to be feruled, Earnest looked savagely at the tell-tale, shook his fist at him, and pointed to the grounds connected with the building.

"This was plainly a threat. What it signified, appeared at recess, when, as Earnest admitted, he kicked Henry a few times, but without hurting him much.

"Then Earnest himself held out his hand, and took half a dozen hard, conscientious blows from Mr. Tome's ruler. He received them without any shrinking, as something expected, and with which he had no fault to find. Two or three tears silently dissolved from pain, were brushed quickly from his cheek, then he turned, and with no sign of disrespect for his teacher, but with a look of ungovernable haughtiness and self-satisfied triumph, he took his seat.

" Henry Logbun carried a few bruises on his person for a day or two, and so careful a remembrance of them while his school-days lasted, that there was no further occasion to beat him for gratuitous tattling.

" But a second rupture grew out of this first one.

James Groby was the largest boy at school. A few days after Doty Tetson's freak of whistling, Groby said to him :

" ' Oh, nonsense, Doty ! you think, of course, there's nobody like your Cousin Earnest. He took your part against that lummox Logbun. What if he did ? Logbun's a baby, if he is big. Earnest wouldn't have tried anything of that sort on *me.*'

" ' Hadn't better give him a chance,' replied Doty : ' you're almost a man, and he's only fourteen ; but if you wind him up, he'll strike like a clock, every time ; mind that.'

" James Groby by no means relished Doty's opinion, that any boy in school would dare oppose him. But the conversation was cut short by the bell, and the boys were soon engaged with their lessons.

" Earnest came in late, and knew nothing of what had been said. That afternoon he was to be very busy. A long and tedious algebraic problem had taken up a good part of his time in the morning, and as soon as he entered the school-room, he sat down to finish it.

" His slate was full of figures. Mr. Tome was hear-

ing a recitation in a part of the room farthest from
Earnest's seat, with his back turned toward it.   James
Groby sat about a dozen feet from Earnest, in an arm-
chair, having a movable board attached, which could be
used as a writing-desk ; and beneath the seat was a
drawer in which Groby kept his books.   Next him was
an unoccupied chair, with an old cushion in it.

" As Mr. Tome was so far from the boys who sat in
this part of the room, some of them had grown restless,
and were throwing at each other such bits of paper, and
crumbs of sweet-meats, as their pockets contained.   It
was seldom that Earnest participated in such vagaries ;
not because he was always obedient, but because he
considered them beneath him, — too small a business.
Now he was so much occupied, that he paid no attention
to anything around him.   He had pretty nearly worked
out his problem, and was eager to finish it.   Several
times, small missiles had hit him, and had caused him
some irritation.   He told the boys that he was in no
mood for play, — they had better let him alone:

" James Groby heard it, and, whispering to a boy
who sat near him, said that Earnest Acton was ' putting
on the man a little too high, and must have his steeple
dropped off.'   Then, catching up the old cushion from
the unoccupied chair, he tossed it directly on Earnest's
slate.   It rubbed out a portion of his figures.   The
problem couldn't be finished, unless by beginning almost
anew, and his day's labor was lost.

" He looked for an instant at his slate, then at the
face of James Groby, who sat laughing at him, knowing
that he would bring no complaint before Mr. Tome,
and fearing nothing worse.   Then Earnest laid his slate

and the cushion on his desk, got deliberately up, and walking to Groby's chair, struck him so furiously, as he leaned on one side to avoid the blow, that Groby and his chair, his writing-board, books and inkstand, all tumbled on the floor in one confused and noisy heap.

" The boys arose in their seats, astonished and frightened. Groby extricated himself from the chair, but was so completely astounded, that he made no attempt to retaliate. Mr. Tome hurried across the room, bidding the boys sit down. By a few inquiries, he learned the cause and circumstances of the quarrel. After expressing his surprise, that one so old as James Groby, should, as he said, ' seek instruction for his mind in the peccadilloes of children,' he addressed Earnest Acton.

" ' My child,' said he, ' you do not mean to be vicious, but you have a temper which I sometimes fear will prove your ruin. You have good qualities with it, and if these should by-and-by yoke it to themselves in the pursuit of noble objects, you will perhaps rise to superiority by reason of this very fault. But if not — if such a force should be connected with evil aims — the misery you will bring upon yourself and others, will be greater than any human being should inflict or endure.'

" Having said this, the good man returned to the class he had left, and never again alluded to the afternoon's outbreak.

" But his words were rooted in my memory. They partly expressed my own vague imaginings. I had dimly marked out in my mind a lofty career for my friend. I couldn't tell what it would be, but I pictured

10 *

it as powerful, while I couldn't believe it would be ruinous and disgraceful."

"Was your friend uncommonly studious," asked Stella, who seemed to desire that Charley should still continue his account of Earnest.

"By no means," said Charley. "His recitations were always creditable, as his lessons were easily learned. Usually one or two depended more or less upon him at classes. But here, he didn't seem ambitious to excel, — only to show that he could do so if he desired. He was a boy. His ambition was that of a boy: it was of a physical cast. Once out of the school-room, he was the head and life of all sports and contests. No one of his age and size could match him in most of them. Was it wrestling? He was always ready. Was it running? Few would attempt to catch him. Had the season come for snow-balling? His own snow-ball was almost as sure as a gun-shot, and as hard as a stone.

"Of course this endeavor for mere physical excellence soon passed away. But now he can enter into, and appreciate all tones of mind, — not only that of the intellectual saint, but also that of the rough boxer; for, to some extent, he has himself been both.

"I must tell you one further instance of his boyish dash, and impudence, and daring. It also speaks of the command he exercised over his school-fellows.

"His cousin and pet, Doty Tetson, had again got into trouble, and was again punished, but, as Earnest imagined, with some injustice, and undue severity. It was just before school was dismissed in the afternoon. As the boys rushed out, Earnest, pale with anger, collected them together, marshalled them up in front of the door, and actually drove them into giving three groans for their respected teacher.

"But for years, he didn't forgive himself for this insult to Mr. Tome, whom he really loved and revered. It was the source of acute bitterness to him, for many days, and more than one sleepless night. His kind preceptor knew him much better than he himself could, and easily pardoned even this indignity, — pardoned it with tears in his eyes. Perhaps it was for this reason that Earnest regretted it more than any other single act of his boyhood. It was difficult to intimidate him; but beneath the rays of kindness, his whole nature would melt."

CHAPTER XIV

"IT is Earnest's theory," continued Charley, "that the record of childhood is necessarily uninteresting, unless the eye is fixed on the future of the child. As 'father of the man,' the boy is engaging. Apart from that, save in our own love of the little one we protect, we pass over his history. It is an account of romping; the chasing of objects symbolized by the butterfly; of heedless endeavor for the gratification of impulses; of loving the nearest objects, but fearing and shrinking from the many; of sportive cruelty toward insect and animal. Each child is a little hunter, a little savage, — afraid of all things, yet, having the strength, he would clutch the stars for his playthings. We scrutinize the early days of the prominent, and of our friends, only that we may see how and why their later days were so vivid and important to us.

"I have told you of Earnest when a child, placing him, to begin with, where every child is naturally placed, I suppose, — in a period of impulse and activity, awaiting higher things. How do you like the picture of his spirit and ability, his faults, his antagonisms, on the low plain, boyhood?"

"Oh! very well," cried Cora, so hastily that Stella

(116)

had no chance to speak ; " very well indeed, for the
edification of philosophers and prize-fighters, and other
such people.   But I thought you told Stella, the man
had a heart.   What was he doing with it all the while
when he was young ?   Didn't he ever love anybody ?
Wasn't there even one sweet-heart who, at least from
pity, could condescend to just a little tenderness for
such an ugly and outrageous boy ?   Why, Charley,
either he was only half a boy, after all, or else you've
told us only one side of a story."

Charley Merlow was silent for a moment, under this
storm of raillery, and then said :

" Yes, Cora, you are right.   You shall have the
other side of the story now, while I am in the humor.
But to punish you for the terror inflicted on me by
your criticism, I shall leave you for at least ten minutes, while I go home and get a letter which Earnest
wrote to me four or five years ago.   He shall speak for
himself on the love-question.   That is a matter I know
nothing about.

" Excuse me, meanwhile," he added, and bounding
to the door, he shut it behind him before Cora could
retort.   But he returned immediately, bringing the
letter.

" Earnest would as soon I should read it to you, as
not," said he ; " for he has often told me, it contains, in
effect, no more the affairs of his own heart than of a thousand others.   Now listen."

· · · " Love, my dear Charley, is a reality the most
beautiful, perhaps, of all.   But there are many follies
and vanities, many affectations and fibs, constantly
clinging to it.   I think it has seldom been deeply un-

derstood or naturally portrayed by the writers. A favorite theory, for instance, is a first love, at first sight,
enduring forever. Has not any one who has once
looked into himself, lived long enough to know better?
I suspect a first love is commonly an illusion vouch-
safed merely to open our eyes."

" There, that will do," Cora interrupted, " it's a
most shocking epistle!"

But Charley persisted in reading.

" 'Tis true, the affections are precocious. I suppose
we-have but a very limited perception of the beautiful,
before we see it in the glances of a maiden. What of
that? By the time she has well aroused the perception, it enables us to see others lovelier than herself.
If we have heart, we shall be thankful to her. But is
our love often ' love forevermore?' Is hers so?

" My friend, open your ear for a confession. I have
a string of loves for you, that, if they were beads, would
reach half round your neck; and if they wholly encir-
cled it, I should not now be jealous.

" When you and I first knew each other, I was four
years old, I believe. Never mind the occasion: you
have laughed at me sufficiently over it. But I insist
that I was simply affording my father's Arab an expert
driver. Well, young as I was, you, my friend, were
not my first love; and I had several of your gender
prior to the other sort. I am serious. Love does not
begin in any distinction of sex; and if we gaze far
enough, I fancy it does not end in any such distinction.

" Before your time, I used to see a little chap, in our
village — I presume he was of about my own age —
who charmed me magically. I was in love with him.

I knew the symptoms. I pined to become acquainted with him; yet I was shy, and scarcely durst approach him. I wanted to do him some favor — anything that would please him, and be accepted. I would have given him my candy — the whole stick — gladly. I wished he might fall off his door-step, that I could pick him up, and comfort him. Yet my fondness was unselfish. I would have thrown myself off, rather than that he should have really been injured in the smallest degree. Poor youngster! I have no doubt he was worthy a better fate than befell him the other day in my memory: so untrue to him had I been, that I could not even recall his name.

"You perceive, my good friend, that you were my second love. We met, and promised, and neither has proved false. This they call friendship.

"However, after moving here to Ironton, I had several passions similar to my first.

"One was for a child whom I courted assiduously for a considerable time, and loved dearly. I gained him as a companion and playmate. He did not correspond with the darling my imagination had pictured him to be, and soon he was deserted. His heart remained whole, and his body grew fat. He is now one of the coarsest, commonest, heaviest young men in the county.

"But when somewhat beyond thirteen, I had *une grande passion*, which lasted me — well, it must have been six months. Here now was an experience to be respected. It was fervid, exalted, even religious. I remember her well, Miss Grey, the dear charmer, as she then appeared. She was a year older than I, which, you know, in a girl, is the same as two or three

years with us. She was pretty, had dark hair, in
ringlets, black eyes, a clear, fresh face, and considerable body. She was rather stout. My ideal was not a
chalk-fed fairy, but a woman with blood in her. I was
not yet Byronic enough even to 'hate a dumpy
woman.'

" I used to see the young lady at church. What
set my heart a-fluttering for her I never knew. There
she was, in the pew, where I could always look at her
— wholesome, quiet, and well-behaved.

" While this love possessed me, there was a revival
connected with the church. My mind had not been
exercised upon religion. I believed what I heard, supposing that the preacher understood the truth, and was
right. I was impressed by his sermons, and trembled
for my soul. Miss Grey, too, was deeply moved. I
was in an agony of fear for her. Hell was depicted in
the most shocking colors. Perhaps I could not escape
it. I felt myself to be an intolerable sinner. But I
prayed in secret, with all my strength, that my adored
might be saved.

" O God! I cried, if either of us, let me be the
sacrifice! I am unworthy ; but spare her innocence
and beauty from everlasting fire !

" I would have given myself to perdition for her
eternal welfare. Was not this love ?

" Meanwhile I was comforted ; I thought I had
found rest among the faithful, and the tempest of my
soul was assuaged. Still, I hesitated to join the
church. I waited to become a little better ; to try
myself a little longer. It seemed that I ought to be
very good, wholly free from guile, to take upon me the

vows and duties of church-membership, to enter the
holy of holies.

" Miss Grey became a communicant. She was confident of her salvation, and I would not doubt it. I
was delighted, and gave thanks with a full heart.

" But the young lady knew nothing of my struggle
or my happiness. Notwithstanding I loved her with
such intensity, I had scarcely spoken to her in my life.
We were almost strangers. Indeed, I hardly durst
speak to her. I supposed that so much sweetness, so
much worth, could not lavish themselves upon my un-
worthiness. Circumstances were such that we seldom
met, except in the church ; and had we been constantly
together, I could not at that time have mustered sufficient courage, it is probable, to display my tenderness.
Daring, to that extent, would have seemed insane te-
merity.

" It was well that this absorption did not long continue. It was acute, even to pain and debility. But
it went as it came, telling not how or why. I looked
upon that lovely face, until it was not so lovely, and
yet it had not changed. Yesterday I saw it, as I
walked the street. It was still pretty and placid, but,
as I deemed, somewhat lifeless. For me, in all save
kindness and pleasant recollections, it was dead.

" I awoke from my religious frenzy even sooner than
from my dream of love. For some time, as you are
aware, there was nothing but darkness and mist in its
place.

" After the pure and silent adoration for Miss Grey,
I attended a school at which there were both maidens
and young men.

. 11

"Here were two pretty girls who severally inspired me with emotions similar to those connected with my former angel, only not so severe. One was slender, gentle, and yielding, whose chief beauty was a kind smile. Her eyes were blue; her hair would be called auburn, if you disliked to pronounce it a still sunnier hue. She is the worthy wife of an industrious shoemaker. The other enchantress had sparkling black eyes, and hair not a shade lighter. Her laugh was round and loud, her person, large and slightly masculine in movement. She also is married. Her husband is a policeman, saloon-keeper, and expositor of 'the manly art of self-defence.' He is much superior to her *quondam* lover, both in the immensity of his mustache and the compactness of his muscles.

"After the reign of the sturdy brunette, my heart was for a considerable time freër and colder. Still, it was once or twice punctured, if not pierced. I remember particularly well, one strangely simple little incident which occurred to set it fluttering. I was in the street of a morning, and met our Madame de Villier's studious *demoiselles*, walking in their pretty file of couples, when a small boy cried out at them: 'Sheep! sheep!' Suddenly, and from sheer fun, as I fancied, the loveliest and most regal maid of the flock, stepped out of it, caught hold of the child, and shook him into a simple bundle of red astonishment. Just then, ready to burst with laughter, I caught her merry, yet most intense and spiritual eye. She laughed, blushed, and resumed her place, without looking back. Would you believe it? — for weeks I could not drive her or the incident from mind, and I have asked myself a hundred times since, if that dash of independence, connected with her dignity and those spiritual eyes, was not indicative of higher phases of the same trait, and of something very near and dear to my own nature.

"Now I am touched by memories which bow my head in tender respect. Affie Brantome — my friend, you knew her. She rose in the horizon of my brightening manhood, after a long night of gloom. For three desolate years I had not loved the world, I had not loved myself, when she came, with a softened picture of the summer heaven in her eyes, to glide into my heart, lighting up with her own faith and loveliness, that too dismal shelter. I have told you the sequel. How could I forgive myself, if I did not know that she has forgiven me, and is happy! How her lingering illness veiled that sunny spirit in clouds of melancholy! She thought it would prevent her from becoming a helpful companion, a useful wife. She had lighted my pathway; her own was now dark. She counted on my love — that it would increase with her misfortune; but she would not live a useless pensioner on its bounty. She remembered my pride: I would bear no coldness, no wavering. Poor child! she sent me chilling letters, though it tore her heart to write them. They gave me a sense of uncertainty. Was she trifling, then, after all? I could not know of her saintly renunciation. I wrote her a few kind words, saying they would be the last. She said, in return, that I did not understand her, that she did not understand herself: — pleading not to be forgotten, yet a little while to be loved; but alas! explaining nothing. I persisted in silence, unbroken, complete. God forgive me! I was but nineteen. Is a boy fit to love, or only to be proud?

" Indirectly, and a long time afterward, the explanation came. It bruised and stunned me like the shock of a fall. I was stung to the core of my being. But to what purpose? Affie had regained her health; and the tendrils of her beautiful nature, which must nestle near to some kind support, had partly twined themselves about another existence. I prayed he might be worthy of that lovely flower, wearing it on his breast more carefully, more sacredly, than I had done. I could not ask it now : it was *his.*

" But I am growing sad. I have written too long, — not dreaming, at the outset, where my pen would carry me. In my soul, I press your hand.

" Earnest."

As Cora brushed away a tear, Charley asked her if he had now completed the story to her satisfaction.

" Yes," she replied, " as far, perhaps, as you can. But we shall yet add a lady more charming than all, as the last on his list."

She looked at Stella. But the young widow's face was buried in her hands, — perhaps in thought.

CHAPTER XV.

ON the second subsequent evening, Charley Merlow came again; and this time his friend was with him. Earnest was still pale. A narrow patch on one side of his forehead, almost concealed by the long, clustering chestnut hair which fell over it, was yet a perceptible souvenir of his late rencounter.

Cora met the young men; but Stella was not visible.

"Cora, where is Mrs. Torson?" asked Charley, who was now always perfectly at home in the house of Richard Clandon.

"Know, Mr. Impertinence," was the reply, "that the lady isn't quite ready to come down stairs. If you wish, I'll step and ask her what she is doing at just this instant:—it might be interesting, it might not. Or if you'll wait a few minutes, tolerating my company meanwhile, then, I presume, my friend will appear. Mr. Acton, now, would be perfectly content with me, I'm sure. But our Charley is very difficult to please."

These last words were addressed to Earnest, with Cora's usual look of merriment; and as he knew the goodness of her heart, her light words and her bright face seemed, just then, two of the most agreeable features of the world.

11 (125)

" You are certainly right, Miss Clandon," he responded ; then, with the gentle look of admiration lingering
in his eyes, he turned toward Charley, seeming to say
by his glance, — Well, my good fellow, you have a
treasure, I think.

The three conversed for a few minutes, when Charley
stepped to a window to see something that suddenly
attracted his attention.   Cora called him, and as he did
not come back soon enough, she started toward him,
with the evident intention of accelerating his movements.   Earnest rose, and as the piano stood at his
hand, he touched it.

"He is very noble and very good, isn't he ?   and
very handsome besides," whispered Cora to Charley,
as a noisy carriage rattled by the window.   " How he
and Stella could love each other ! "

Then she returned immediately to Earnest, pulling
Charley by the sleeve.   She had heard a boy in the
street, whistle a tune, that morning, she said ; and
now, while two or three notes that Mr. Acton had
struck, reminded her of it, she must try to play it.
So down she sat at the instrument.   But she was unable to recall the whole of the melody, and Earnest,
who had also partly caught it, somewhere, aided her
by humming portions she could not remember.

When she had run it over once or twice, to her satisfaction, she struck off into some sprightly operatic
music, playing with precise execution and good taste.
Earnest told her so, frankly and respectfully.

• " Oh, yes ! " she said ; " I'm among the champions
about here of the so-sos.   But I'm glad I happened
to play for you in advance of Stella — Mrs. Torson

I .mean. After listening to her, one never asks anything more of poor Cora. The child may go talk nonsense then, — a feat in which she has few superiors. But Stella is a genius. She carries music to a science. She will make the ocean roar, or the elephant tread for you, on the piano ; or she will make the saint pray and the lovelorn maiden moan. Then she will give you a sound that will correspond to a toothache you felt sometime, and you wonder if it's going to begin again. Or, in strict truth and soberness, her playing is the most expressive I ever heard, except from one or two great artists, the best in the country. I've heard her play when I've even preferred her to them. But — and now I'm going to put in a modification, for they say a lady always finds one, when she extols another lady — Stella has a big hand. The man, though, who gets her heart, will find that bigger. Bless me ! I wonder why she doesn't come down ! "

While Cora was thus entertaining Earnest and Charley ; chatting, joking, flying from one subject to another ; and never forbidding the mouth to utter the thought, the fancy, or oddity that popped into her mind ; — Stella, alone in her apartment, was very differently engaged.

When Earnest and Charley came, they had been expected. As their voices sounded in the hall, Stella had begged Cora to go down and meet them alone.

" I want a few minutes, dear, to myself," she said : " then I will be with you.

Cora did as her friend desired. Meanwhile Stella had tried to dream out of a problem, its yet impossible solution.

The truth was, notwithstanding her declaration to Cora that she did not love Earnest; that she could not love any one so suddenly; she felt an indefinite, prophetic dread of meeting him, though she would not give herself up to it.

"No," she soliloquized, "I have seen him but three or four times in my life. Surely I am not so weak that I need fear meeting him as many times again, before permitting myself such a thought as love. And in any event, is there more than one course? — to walk on till I see when and where I ought to turn? And what if I should love? Where is the danger? Who knows that he would respond to my longing? His heart seems to have passed away from special objects, to a mellowed kindness for all who are noble, and gentle, and fair. But yes, it would be so! He is young; he is generous; he could not repel a heart knowing his, if it painfully leaped out to meet him. It is only too easy for such a soul to love!"

Then Stella experienced once more the heavy, clogging sensation over her heart, which she had felt before her marriage, as she looked out of the window from her father's house, into the sunshine, which blackened instantly to cloud and gloom.

"I *know* it," she murmured: "he can love; and I can love only him. Yet neither of us *must* love. The reality of my youth's dream is before me. Can I myself now drop the veil to hide it from my sight? Yes, I am strong enough to do my duty; I can."

Stella sat awhile in deep, silent meditation, then she bent her body, and bowed her head; but her spirit rose on high.

" My Father," she murmured, " let my soul grow calm by approaching Thee. I know not what to ask; Thou knowest all things best to give. Guide me to see my life's duty, and, seeing it, to shrink not away. Let the example of the world's greatest spirit be ever near me. He was thy noblest Son, my loftiest Brother, by giving all to Thee. In his spirit, grant me to live, grant me to die, — asking no dearer pleasure, no sweeter reward."

Stella rose, and soon joined her friends in the drawing-room. Her face was thoughtful and a little sad. Her brow was very white — almost pallid; but a flush was on her lips and on her cheeks. Her hair was, as usual, plain and glossy, brushed " madonna-wise." Her dress was a black silk, elegantly fitted, but as plain as her hair. It was finished at the neck and wrists by the simple lustre of pure linen — the collar and cuffs. A white, fleecy knit shawl, almost as soft and delicate as lace, was thrown across her shoulders, and yielded pliantly to every motion. Small golden crosses, enamelled with a blue like the azure of her eyes, and closely set with little pearls as the centre of the skyey tint, — these for ear-rings, and a larger cross of the same kind for a breastpin, were her only jewels. She was very fond of the Christian symbol; and in some color — black, or blue, or the gleaming yellow of plain gold — it was almost constantly worn upon her person.

" Why, how long you've staid away from us," said Cora, as Stella entered the room.

" I began to find myself very dull to the gentlemen without you," she continued, as Earnest and Charley advanced to meet her friend, who extended a hand to each of them, — the right to Earnest, as he happened to be on that side, the left to Charley, who did not wait for the other to be disengaged.

" I was not aware it was long," replied Stella. " As for the dulness, it seems to me, the gentlemen's faces and their merry voices flattered my Cora wonderfully, if she had really lost the least particle of her *esprit*."

" Tut, tut !" persisted Cora, " don't you know it's shocking to contradict people ? "

She said this with one of her ever-ready kisses, still declaring that Stella had been up-stairs such a great while, that she couldn't tell without tasting, whether she yet loved her or not.

From Stella's solicitous glance at Earnest's forehead, and her inquiries after his health, the conversation turned once again to the affray on High street, then especially to Jerry Kay.

" What a kind-hearted, quick-witted, demonstrative old blarney he is," said Cora. " I think he's the most Irish specimen of Ireland I ever saw. What fun it is to hear him swear ! I know it's dreadfully wicked in me to say so ; but whenever I hear him, I can't help laughing. I couldn't to save my ears. Stella, why do people swear ? "

" A fair question, truly," replied Stella, " but not so easy as some others, it may be, for me to answer. I believe, however, if you really want to know, there are reasons for the practice in human nature, as there are such reasons for all other human practices. I might give you my opinion, but I should prefer to hear one. Mr. Acton, suppose *you* tell us why people swear."

Stella spoke thus, partly because she wished to hear Earnest talk; partly because, in spite of herself, and needlessly, as she knew, she felt slightly awed by his presence and bearing. It was perfectly simple — even childlike; but there was a certain depth, a certain directness in his most careless actions, in his very motions, which others might not perceive, but which she could as little fail to see. The perception might increase rather than hamper her own powers, — she would be sure of being understood. Still, she wished at first to listen, rather than to speak.

"I am disappointed;" was Earnest's answer to her request. "I expected to hear a much better response to our friend Cora's question, than I could myself offer. I will obey you however; but you must promise to correct me if I should err.

"Swearing," he continued, when the promise was given, "is confined to no locality, I presume. It is a failing of mankind. Men swore by the gods, as they also worshipped them, before their minds rose completely to the conception of one God. Or they swore by some special deity, or by Jove, the 'Father of gods and men.' The name of Jehovah had evidently been used with lightness, before it was necessary to write the commandment: 'Thou shalt not take the name of the Lord thy God in vain.' Profanity seems to me the reverse and dark side of prayer. We instinctively believe in a power above us. We call on it to bless us. If ignorant and filled with hate, we call on it to curse the objects of our hatred. If wrapped in excitement, even over trifles, we are apt to feel as though nothing we conceive as limited, can represent our agitation. So we appeal to the Boundless. An oath is thus a recognition of God, in a low and hasty manner. But our reverence demands that the All-High shall be recognized loftily, — never as we bandy trifles. The third commandment is an inevitable decree of the soul, — as inevitably broken by frivolity and heat.

"But the man who thinks and defines, putting things in their places, has no need to invoke his Creator as he brushes away a fly or describes a toy. We say ' the gentleman does not swear.' The ' gentleman ' we account to be thoughtful and cool.

"I have noticed that the French swear glibly and commonly; the Irish, invariably. These people are hot-hearted, enthusiastic, and light. Their profanity usually means nothing more than that they have a word to say which they cannot say strongly enough to suit them. It is so with our kind old friend, Jerry Kay. He intends no harm, but can hardly breathe without mentioning God or the Devil — the highest good, the greatest evil. Well, the human spirit itself can scarcely throb in any direction, but it shall instantly come upon these : — reverence and love in their own way, violence and anger also in their way."

"Thank you, Mr. Acton," said Cora, when Earnest had concluded ; "I've found out then, at last, why I do really ache sometimes to say — well — ' fiddlesticks ! ' I thought there were roots for it in my blood ; I rather suspected the roots were a sort of natural growth in blood generally. They sprout especially in mine, I see now ; for somewhere, at the other end of my pedigree, the Clandons were French-Irish. Charley, don't you like Irish girls ? "

" Certainly I do," replied Charley, " and French girls too."

" Well, then," said Cora, " come here, and sit by me a minute, which you haven't done this whole blessed evening. Mr. Acton, as I know, likes the Germanic blood, or the old Grecian. That means Stella. Come, let us arrange ourselves according to our attractions for blood, — not gentlemen with gentlemen, and ladies with ladies, as some evil genius has now assorted us. It's dreadfully stiff. For my part, I always liked to sit with the boys, even for a punishment at school."

With this, she took Stella's arm, and pushed her gently into a chair beside Earnest, at the same time taking Charley's arm and pulling him into the chair beside herself, which had been occupied by Stella.

Both obeyed easily ; for everybody obeys a humorous, capricious, irresistible young woman.

" Now," she exclaimed, " this group pleases me. We'll resume, if you please, our researches into blood, with its morals, manners, and customs."

But they had not conversed long, before she was ready for something else.

" Stella," she said, " I told Mr. Acton, before you came down, about your musical proclivities. My criticisms were very impressive : were they not, Mr. Acton? And haven't you been dying ever since, to hear her play ? "

Earnest said he was at that very moment on the point of requesting her to do so ; and now, that the opportunity had been given him, he must urge her.

" I need but little urging," Stella replied. " I am so very fond of music that I am always glad to be at the

12

piano, when others are really glad to listen. Cora,
what will you have? "

" Oh! a jig for me, by all means!" Cora answered.
" But I think Mr. Acton wouldn't like that. He's
been telling me that he likes the German music, considering it equalled in power and richness only by the
profundity and research of German literature. I believe that's your opinion too. Well, suppose we have
a touch of Mynheer Meyerbeer, to begin with, — say
the ' March ' from the ' Prophet.' That's Teutonic
enough to charm the glass out of the windows."

Once on the stream of music, with Stella as pilot, the
minutes passed to Earnest like seconds. He was
entranced. Charley Merlow was again completely
amazed, and Cora was radiant with delight at her
friend's success.

" A queen, isn't she!" was her exclamation as she
and Charley stood listening together.

If Stella was now absorbed in the elysium of har-
monics which she seemed to create, Earnest would
have been as deeply so, if it had not been for his interest in her on whom such felicity depended. At first
he could not give his thoughts wholly to the music;
for music itself appeared to be embodied in her. He
saw at once that Cora had not exaggerated her merits.
He acknowledged to himself that he had seen no one
who could at all compare with her, except, as Cora had
asserted, one or two public performers, and they among
the most noted in the world. It would have been difficult to convince him that even these could have excelled her, unless, possibly, in their own favorite efforts.
But she played everything, from ballad to oratorio, and

all perfectly. Yes, *perfectly*, in as far as that Earnest could ask for nothing more, in conception or execution, than she was able to render.

In his reading of different authors, Earnest had tried to understand them, not through prepossessions of his own mind, but by creeping into their minds; — by sympathizing with them for the time being; by making *their* outlook *his* stand-point of vision. A book which he esteemed worth reading, he thought deserving of this compliment. The writer once permeated, once comprehended as he comprehended himself, then the reader must judge as to there being a higher outlook than the one just occupied. Earnest now fancied that Stella had done the same in music. Her performance seemed different from that of others, not merely in the faultlessness of the touch, but in the inmost sense of the theme. Her style was her own; yet it was evidently nothing but the most sensitive and accurate appreciation of the grand masters of the art, most dexterously declared by her fingers instead of her words. She had truly " thought to music; " to her it had not been merely a sensuous revel.

To Earnest, sounds were representative of things. He had not made music a study, but he could never listen to it without knowing that he had come in contact with one more phase of that intelligence which is the centre and substance of the universe. He perceived that it expressed his joy, his sorrow, his worship, his mirth. It uttered his attractions, his repulsions. He had asked if gravitation had a heart, and this were the murmurings of its love. He had sat in church when he could bow to God only through the prayer of the organ ; and as some receptive, melodious nature which had no utterence at the lips for its aspirations, but could praise Heaven for blessings, and beg their continuance, by the thanksgiving and the supplication of the key-board, — as genius had thus directly communed with the Father, and Earnest had heard it cease its petition, that perhaps some fleshy face and husky voice in a surplice might say : " We will now *begin* the service of God," — the young man's soul had sunk within him, and all worship had fled.

As Stella now sat at the finest piano that Richard Clandon could procure for his daughter, pouring out all the harmonies of which it seemed capable ; as Earnest stood admiring that superb woman, — how soon and how easily they understood each other ! how impalpably, yet how surely, their spirits conjoined ! She struck up the wild, terrific battle song of *Rouget de Lisle's*. The storm gathered on Earnest's brow, the spring of the tiger seemed flashing from his eye, and his right hand was clenched, as though a sword was in its grasp. She looked up into his flushed face, anticipating, yet almost recoiling from the effect she had produced, and suddenly that epitome of the French Revolution died from her fingers. It melted into an operatic aria of love and hope. As she looked again into his face, how different must have been the emotions it expressed ! For her eye, all softness, turned away, and a deep blush was on her cheek.

CHAPTER XVI.

AGAIN the friends met at Richard Clandon's.

It seems that after Earnest and Stella had been drawn so near to each other by the charm of music, on that early April evening of our last chapter, Stella had spoken of her pleasure in meeting one with whom so close a communion of the kind could be established. Earnest, in return, had applauded her gift with simple directness and fervor. He had said what he thought, with no strain at personal encomium, with no fear of it; but as though the gift itself were above all persons, and separate from them. She had alluded to his poem, to Charley's remarks on it and on him, and to having somewhat interested herself in his history.

"I find we are both given," she said, "to looking for a life deeper than this life, — for the undercurrents of affairs about us. Let me ask a favor of you. I always have a strange curiosity to know what picture of God and man is painted on the thought of a person who strikes me as in any way remarkable for good or ill. I regard it as the index of his actions. In *it* I look for *him*. You like to talk, I know, on subjects which men have deemed the highest. Would you

(137)

think your time wasted in talking upon them to me ? I
wish you would promise to do so sometime."

It was pleasing for Earnest to give the promise she
desired. It might have been a fancy of his, but he regarded his inward experience as in some degree a
mirror of great facts and tendencies about him, as Charley Merlow had intimated to Stella. And why should
he decline to hold this mirror up to the fair, sympathizing friend whose image had already sunk deeply into
his heart ?

When now they met, Stella soon reminded him of
their last conversation.

" I have not forgotten it," he said, " but with your
permission I must modify my promise. Such an account of myself as you wish me to give, requires
compression and exactness, or it cannot be worth your
while. It must relate too, you know, to the deepest
questions that have ever engaged the human mind.
Now if our friend Cora were obliged to listen to it, she
would scarcely hesitate to call it dull, I fear ; and perhaps obscure and heterodox besides. Then the experience is such that I should have to speak of myself in
connection with some very strong minds and illustrious
names. Not at all in *comparison*, of course, so far as
strength and action are concerned ; but as having been
in, and passed through — although in my youth and
weakness — the general phases of thought and feeling,
which they, in their might of personalty, represented
to the world in their time and place. To any one not
having the clearest perception that great men are always representative of ideas and epochs of history, —
that they are merely strong embodiments of a common

progressive humanity,— I should labor under the disadvantage of much apparent egotism. In conversation, too, my narrative would be almost interminable, as it would lack order. But not long ago, I wrote out a summary of the matter, as well as I could, for a young friend, who was earnest, inquiring, and thoughtful ; but sceptical . to the last degree ; and who yet needed to believe in *something*,— needed some faith which could be reconciled with his reason, and on which he could rest. Mine was radical enough ; but I gave it to him for what it was worth, and at the same time pointed out to him those who had helped me reach it. I have brought the paper with me to-night. It is rather long, and would be tedious to many. But you may take it, if you wish, and read it at your leisure, or brand it ' heavy,' and return it to me unread."

Stella accepted it gladly, and after Earnest and Charley went home, she sat up late, and read it very patiently, as follows :

" At sixteen years of age I was at school. During the last year I had lost my boyish vivacity, had grown thoughtful, retiring, and was sometimes much depressed. I had begun to perceive, to reflect, and consider. Who was I? What was around me? What should I do? These are hard questions, and, in general, the last one only is persistently put. But they had all occurred to me, and I could not rest without an answer.

" I did not consciously say so : I merely opened my eyes, commencing a secret and silent questioning of men and things. I felt strong impulses, premonitions, and powers. I had been a leader among boys. But now

circumstances and regulations displayed their checks. I
was in a world of fashions, precedents, establishments.
Wealth was the special crown of endeavor, and every
one was seeking to wear it. It was a despot. It or-
dained castes, like the Hindoo theology. It was the
great Bramin of American society. I saw that it
partially excluded me from certain circles into which
some of my companions might enter. These circles
dubbed themselves the highest, and people accepted the
assumption. My father was not rich : he had accumulated and lost : comfort was left, 'not opulence. Even
then, I did not care for the magnates of society, as I saw
them, or for their favors. But to be excluded, looked
down upon, slighted, by those whom I could not regard
as my superiors, if really my equals, enraged me beyond
measure. Madame Roland herself never hated the
supercilious rich more fiercely than I.

"Pardon me ; but I fancy that if my insight had been
less clear; I should have now started with the rest, in
the foot-race for dollars. In a country free to my exertions as to those of others ; a country not yoked by a
titled aristocracy, only by' a moneyed class, — why
could I not climb the Mammonic hill? So I asked
myself. But I turned, scanned the hill, and pronounced it a lie. I said there was no hill, no height
there, — nothing but an ant-heap which small eyes had
magnified to the Andes. I said that nothing was high
but lofty manhood, which was all running to claws for
the grasping of ingots.

"I was not wholly wrong ; I was not wholly right.
I was ambitious, imaginative, enthusiastic. The petti-
ness of the rich, and their meanness in accumulating

wealth, caused me to detest them, to wonder at the respect paid them by others, and at the airs they took upon themselves. They seemed to me among the least of civilized men. Of course I could not yet perceive their place and use in the world, though it is as definite and necessary as any. But, as I have told you, they sometimes preferred to walk alone,—not at my side. Once in awhile they tossed me a sneer. How I scorned and cursed the presumption. They were superficial and selfish; I had already thought and loved. I was really as snobbish as they; only I would not recognize their special idol. They bowed before lucre; I before culture and intellectual strength. My worship was the better, but not the best. That, I could not yet perceive.

"Thus I doubted society, spurning its notions and ways. Its ideas of life were not mine; nor its ideas of death. Even the God I heard it proclaim, I could not worship. But I was unable to peer through the objects of my antagonism, and through my own position in the midst of them. So I sank into gloom, without a guide.

"My father, a man like the spectral Dane,—

> · · · 'take him for all in all,
> I shall not look upon his like again,'—

could neither gratify my longings, nor teach me the wisdom to forego them. His kind, self-sacrificing, trustful heart, had no experience by which to interpret mine. He was astonished at what he had never before seen — settled misanthropy in a mere boy. He was cheerful, upright, and simple-minded, with such perfect faith in the ultimate right, that he did not ask to *see* it. He was a good man, without caring a great deal whether he was regarded so, or not; an honest man, who would have been just as honest if there had been no courts or jails in the universe, — simply because he felt it sweet and pleasant to be honest; and he was practically a Christian man, without knowing or believing much of ecclesiastical doctrine, but conceiving, in his tender, upright soul, that the Golden Rule contained the substance of religion. In short, he was a natural man in an artificial epoch. He could not help me. Who could?

"About this time I became interested in the strange, sad poetry of Byron, which appealed directly to my disconsolate, combative state of feeling.

"Prior to becoming acquainted with the 'noble bard,' and while at school, I had gobbled my share of the common novels very properly termed of the 'blood and thunder' description, and a few books of better quality. Of the novels I soon forgot even the names; but if they had all been piled together, and called 'The Long-Bearded, Big-Booted, Bloody-Branded Rover, or the Magic Jib-Boom of the Bay of Biscay,' this appellation would perhaps have rendered a general notion of their calibre.

"When about eleven years old, I had delighted in a well-known sporting paper, and had read accounts of the principal English, Irish, and American pugilists. Then I was ambitious to be short and thick-set, a person of superior muscle, handy at 'straight-out' blows, 'upper-cuts' and 'under-cuts.' I did not quite want to go into the 'ring,' but imagined it would be a positive accomplishment to have the prowess and the 'science' to go there, while yet remaining out.

"This view of things soon passed away, as also the desire to become a sailor, — with which 'the Magic Jib-Boom of the Bay of Biscay' had inoculated me to such an unwholesome degree, that like many another foolish lad, I occasionally determined to pack up my trunk, depart from my dear old father and loving mother, and become a second and mightier 'Jib-Boom.'

"The ring and the sea having faded from my vision, the martial hero appeared. Napoleon — what a man was he among the giants! though Murat, his dashing marshal, with the high, waving plume, seemed in some points the more dazzling leader.

"Thus my reading had advanced from the idea of strength marvellous and monstrous, to the idea of strength more natural. But still the heroes of my collection were all strong men, not necessarily good ones. There were no saints among them. They were upright and generous, and truthful enough; — because it would have detracted from their greatness to be otherwise; — good fellows as well as mighty, but not too much hampered by any strict sense of duty.

"The heroes we worship, are our ideals embodied and accomplished. What I was at this period, in my central tone of mind, in my feelings and wishes — without, of course, any ability to execute them — Achilles, and Alcibiades, and Themistocles, had lived and acted in Greece, Cæsar and Antony in Rome, and Napoleon in modern Europe. These were all powerful, selfish men of the world, who could secure what they sought in it, and who could do as pleased them best.

" At this time I encountered the fiery soul of Lord Byron, through his ' Harold ' and ' Corsair,' his ' Vision,' his ' English Bards,' and his ' Don Juan.'

" Here, again, was depicted, in the most wildly fascinating colors of feeling and imagination, mere strength — ambitious, dark, wasted strength. Yet the devil in such guise seemed more beautiful than an angel; and who but Byron should thenceforth be my criterion of greatness; and what but poetry was worth man's while beneath the sun.

" But it was decided that I must engage in some kind of business. I was offered a position in a mercantile establishment, and took it. My duties were light, and I had several hours of leisure each day. Sometimes, in fact, I could have almost the whole day. Without neglecting my business, I was sure to occupy the spare time, book in hand.

" Here my outward life was floating along in the quiet, ordinary channel. But my mind and heart were rolling, surging, and tumbling, far out on a stormy sea. My body was amid the surroundings of commerce. My soul was scudding on chaos, impelled by one restless motor — ambition, toward one goal — poetical glory.

" How could I be happy? When alone, if not applying myself relentlessly to some book, I was sure to be munching my sorrow. I took every occasion for retirement that I possibly could. I seemed out of place in the world, and the world seemed sadly out of place itself.

" But was such a state of mind independent? Was it not derived from Byron's influence?

" The writings of Byron first brought to my mind

a keen inherent taste for literature, and especially for
poetry. Then followed the ambition to convert the
taste into a power. From the exercise of the power, I
desired greatness, glory. So far, then, the influence of
Byron merely discovered to me what finally appeared
to be my ' effectual call,' my dearly beloved, my chosen
pursuit.

" But why the melancholy? Was not that the fruit
of the bard's morbid hold upon a young, plastic mind?

" No. Byron's influence was again a stimulant, not
a cause. It only came to properties ready and waiting.

" What covered Byron himself with gloom? He
broke into a world which he regarded as foolish, frivolous, and unkind; its people little in aspiration and
endeavor — ' tickled with a straw '; large in selfishness — grasping each at the all of every other man.
Their pursuits, so important and engrossing to themselves, seemed to him the mere strivings of children for
a larger kind of toy-houses than their infancy delighted
in, and for a play-ground increased in extent while
diminished in innocence. Their conception of God
was, to him, a variable and dubious ogre; and their
conception of their own relation to their Creator, a
matter of mere assent to uncertain formulas, — a thing
of belief, which he could not believe, — a matter of set
devotions, church-presence, and water-drops. And he
himself — what was he? Where was his place in this
odd, interminable labyrinth? How was he different
from the rest? unless, indeed, in knowing that they
could not be right, — that they were far from wise, and
that he, too, was more distant from wisdom than even
from sympathy and harmony with them. Was he not, .

13

in fact, more miserable, more pitiable than they? They could rest secure in their credence, and satisfied with their vocations. However sandy the foundation of the one, or trivial the pursuit of the other, to them, these things were stable, and important, and real. While he, searching for absolute truth, could find no resting-place for the sole of his foot; enamored of perfect beauty, must everywhere drag with him, in quest of it, a poor body touched with distortion; and loving justice and right, as the ideals of his inmost soul, must still be as painfully conscious of incumbent flesh-pots, of muddy promptings, and selfish, savage passions, as any honest parson that ever accepted the notion of total depravity, or dreaded an outward, personal, hotly-located Devil.

"Strong, wilful, sad man! — a groping colossus amid a thousand wondrously charming mirages, where, for want of an abiding, greenly-growing faith, all was still a desert! He stood on the crust of the world in his time, knowing that beneath him it was hollow, — the philosophy, theology, ethics, all mummies dead and buried, but wrapped in cerements still costly and venerable, which to him were curious, like all idols of man's historical worship, yet which could not seem more than dreams, and could inspire no higher sentiment than an occasional half-tremor of fear, as at the possible reality of ghosts. Yes, he stood on the surface of creeds and customs, and stamping with his heel, broke them through, beholding their shallowness and falsity. Then he strained his eye toward the heavens, trying to see an angel who could yet explain to him how this might be, and be well; — how altars might crumble and fall, and still the altar of worship be ever holy;

how creeds might totter and tumble, and belief still be man's halo of happiness; how systems of religion could be false, and religion itself be true; how imperfection, sin, misery, could universally abound, and man still be the child of God, created for a blessing to himself, and a joy to the spheres. He strained his eye to the heavens, but the heavens gave no sign. He had not yet the innate charm to invoke the angel, and she could not come. He rolled and tossed on the waves of doubt and denial, scarcely even approaching the *terra firma* of faith, until just as he was called away from the shrine of muse and sage, to a realm which faith alone, as it seems, can discover and vivify.

" It was left for other and later minds to accept the same doubt and denial, — to perceive the barrenness of creeds, and systems, and establishments; — then to reconcile this perception with a higher, a purified belief. Byron in youth, Goethe in youth, were the. symbols of an inevitable dissatisfaction, an unavoidable scepticism, which the ripeness and decay of old institutions necessitated for the regeneration of Europe. Byron, the young man, flamed high, and then went out, while the symbol was unchanged; Goethe, the old man, lived to see that the youth, Goethe, was miserable and fantastic, because, perceiving the falsity and rottenness of the world's standards of truth, he could not see beyond his own scepticism. But to the old man, truth was not doubtful or dead, while many things which had been commonly accepted as truths, were forever inhumed.

" But what could a poor child, like myself, know of all this? Before I could comprehend it, my own mind

must be lifted into the sunlight. I must be dashed
against some sharp, ragged juts of experience; must
often be thrown violently in upon my inmost soul,
to wonder, and reflect, and suffer; must mount high
on many a towering peak of thought, borne up by
other intellects, as a traveller on the shoulders of some
clear-headed, sturdy guide. Now I was a boy. I had
thought, and felt, and read enough to doubt, to discredit, to hesitate. I had stumbled on questions I
could not answer; had wept and despaired over
defects, sins, and sorrows — my own and others' —
which I could not penetrate and solve. In short, my
tone of mind epitomized in miniature the chief phase
of the general advance of mind in the last half of the
eighteenth century, and the earliest part of the nineteenth. This epoch was strangely foreshadowed in
Shakespeare's character of 'Hamlet'; Britain incarnated it in Byron, and Germany in the early manhood
of Goethe and Schiller. Voltaire was a partial embod-
iment of it; but the sprightly Frenchman, though the
essence and full-bloom of intellectual scepticism, had
scarcely the central earnestness of nature to be un-
happy about any thing. Germany, however, possessed
this trait in a most remarkable degree. While doubting to the depths of negation, the German soul grew
sorely sick of doubt. It *must* break through denial, to
something better, or *die*. So Germany built up the
new faith of to-day; and her children have been those
' semi-Greeks ' who ' think for Europe,' and for mankind.

" Their thought is now the thought of the nations.
Byron passed away from Britain; and what he might

have been had he longer lived ; what Goethe was in
mature years ; — came largely to life in an odd, sono-
rous, angular Scotchman, Thomas Carlyle. France,
whose *Père Bonhours* was suspended over the pool of
oblivion by a single thread, according to that same
Scotchman, in memory of having once asked : ' *Si un
Allemand peut avoir de l'esprit ?* ' — France received
the new wine into her very best mental bottles, from
Madame de Staël to Victor Hugo ; and it has become
even a popular beverage, spiced as only France —
nicely discriminating, critical, executive France — can
flavor the riches of her sunny vineyards. In America,
flowing especially through the deep, deep, but clear
crystal goblet of Emerson, and through the broad,
heavy Saxon mug of Theodore Parker, it has done
much more than editors and the clergy know, to
shatter unsightly decanters of Church and State, and
to infuse into the gigantic young Republic, freedom of
body, freedom and vigor of soul.

" I said that the frame of mind which enveloped me,
and which I have been trying to describe, was a sort
of summary and likeness of the first part of our
century.

" I had lived, as it were, within myself, the history
of the world's life, up to a certain stage of its development.

" Man, as his records portray him, was at first a
simple, cruel, superstitious, pettish being, robust and
shaggy in body, and constantly at war, family with
family, tribe with tribe. Large physical bulk, with corresponding force and activity — ability to crush enemies — was the desire of the aspiring, was the one constit-

13*

uent of greatness. Some Samson or Hercules was the great man, the admired of swains and maids. Mankind took one step forward, and force of mind, applied to the same end — war — constituted greatness and achieved glory. The man who could plan an ambush, invent an arrow or spear, was plainly more powerful than one of huger body, with his weighty fist, or a club. Bigness of proportion — brute bulk — was first eminence ; then came a sort of cultivated animalism of the intellect : — first the fighter, whose art lay in his height, his arms, his thighs ; then the handy bowman, or swordsman, or organizer of men into companies.

" In my feelings, in my ambition and imagination, I had been each of these. The pugilist, sporting-paper in hand, proud of his ' manly art,' is nothing more or less than primordial man the savage, of I know not how many thousand years ago. The alphabet and broadcloth have not essentially changed him. When I pictured myself as ' The Long-Bearded, Big-Booted, Bloody-Branded Rover,' fighting for fame, for revenge, for riches, I had advanced one degree, and become the fillibuster — Romulus, or Norman William, Spanish Pizarro, or William Walker.

" Then I took another step.

" In recognition of the absolute supremacy of intelligence, the pen had been declared mightier than the sword. I, too, felt that it was greater to think, to know and declare, than to wield the blade of the soldier. Now I was in the realm of intellect, looking down upon physical ambition and force. I wanted them not; but longed to command fame and power through the exercise of thought and feeling. How far had I grown in

my wishes and objects ? From the savage to the man
of letters. It seems a good distance. But ambition
was the incentive ; glory, power, the end. For fame I
would have brandished the pen as ferociously as ever a
Carib his club, or a Gallican his battle-axe. Not quite
indiscriminately, right or wrong, against friend or foe ;
yet almost any way to accomplish the purpose.

" Here was a ' power-man,' — a Mandingo carried
up into the sphere of intelligence and refinement.

" It is a most unfortunate temper of mind. It is an
exalted mental cannibalism. It is still mere strength,
grasping for its object — fame, wealth, enjoyment,
power : — not literally eating up the body of its victim,
not necessarily delighting in his torture ; — for the
senses have become sublimed ; — but heedless of any
fate that may befall him, willing to submit him to any
fate, if only he stands in the way. What cares it, really and inherently, for man or woman ? ' Self ! self ! '
is its cry, — ' Give ! give ! ' — ' What I crave, that will
I have ! '

" Yet such, on the one hand, has been the shout of
men, the shout of the ages, from barbarism to the highest civilization.

" On the other hand, there has been a censor and director — conscience, religion, God. Men have asked,
when self demanded a thing, ' Shall I do it ? Dare I
take it ? ' They have said, ' There is One above ;
there is duty to him. Is it not better to forego this
pleasure, to resist this temptation, than to disobey Him
who must know and order best ? ' They have bowed
and believed ; they have constructed systems of faith ;
they have obeyed.

" But they have grown also. The faith, the truth of one age, has been the doubt, the falsehood of the next. And the breaking-up of a special faith, too often, perhaps always for the time, brings universal misgiving and disbelief. Men deny a certain conception of God, a certain standard of right, which they perceive to be *not* God, *not* right; but alas! they often see no farther than the contradiction: they doubt God himself, and are not clear that right exists. Still, sense clamors for its dinner, the body for its joys, the mind for the indulgence of its appetites and tastes. Now where is the censor, the director? What voice shall say: ' Peace; be still?' At most, nothing better than the higher attributes of selfishness — refined calculations and fears — can control and rectify. Humanity may then be courteous, dignified, sparkling; it cannot be conscientious, it cannot be good. ' Voltaire,' said one who knew, ' was the *cleverest* of all men past or present; but a great man is something more, and this he surely was not.' No, the doubter, the denier, cannot be truly great, but merely strong and smart. Cultivated antagonism is dexterity, not ability. Ability journeys with the stars in celestial orbits. It sits in God's hand, and moves with that. Where *that* moves, let not mere power — man's selfish strength — be stationed, thinking to stand. It must bow low, and supplicate for light; or it shall fall crushed, bleeding, dead ! "

CHAPTER XVII.

STELLA leaned back in her chair, wrapped for a few minutes in deep meditation. Then she took up the manuscript and resumed reading.

"I have endeavored to account, from my own experience, for the cause of the sadness, violence, and discontent, which have pervaded so many minds and so much of our literature, in recent days. It came unavoidably from the growth of mind itself, which had become too large for its ancient forms of belief and action, but was destined to grope awhile sullenly in the dark, before it could clothe itself with better. It is necessary for every soul to feel that it is of use in the world, and to hope confidently for its future well-being, if it is to have present content. How much we are dependent on faith! It smooths all our actual ills into future blessings. The poorest faith is better than none. But our faith is always dependent on our perceptions; even if we perceive nothing more than good grounds for trusting our neighbor, and believing as he does.

"When thirteen years old, being of Puritanical, orthodox stock, I was a Calvinist, just as I should have been a Mohammedan, if born in Constantinople, and my mother had attended a mosque. That is, the

weight of local circumstance was upon me, and I took
its assertions for granted.

"The first time I distinctly contradicted it, was
directly on this point of sect. A well-meaning man,
with a low forehead, preached the everlasting perdition
of all Pagans, Romanists, Jews and sundry, reserving
a contracted, insipid heaven for the mouthful of men
and women belonging to his own denomination. I
was not quite fourteen. I asked myself — doubting
for the first time — if the minister could be right. I
never insulted my God but once by so foolish a question. In twenty seconds I had broken forever from
my accidental church.

"But I was driven to think. If here was not the
truth, where should I find it?

"I never doubted, for an instant, the existence of
God. I could not doubt it, though I knew not the
reason. It seemed as much a fact, as my own existence. I should have doubted both, if one. I have
since read many writings on the subject, among others,
those of that wonderful anatomist of the human soul,
Immanuel Kant. I have seen that our faculties rest
directly upon the idea of God, — that they cannot take
a step in consideration of themselves, or in any direction, without it, — that it is the one pivot whereon
each and all of them swing. But at the time of
which I speak — in my boyhood — it was enough for
me, as for the world, to *feel* the fact; I did not ask
why. Neither did I demand why there should be religion — man's duty to God. Its germs and promptings were in the core of my being. I might as well
have ignored the whole of my nature as this part. It

was only the theology that I began to rebel against. But they told me the theology was religion — the Christian religion. I must believe it, or be harried along into the pit, with the Pagans and Catholics. I concluded to go, if that was the understanding. But it did not trouble me much. The doctrine was too absurd, too horribly wicked, to inhere long in a healthy mind. It was a sort of pip, to which, at the time, as a young chicken, I was liable.

" Yet now that I began to interrogate them, many other doctrines seemed no better. Then came my disavowal of money as the measure of worth ; my longings for intellectual power and fame. They could not be gratified ; and it was well. The period of negation and subversion had been fully represented. Constructive minds were already in manly vigor, though I knew not of them. Within a day's ride were two of the loftiest in the world. But it was to be several years before I could grope my way to them, as there was no sympathetic soul to guide me. So what with my ambition, my doubts, and the knowledge of my sins and imperfections, down I dropped into the misanthropy that I have referred to.

" Poetry, as a pursuit and solace, was here paramount. I loved Byron and his thrashings of hypocrisy, with all my heart. I liked thrashings in general. I thought the world needed all it ever received. I ached to thrash it myself. But instead, it was giving *me* the knout, as I needed.

" No modern poem helped me much, except ' Festus.' For I craved something that would lift me to a sight of the axis of the universe. Then I could perhaps discover why I was whirling around it. 'Festus' is a fair attempt to do this. It has been a strenuous aid to many. It is the crystallization of Universalism, and the doctrine, like the crystal, sparkles with manifold hues of love. But the book and the teaching are theological and mythological. They are the half-way-house between 'Orthodoxy' and rational Christianity.

" Meanwhile I read some of the sceptical writers of the eighteenth century. I could not but credit many of their statements. But they appeared cold, suspicious, mental. They did not sufficiently distinguish between religion and theology ; but inclined to ridicule both. I read some of the chief ' Evidences of Christianity,' ancient and modern ; but never found one that gave me any satisfaction.

" At last, a plain, quaint man put into my hands a book of Theodore Parker's sermons. Theodore Parker ! Who was he ? I had seen· his name in the papers ; I had heard him called an ' infidel.' That, I knew, sometimes meant a man who doubted miracles ; sometimes one who doubted the 'Fugitive Slave Bill.' I had heard Beecher called an ' infidel ; ' but on reading his discourses, had found only a great, munificent heart, near to God and man, but not very different in leading ideas from my first good parson. It seems astonishing now, that I did not sooner find something to lead me to Theodore Parker. But I fancied him a clever preacher, like Beecher or Chapin, — stronger, broader, better, but not much *higher* than others. I loved these men ; but they had not the kind of light I needed. My friend loved them too. But he said, as he gave me the volume of sermons : ' You will find your doctor here.'

" He was right.   Here, indeed, was the first glimpse
I ever had of an American giant, standing up, head
and shoulders, with the loftiest thinkers of the human
race.   The others had been cramped and insulated.
I had now come upon a spiritual cosmopolitan.   Horsed
on a score of languages, he had sped through the
literature of all times and all places.   What men
had anywhere thought, what they had felt, what they
had done, that he knew.   Could Napoleon sit on his
horse sixteen or eighteen hours a day ?   Here was an
iron man, who could keep the saddle of letters as long,
day in and day out, preaching, praying, and feed-
ing the poor besides.   Where was the scholar out of
Germany, or even there, in the land of students, who
was so intent and so laborious ?   Had there been col-
leges in New England or Old ? libraries at Alexandria
or Rome, Paris or London ?   Their use was plain.
Here was a mind that engulfed them like a maelstrom.
He had watched the growth of his race from its babyhood to the year of our Lord 1855.   It was refreshing
to get into the wake of this ' Great Eastern.'   Of
course I had no silly fear of going down in so tremen-
dous a vortex as his intelligence.   Only snivellers told
me that great knowledge made great demons and fools.

" It would take me too long to enumerate the particulars of the change through which my mind now
passed, and to mention all the sturdy aids to its reflection.   Theodore Parker, however, immediately guided
me to the books and the men I had been groping to
find.   He knew them all ; and still better, he had com-
pressed their labors into his own.   What gave him a
great advantage, too, was that while the best new

14

thought and research glowed in his furnace, he could pound as no other man, with the olden hammer of Scotch logic. His facts were all in order and degree. The executive English and American mind needed this. It could understand him, while it could not grasp the single deeper intellect, which he himself pointed out as such, saying, as he referred to his friend Emerson: 'America had seen no such sight before.' Surely our land had not. 'That great, new star, a beauty and a mystery,' was the one orb which shed a brighter, a keener effulgence, than the mammoth reflector at Music Hall.

"But many minds, I think, have seen Emerson through Parker. Many have received all the former's light they could contain, by means of the latter, while they could scarcely have received any of it without him.

"A Boston merchant of practical sense, and a good reader, once told me he did not believe Emerson ever knew what he wrote or talked about. I considered it preposterous to discuss the matter, and so asked him what he thought of Theodore Parker.

" 'Theodore Parker,' he answered, 'was the greatest man that ever lived; he knew everything.'

"The difficulty was that my friend the merchant, had a tough, formal, Saxon head, and could only perceive truth by means of authority and the customary arrangement. Ordered as it came immediately from intuition, and in Emerson's hydraulic pressure of style, in which sentences mean centuries, it was impossible for the man to comprehend it.

"Well, Emerson and Parker became my sages, as

through them I could behold a universe fit to live in, and a God large enough and good enough to be really the Father of all his creatures. With the service of an extra language or two, it was easy to consult and compare other vast minds. In fact, the busy brains of scholars were bringing every Grecian, Roman, German and Frenchman, to speak first-rate English; and as I was after thought, not its clothes, I always struck for the substance where I could obtain it most readily.

"In five or six years from the day I stumbled upon the question of perdition for pretty nearly the entire race of man, I had gone over considerable ground, clearing up that matter, with several of its surroundings. I could take my 'catechism' to pieces and put it together again, so that it was intelligible to me. I had ascertained when, how, and why, its component parts came out of that human nature which was my human nature.

"I had found, to begin with, that 'Religion is no more to be confounded with Theology, than the stars with Astronomy.' Religion is always duty to God as best one knows. Theology is always man's conception of God; and it varies according to the wisdom or folly of the man. But to perform our duty to God, we must have some idea of Him. So far, religion is dependent on theology. Yet as soon as man acknowledges himself to be finite, and God to be infinite, he owns that he, the finite, cannot possibly have a complete conception of the Infinite, — only of some of its attributes, as wisdom, justice, goodness. This is the end of theology, which is the attempt of the mind to construct God, and which, in one direction, invariably leads to idolatry of a physical or spiritual kind. Theology is itself the breaking of the first two commandments. It carries the soul, however, — if not to the possibility of defining and picturing God, yet to an idea of Him as all-wise, all-just, all-good : that is, Self-conditioned Perfection. Let us not try to name it. It is ineffable. Yet if we mean this, we may call it God.

" If we have found, then, that perfect wisdom, justice, goodness, is that of God which we may know, what is Religion ? Is it not the imbibing by us of these attributes ? — the resignation of our nature to their nature ? — the approach to God by receiving God into us ? Underlying all nominal religions, all forms of worship, I found such to be their essence and intent.

" My Sunday-school teachers had told me that the Jews alone, of all ancient peoples, were believers in One God. I found that the foremost souls of all times, had looked to one source whence all things proceeded, quite as certainly as had any of my mistaken instructors.

" The contemplative Bramin among Hindoos, the scientific priest of Amun or Osiris among Egyptians, believed inevitably in the existence of One Supreme God, and did not attempt to portray Him. But the creative, the conserving, the destructive attributes of this supreme One, were imaged in every variety of form, and before these images the people bowed down with orisons. The aristocratic priest despised the masses, deeming it hopeless, even wicked, to teach them religious truth, except by solemn ceremonies and mystic symbols. Moses came. He was the religious democrat of antiquity. He was the adopted son of a king, and so educated, it is said, in the inner sense of the Egyptian worship. At any rate, like every thinker, he pierced through all emblems to their centre; and taking the conception of One God, made him the special deity of the Hebrews, as he had been the God of Abraham and of every other lofty soul. The conception was doubtless somewhat changed, somewhat purified in his mind. But the principal change was in popularizing it, — in setting it up for the adoration of a whole people. And more than a thousand years elapsed, before the children of Israel could fully adopt it, permanently casting aside the idols which Moses had condemned.

" There has been Fetichism in the world; there has been Polytheism. The Egyptian prostrated himself before a winged bull, a serpent, or a cross. The Persian saluted the orb of day at his coming. The Chaldean kissed his hand to the starry host of heaven. Often both priest and people mistook the symbol for the sense, as now they do, in all nations and under all forms of religion. But there never was a Moses, a Minos, a Zoroaster, a Confucius, a Budha, a Pythagoras, — never a great leader and type of a momentous epoch, — who did not reach the import of all rituals, all representations, and bow lowly to the one God.

" Having learned the fact, I was no longer troubled with the notion of a haughty and jealous Deity, the patron of a chosen people. God had chosen all the peoples to do his will.

" In fact, it was not so very difficult to dig to the bottom of the many doctrines which had perplexed and stung me. I ascertained that they had all some-

14 *

thing to rest on. They were true in essence, false in the acceptation. They were in nowise 'mysteries,' which could be accepted by faith alone. They were fundamental facts of the soul, which had been warped, at different historical epochs, into special and local phases.

" The Trinity, of all doctrines, contradicted most emphatically my favorite study of geometry. Three Gods in one; and each part equal to the whole! The conception turned one's mind upside down. Yet it was true; and now I could assert it. There is God the Father, — the infinite wisdom, justice, goodness. He has created man to receive these properties infinitely, and thus to be His infinite Son. The universe is infinite in its means of suggesting holiness to man, and of impressing rectitude upon him: it is the infinite Holy Ghost.

" The Incarnation, really a part of the former doctrine, had also afflicted me. I found that five thousand years ago, it had been believed in India. There, devout, ascetic, mystical men, had retired from the active world to the forest and the mountain, devoting their lives to contemplation. They deemed matter and its forms an illusion. Man's highest good was to crucify and ignore the flesh, and to be absorbed into the one only Being and Reality, Brahm. They imagined that by prayers, and penances, and austerities, they could become incorporated in the Divine Essence, could incarnate God, could *be* God, as it were, while yet on earth.

" This was the grandest effort of piety, the most exalted dream of poetry, then or since in the world. On

the threshold of time, the sons of God lifted their
hands to Heaven, saying : ' Our Creator, let us come
to Thee. Let us come into thine inmost spirit, thine
inmost life ! ' What other prayer is worth our while ?
What other prayer has been uttered since, which this
supplication does not include ?

" Our doctrine of the Incarnation was virtually a
portion of Asiatic theology, probably before the race
could write their record. It inheres in human nature
itself, and if we could trace it to its origin, we should
doubtless find it as old as man's aspirations for the
Better, for the Best. From India it appears to have
travelled to Egypt, or wherever there was a brain fine
enough to hold it; from Egypt to Greece, with Pythagoras and Plato; from Plato it entered the heads
of the Hellenistic Jews; and from the author of the
gospel *John*, was finally reflected, with a special application, into the Christian Church. Its essence and
meaning is, that man's nature may draw upon all the
omnipotence of the Divine, and by faithful obedience,
may become that which it serves.

" As I think of the age and venerableness of our
crude theological tenets, if understood in their deepest
and universal sense; still more, as I think of their
underlying truth and value; I do not wonder at the
tenacity with which strong and good men have held
them. I do not wonder I was told to *believe*, not *inquire.* The Christian Religion, which is pure love to
God and love to man, — containing the most blessed
benefactions of morality, of mercy, of fidelity, ever proclaimed, — was destined to wear for a garment through
the centuries, all the great philosophical truths of the

human intellect. If the garment has proved coarse when the times have been rough, — if it has been a wolf-skin to the wolves' eyes of our shaggy Scandinavian sires, — what matter? It was to serve them as they needed; then to be of finer service to more refined epochs.

"As the doctrines I have referred to were relieved of locality, and bore universal significance, the others were soon enough cleared up.

"The Atonement, I had been taught, was the sacrifice of the Divine Nature to itself, for the good of men. God sent his Son into the world, to suffer and die, that the world might be saved. This idea, too, I found to be as ancient as any primeval records. In the Hindoo theology, Vishnu, representing the preservative powers of God, had often been incarnated in mortal shape, to fulfil some beneficent mission on the earth. Said Nareda to Crishna: 'Men, who are buried in the pit of their passions, have no possibility of escape from their control, except by thy mercy in consenting to be born into this transient world!'

"True enough! How shall we receive the spirit of God — our sole salvation — unless some loftier brother, by containing more of it than we possess, brings it down to us? But shall we accept it gladly when it comes? Oh, no! We are dead in Mammon and in mummeries. We shall say that our more gifted brother is not of God, but of the devil; for we cannot understand him. We shall slay him, or banish him, for interfering with the little gods we had been accustomed to regard.

"If a Budha comes to love the poor Hindoo; to throw the yoke of caste from his neck; to elevate him to a

more spiritual adoration ; — the groveller will turn to
crush the saint or his disciples, — to annihilate them, or
drive them into exile.   Yet it shall be seen, in two or
three thousand years, that a third of the whole human
race shall worship God in the name of Budha, as we
see to-day.   If a son of wisdom and sanctity is born in
Athens, believing that absolute justice is the one thing
to live for, he must go straight to prison, and drink
hemlock.   Then, for a recompense, the sage of every
generation shall borrow weight from him, and civilization shall convert his thoughts into laws, for the government of nations.   If the most loving heart ever in flesh,
descends into Judea, they will crucify him between two
thieves, and afterward, impressed with his heavenliness,
will declare that it was the Creator himself who came
down to suffer and die.

"Yes, persecuted sons of God are ever atoning to
Him, with his own goodness embodied in them, for the
sins of all the children of men.

"Why dwell on the other doctrines that in my childhood I had heard preached?   All the principal ones
were sectarian applications of universal truths, which
had always existed where there had been souls to aspire
and minds to reflect.

"Even the monster of Everlasting Punishment, which
I had so detested, I observed to have a true side.   It is
this.   Our souls are finite.   If so, we must sometimes
err, we must sometimes sin.   Only the possession of
absolute perfection could enable us to avoid doing so.
But then we should be God.   When we err, or sin, the
retribution must follow, — in this world, in any world,
in all worlds.   It is our discipline ; it helps us to improve

upon the last act. In this sense, indeed, we are perpetually punished, but perpetually blessed, as well.

" The doctrine, however, as established by the Romish church, was unique. There was no such mad cruelty in the former Paganisms. Rome had become the earth's cess-pool of blood and crime. The notion emanated from the interpretations of this Roman people, without imagination, who could perceive no second sense in Oriental symbols, who for their daily pastime tossed men and women to wild beasts, and whose hearts fluttered with ecstasy, as human heads, limbs, and entrails were torn and strewn before them by the teeth and claws of lions or tigers. Through no other medium could the merciful teachings of Jesus have been dragged and harrowed to such depth of distortion.

" Still, it is God's way that nothing is lost. The doctrine had its use. For several centuries, many rough-riding ancestors of some House of Lords, were doubtless flogged into mercy to the poor, if not sympathy with the free, by the threat of being everlastingly flayed in Hell. And many a baronial or kingly foot-pad was crushed by it into something like justice in governing his people. It was a requirement of the times. Savage men needed savage restraints. Now it is empty, cumbrous, and almost ludicrous.

" But, my friend, Christianity itself is not at all shaken or impaired, by riddling the doctrinal coat of mail which has so long encased it. To the powerful deniers of the last century, it sometimes seemed to fall, as they stripped off contradiction and mythology, shred after shred. But criticism has only left the person, the character and mission of Jesus, as bright and

hallowed as ever, while it has rendered them clearer
and dearer, as being wholly consistent with the mind
and soul of man. Simply by a comprehension of the
Roman Empire in the year 1, it has disburdened
Christianity of the miraculous, in the sense that a
miracle is ever a monster which breaks a natural law;
and at the same time it has relieved the manhood of
Jesus from all mythical and abnormal apotheosis.

"Nineteen centuries ago, almost the whole known
world had been sucked into the dominion of the seven-
hilled City; and the talent of practical, executive
action, rendering such absorption possible, had engrossed about all the physical and mental energy of the
epoch, leaving scarcely any material for the embodi-
ment of imaginative, intuitive, spiritual natures. Old
faiths were breaking up. They retained but a slight
hold on the learned, but were regarded as a necessary
part of State. The people — the populace — the vulgar — have now no parallel on earth. They were
submerged and overwhelmed in ignorance, superstition,
and every unspeakable abomination. Miracles were
universally credited, and were inevitably attributed to
the exponents of all religions. Magic was as eagerly
accepted as it is now contemptuously discarded.

"At such an epoch Jesus appeared. He came in
the midst, and out of the Jews, — a people who, even
then, were a proverb for backwardness and superstition.
But they had held, through all dangers, trials, and difficulties, to an unswerving and sublime trust in their god,
Jehovah, who was to unite their divided tribes, exalt
them to material power and splendor, and give them
regnancy over all nations. Jesus incarnated this

national trust; but in him it was elevated to the bounds
of utmost spiritual insight, and was modified by the
most loving heart ever in flesh. So the haughty and
narrow Jewish conception of God — the Jehovah — became in his mind the bounteous and merciful Father of
all mankind. Furthermore, 'he saw that God incar-
nates himself in man,' — that man's nature is a germ
for the infinite reception of God's nature: and never
for an instant questioning the great truths which his
spirit prompted him to teach, he declared that the authority for them was God himself. He proclaimed the
Father's truth. In that truth, then, the Father and
he were one.

"But who was rightly to comprehend this sublime
'Poet of the soul?' The whole epoch was sunk in
the lust of aggrandizement and the grossest materi-
alism. Probably there were not twelve minds on the
earth of sufficiently celestial texture to understand the
thought of Jesus precisely as he understood it. More
than once, it seems, he sickened and grieved at the ob-
tuseness of his very disciples. Then, when the innate
sweetness and truth of his precepts began to force their
acceptance, — first among the poor and lowly, who
needed in that age of shocking corruption and innumerable rituals, some religion that could touch the soul and
purify the life, — then all the notions, exaggerations, and
subtilties of the time, began also to creep into the most
natural and beautiful faith ever breathed to mortal
ear. Then, for five centuries, the immense fabric of
theological dogmas was gradually constructed. Men
talked, and wrote, and contended about it, differing as
much as they differ now. They bruised each others'

faces in street-fights; they skewered each others' bodies
in pitched battles. At last it became a thing settled
by authority. What authority. Practically the Roman State. It rested on what? The votes of a majority. It was a necessity of the time. Now it is
neither necessary nor true; and therefore is so fast
dropping away.

"But the religion of Jesus, — that perfect faith in
God as the Giver of his very Self to man, — which
includes the Golden Rule, the Sermon on the Mount,
the Lord's Prayer, the fidelity of the blood which
dripped from the cross — symbol of man's last sublime
duty to his Maker: — we need not fear that this religion can pass away from our faith. Its stability is its
truth. It is founded on human nature, which is
founded on God. It is, in one sense, the condition on
which every loftiest soul has been born into the world.
Plato was the philosopher of all time, because he saw
and expounded through the intellect, what Jesus perceived and declared through the heart. Socrates was
wise and grand, because he too went down to death
for the same essential justice that Christianity affirms.
Budha has four hundred millions of followers, because,
long before Christ, he taught something of Christian
mercy to the downtrodden children of Asia. Confucius was the sage of China, because some of his best
precepts are Christian commands.

"Let us truly understand this religion, my friend,
and we shall never be deprived of a bright, serene,
immovable faith."

15

CHAPTER XVIII.

"A RATHER strange-thinking, plain-speaking individual, that same Mr. Acton," said Cora, after Stella had finished the manuscript, which, notwithstanding Earnest's warning as to its heaviness, had been read aloud at Cora's request.

"I wonder how one dares attempt to unriddle the world. Why not be as good as we can, without talking about it? Now I shall lie awake half the night, perhaps, and who knows but I shall be disputing, pretty soon, with Pa, and Captain Bub, and my minister, Dr. Bugle himself. How Earnest takes everything to heart! I never would have bothered myself with all those questions. Yet his experience, he declares, is the experience of thousands. Do you think so, Stella?"

"I don't think it is literally so," Stella replied; "I don't think he means that. I think he means thousands have had the same doubts as his, with the same consequent gloom, which they have passed through, to arrive at a similar result. Besides, every one has his own special imp of darkness to harass him in life, in addition to the foolish beliefs and fancies of the world. With him, it was early ambition, the want of riches,

(170)

which he yet despised for themselves, and a painful consciousness of his defects. My demon has been, as you know, a very different one, in most respects. But the great object in life, appears to be the finding of a faith by which we can overlook our present misfortunes in the contemplation of future benefits, and can have a smile and an eye-full of kindness for God's other people whom He has placed beside us. Your Charley's friend has found such a faith; I have found it, though not precisely in his manner. We are now ready to live; we are ready to die when it is best we should. Perhaps there is more to be attained; but I scarcely know what. It is pretty nearly the whole story of our lives, whether they are great or little.

" But Cora, my dear, let us go to bed and to rest. To-morrow, perhaps I shall leave you. If not, I shall go the next day. I begin to feel that I ought to be making my way homeward. My silent retreat beckons me to return to it, and there think over some matters carefully and alone. My heart would keep me longer here with you; but I had better go. Furthermore, sweet one, I am losing you in another, who is beginning to look too steadfastly on me. Kiss me, Cora, and forgive me; you know what I mean. So make up your mind for a farewell to-morrow noon, or the next day morning, unless you will forsake Charley and accompany me."

" Cora was in tears in an instant. She loved Stella with an almost childish devotion, and could not bear to part with her.

" I would go with you in a minute," she said, " if I could. But Captain Bub is coming home on a fur-

lough, this week or the next, and of course I ought
to be at home with him. He has been away almost a
year. He's a dear, good brother, and very fond of
me. He wants me to go everywhere with him, when
he's here. I wish you would stay a little while longer.
I can't go with you. I could write to Charley, every
day, and that would do for a week or two; but Pa
and Captain Bub wouldn't dispense with me. Come;
you haven't been here but a little more than two
weeks. You ought to stay two months at least. But
I know there's no use of talking. What is said by
Stella, Stella does. I wish she were a trifle more
yielding, like poor Cora, whom she will certainly kill,
some day, by persistence, and absence, and conscience,
and such things."

   .   .   .   .

Yes, Stella had determined to return to Boston. But
why so suddenly? What so hastened her conclusion?

It was a very simple incident of the evening. After
Earnest had handed her his "sermon," as Cora failed
not to call it, the conversation was turned to light general subjects, and then to literature and music. During
the latter part of the evening, Stella had sat at the
piano again, and played, while the friends had gathered
about her and listened. When she had concluded,
Earnest casually took up a book, and after turning the
leaves mechanically for a moment, he looked at it. It
was a collection of Robert Browning's sweetest poems.
Earnest was excited. He turned to the short poem,
" Evelyn Hope," the gem of its kind in the English
language, then put the book aside, and without a pre-
liminary word, commenced to repeat the stanzas. His

friends sat motionless, and scarcely seemed to breathe. Stella placed her hand on her forehead, and gave herself wholly up to the emotions of the piece. She seemed to die, and to pass into other spheres, while one who loved her was revealing his heart. When Earnest — his voice melted to the tone of utmost purity and tenderness — came to the lines, —

" I loved you, Evelyn, all the while ;
   My heart seemed full as it could hold ;
  There was place and to spare for the frank young smile ;
  And the red young mouth, and the hair's young gold, —

Stella looked up into his eye, which was beaming upon her face. Could she be mistaken? Was it not love that was there, liquid and light, willing her to approach and linger in it? 'Twas with the greatest difficulty she could keep her seat, she so longed to throw her arms about his neck, and lie clasped to his heart. He finished the poem, and she dropped her head, unable to speak. From that instant, she resolved not to remain at Ironton another evening. The strong-souled Stella shuddered, and felt an absolute dread of being charmed beyond the full control of her will and judgment. How she loved the spell! But she must go home, — yes, home, to consider, to wonder, and now once more to mourn.

" O God!" she murmured, " would that I had found this at seventeen ; but not now, not now! "

They could not prevail on her to remain. The next day, at noon, Mr. Clandon's carriage was on its way to the depôt, and Cora's friend was about to leave her. Through a note from Cora to Charley, Earnest had received an intimation of Stella's departure. He was surprised and saddened. He could not refrain from presenting himself at the cars, to bid her farewell. He looked into her face for the explanation her words did not offer. Tenderness and regret were in the blue eyes.

"I am very sorry," he said, "to lose, so soon, a friend whom I do not know where to replace. Permit me to say it, Mrs. Torson, — I have spent a few of the happiest hours of my life with yourself and your friends. If anything should come to me that I should think you would take pleasure in, may I write you a line?"

Stella could not refuse.

"Yes," she answered; "and you will visit Boston sometime. Come and see me. No one will ever be more welcome."

Thus the friends parted.

Stella told Cora that she might mention to Charley the facts connected with Mr. Torson's will. She might also acquaint Earnest with them, if she pleased. He could then draw what inference he might from her hasty departure, "though the Fates know," said she, "that it will not be unfavorable to himself.

"Neither will he regard me as volatile and capricious, for hastening away with some of our plans and pleasures unfulfilled. We all had several walks, and talks, and rides which I counted on. But here is the end of them."

She kissed Cora, and stepped into the cars. In another minute the train rolled away.

CHAPTER XIX.

STELLA arrived safe at her Boston home, though on her way one of the cars was thrown from the track, causing a temporary delay and inconvenience to passengers, while no one was harmed. The accident was mentioned in the Ironton papers a day or two afterward, and the mention was noticed by Earnest.

He had been sad and restless, in spite of himself, since he could no longer pass an occasional evening with Stella. She presented herself constantly to his thoughts. He read his books, but her image was between his eyes and the page, which now conveyed to him only half its significance.

As yet, Cora had said nothing concerning the will. He knew, however, that there must be some mysterious circumstance linked with Stella's procedure, and he connected himself with it. For he did not require words to arrive at human feelings. He was certain that he had seen a more than ordinary tenderness in those glances which had met his; had heard a more than ordinary tenderness in those tones of voice, as she addressed him. He was not to be deceived. Stella had told him she loved, as plainly as though her articulate vows had been communicated to him. He, too,

(175)

had silently avowed the story of his heart to her. He knew that he had done so. He felt that she knew it.

As he read of the slight accident to the train of cars on which she was journeying, — an accident which, as the papers stated, might very easily have proved serious, — an irresistible tremor came over him, as though he had heard of a worse fate, — as though some one had told him that his beautiful friend had been crushed and mangled, and snatched away from him forever. What if it had been so!

Then he sat down to write her of his happiness in learning that she had not been injured. His note was merely expressive of kindness and the loneliness of her friends, one and all, since she had left them. But in it he enclosed a few stanzas of verse, which he said he had picked up recently, and which he had thought might interest her for the moment. He did not say *how* he had picked them up. Probably there was no need of doing so.

The note was dated the 10th of April, 1861. The stanzas were these : —

> " I sat in the silence alone, —
> The peace of my quiet room ;
> I looked at the picture that hung on the wall ;
> There were trees and a child and a tomb.
> But something came and veiled the view :
> How softly, friend, — 'twas a thought of you.

> " I turned to the book in my hand ;
> On its page were names of the great ;
> Ideas that would soften savage men,
> Words to be laws of the State.
> But there on each line — it would peep through —
> Again, my friend, was a thought of you.

"I passed out into the street;
  'Twas a sunny April day;
  There were couples walking arm in arm,
  There was leisure, was haste, was play.
  I fancied now would be something new;
  But no, my friend, 'twas a thought of you.

"I was met by a gentle maid,
  Whose locks the air-breath fanned;
  On her cheek she carried the summer rose,   .
  Though a daisy was in her hand.
  She smiled and spoke; but her eyes were blue.
  I looked, and then — 'twas a thought of you.

"I walked on the distant hills;
  I gazed up into the sky;
  Goodness and beauty lay stretched below,
  God and the boundless on high.
  There was Heaven. I wonder if Heaven knew,
  And forgave me still, for the thought of you."

CHAPTER XX.

IT was nearly two weeks before Earnest received an answer to his letter. But, in the interval, what a startling change had overpowered the whole nation! Fort Sumter had been bombarded! The cannon which first opened its mouth against those walls was the symbol of destruction to the Union, to republican liberty, to the natural laws of God to man. A few saw all this at a glance, and knew that the second great hour of American history had at last struck. The many saw that the Union, the great idol never to be questioned in the instinct of the masses, had been threatened, and was liable to be thrown from its pedestal. This was sufficient for them. The land, east and west, was in a blaze of indignation, a storm of anger. Massachusetts was rushing through Baltimore to Washington ; New York was close behind her. God, Liberty, Union, had come to mean something. Religion invoked its followers to take up a cross, — heavy, sad, dreadful war. They said: "We will: God help us!" The great "revival" had been granted of Heaven, and a practical salvation was at hand. It was a salvation of self-sacrifice, of manly deeds, of noble duty. There is no other. The day of grace had

(178)

dawned, and the American people seemed worthy of its resplendence.

To Earnest, the outburst was not wholly surprising. He was young. He had trusted the intentions of men. He knew that commonly their vision was very limited, their views were very narrow. But he had been sure that Americans loved America; he had been sure that they meant to love liberty. They had been so warped and confounded by the littleness of politicians, and the grovelling ambition of strong statesmen, who were yet not strong enough to be great, who were too selfish to be true, that they knew not whither they were drifting, where they should find justice and safety. But all the time they were bent on these things.

A few at the North really gloated over aristocracy and slavery, — believed them necessary and right. These were virtually Austrians and Turks, accidentally born under American institutions. A few others accredited nothing in heaven or earth but a fat pocket. These were of no special nationality. They were poor fellows whom every thinker saw to be lingering in the quadruped condition, attempting to be men, even supposing they were such. But the fox, the jackal, the spaniel, peeped out constantly under their pinched brows.

There were these two classes. But the American masses looked steadily at Mr. Jefferson's Declaration of the Rights of Man. They trusted it would be fulfilled. They had determined it should be fulfilled. But they thought the Constitution good enough to make its Preamble veracious. If not at once, then sooner or later.

Earnest had scarcely ever talked with a sturdy, honest man, of any vocation or any party, who did not thus reconcile his present political action with the future welfare of his country. He had seen and conversed with many such persons. He had met, too, the sharks, and the rhetoricians of the wind-bubble. But on these he had wasted no time. He had paid but little attention to the mere forms of law and legislation, while he had studied closely the substance which these forms are ever striving to comprise, — progressive human life. He knew himself; he knew others. He prophesied, therefore, that in case of actual collision between the North and the South, there would be an uprousing of the people, and a merging of parties. Cunning graybeards, versed in what they termed practical knowledge, told him he had better wait and tremble; that the masses were chaff, blown one way as easily as the other. Young attorneys reiterated the advice and the assertion. These had felt of their own pulse. Earnest had laid his hand on the nation's heart.

How he rejoiced in manhood now! How his soul leaped out to the people, who more than affirmed all the soundness he had declared them to possess!

Now, also, he saw the use of the watchword *Union!* which mealy hypocrites had so often mouthed, as they favored meanest measures and filthiest harpies, that the word itself had been coated with a secretion of their own slime. By it they had meant lust of wealth, lust of power, lust of rapine. They had meant the assassination of freedom, — the confederation of two hundred and fifty thousand autocrats, to despoil man of his birthright and make him a slave.

Here was the revulsion. Now again it was *Union, Union, Union forever!* Ah, yes! and now it was a cry to devour the hypocrite and the assassin himself.

In itself, and for itself, it was a low war-cry — the shriek of divers and dippers — mud-fowls in quest of worms. It deceived Europe. We seemed an army of peddlers, who had thrown off our packs and gone to a rat-hunt in our stinginess of corn; an army of snakes, full of venom now that we could no longer burrow in all of our accustomed ground-holes; an army of alligators with the jaw thrown back when certain bayous were denied us to batten in.

Well, how many of us were ourselves deceived. We must do justice to our tough democrats. They had heard so much of Union! that they supposed it meant, under God, everything good and great. They supposed it synonymous with the integrity and sense of Washington, the genius of Jefferson, and the grip of Jackson. When the Hon. Vulgar Loudmouth bawled *Union!* they imagined he talked of liberty; not a mutton-chop and his glass of brandy.

This was the rule. Certainly there were many who were ready to fight for the mere acres of ground, — who conceived there was nothing better to fight for. Their shout of *Union!* was the wrath of man praising God, — mud turned into divine muscle. The end to be attained in God's design, in good men's efforts, was human freedom as the immediate foundation of incalculable human advancement. What a spectacle! — to see for once, saints, scholars, hucksters, hunkers, and thieves, all lending a hand to Heaven!

Earnest felt it was the one sight of a lifetime, and he

16

threw out all his faculties to the view. He had almost forgotten Stella. But now her letter was before him, and her sweet face rose from his memory, serene, intelligent, sensitive, grand.

Yes, he would leave the gathering storm of war, and dwell for a little while with his thoughts, and with the image of his friend. His eye ran hastily over the letter, as if to devour its substance at a glance. Then he would read it more carefully.

But here were some verses. What! was Stella favored of the Muse? Was this another of her accomplishments? Her letter stated it was not. She partly apologized for sending the stanzas.

" My friend," she wrote, " the floodgates of principle have at last opened in battle, and as there is no other way for them to open, God be praised for this way! I am here among the sons of the Puritans. I am not ashamed of them. They were not dead: they slept. I had sometimes feared the old blood was all out of their veins. But in these last few days I have seen Otis, and Adams, and Hancock, striding about our modern Boston. What else than they and their spirit have I beheld here since the 12th? It is so with you; it is so in all parts of the North. What a time, after all, is this we are fallen upon! What history must the country now inevitably write during the next five or ten years! But I will not look forward. The present is enough.

" I have done little but read the daily journals since I left you. A few times I have sat down to my piano. The wish came over me to throw something of the passing hour into music. I made the attempt to thunder, and threaten, and proclaim, sounds descriptive of the outburst around me. Then I tried to adapt the sounds to words. Perhaps the words are lame. I feel that they at least need the music to render them complete. But I send them to you. Try to make me some better ones. Then you and I can have a song for the times."

"I think I shall not," said Earnest, as he read them. They were these : —

> "It has come! it has come! — the cannon's grim thunder —
> From threatening clouds that have flashed in the South!
> Columbia, pallid with wrath and with wonder,
> Darts fire from her eyes, fiery words from her mouth!
>   They have shot down the stars,
>   O Spirit of Mars!
> Now cover, ye stripes, the palmetto with scars!

> "That lazy-leaved tree has borne fruit for the nation,
> That's poisoned its breath with a feculent lie!
> And now that for crime, it would sever relation,
> My banner, with thee, cut it down! let it die!
>   They have hated the good,
>   They have thirsted for blood:
> Let them sink, if they must, in the reddening flood!

> "Strong sons of the North, ye are roused from a slumber
> That long has been rusting your glory away.
> Ye dreamed not of battles, nor counted the number
> Of deadliest foes ye were destined to slay.
>   Ye were drunken with gold!
>   But oh! ye are bold!
> And your grasp is a fate to the purpose ye hold!

> "Ye meant in your hearts that our country should never,
> No, never bow down to the whip and the chain!

But ye've borne and forborne till I marvelled if ever
Your blood could be nettled by insult or pain.
    For ye waited to see
    If the struggle *must* be:
Now God pity him who encounters the free!

" He has opened the death-dance, to wanton the longer
With her who has ever been mother of wrong.
Then war to the hilt! — with a will that is stronger
To burst all her shackles and scatter her throng!
    There, down let her fall!
    Here, put on the pall!
It is woven of groans and the curses of all!

" Yet ever remember, O Sons of the Union!
For better than vengeance your legions pour forth:
The Southron ye meet in yon gory communion,
Shall die or succumb to the men of the North!
    But your flag is unfurled
    Not that down he be hurled,
But for life, and for freedom, and peace in the world! "

CHAPTER XXI.

SOON after Earnest had read Stella's letter, Charley Merlow came into his room, and told him the circumstances connected with her marriage, and her deceased husband's will. Cora had narrated them in full to him on the previous evening.

"The secret is out, my boy!" he exclaimed; "and now I scent the sole cause of her fury to regain the classic cow-paths of Boston. A certain dear fellow, over here, was making himself felt as such to my lady the Torson. She has a heart. She fears it is flesh. She would tuck it away out of danger. She is conscientious. She is sensible. She has looked in the glass. She knows she is somebody, — quite somebody, with several attractions, — and doesn't believe you are blind. Well, there *was* a little conversation, I noticed, between your eyes and hers. They had a way of sparkling to each other that was growing serious. A minus A equals 'ought,' as the boys used to say at school. Heart minus the possibility of hand, equals *ought not* plus a journey to Boston for consideration of the matter.

"But you and she were made and foreordained for each other from the beginning. Neither of you will

16*   (185)

be content alone. She doesn't care a pothook for
wealth; and her position, forced by the will, has almost
made her hate it.   There's money in your brains, and
bread to be had outside the bakery of Jabed Z. Torson.
The question, 'then, before my side of the house, is
how to send his will to the devil.   Furthermore, if one
storms Hades, I don't think he should be too tender
about the sort of fire he uses.   Why not slop a dipper-
ful of his own brimstone into his black majesty's very
face?   But " —

" Charley, Charley, you are going wild," interrupted
Earnest.   " Listen a minute.   You say the will de-
pends almost wholly on her word ? "

" Yes."

" Then may she break that word never !   You say
her parents rely on her.   Then Heaven prompt her to
stick by the money !   You say that, if she disregards
the will, the property will probably slide into doctrinal
tracts and pro-slavery pamphlets.   Well, that is not
of so much consequence.   The flag that was shot down,
the other day, is all that ever gave slavery any real security in the country.   It will die now in ten years, —
perhaps in five.   All the corruption of earth can't
save it, to say nothing of a ghost's bank-account.   The
other matter, too, is of as little importance.   God's
great truths of faith and life vibrate to no pedant's
whim or his purse.   Still, a personal inclination to anything but a duty, cannot outweigh a third of a million
dollars.   I should advise that noble woman, whom ·I
will own that I love, to think well, before allowing her
fortune to pass into other hands.

" My dear Charley, we will *not* send the Torson's

will to the devil, for our own convenience. But I shall
have a little talk with Stella in a few days, and tell her
that I have not done myself such injustice as to see
her and keep my heart. The regal woman ! How I
long to be with her once more, if only for an hour ! I
shall not ask her love. I shall not ask for anything except to be followed by her eye and her heart, as I walk
away from her with a sword by my side. Yes, one
thing more I shall ask, — that we both live to hope.

"For, Charley, I who have outgrown all ambition
for feathers and the stuff they call glory ; who now
wish to live only for knowledge and truth ; I too must
strut off, like the rest, with gilt buttons and a cockade.
The times have brought us to this. How dearly have we
paid for our fostering of slavery, which now threatens
to devour the best fruit that Christianity has borne for
the ages ! And slavery knows no other argument than
war. It is a wild beast. To kill or be killed is all that
is left to civilization, religion, justice, peace. War is
wrong. It is the one great wrong next to slavery. But
my country is not going to war. It has shuddered at
the thought for years. I mean the nineteenth century
at the North. The middle-ages, at the South, have
hugged the sword, of course, and have compelled us to
wield it against our will, as in Mexico.

"I say my country is not going to war. It hates
war. It has risen above the spirit of military strife.
It loves peace, industry, culture. It is going forth to
slay a wolf, whose red eyes it now plainly sees, and
whose red jaws are agape to craunch the very life of
American principles. The wolf would eat up liberty,
light, and the sons of God. Not in hate, then, but

sorrowfully, and as mercifully as possible, these must eat *it.*

" There was never slavery that did not bring war ; and now it has fallen upon us. But we shall crush the wolf, and then our wars, as I think, will be over. We shall want no more of battles ourselves, and other nations will not dare to force them upon us.

" Yes, Charley, since I was eighteen, fighting of all kinds has had no charm for me; unless the fighting of truth with error and ignorance. But now I shall go South, and with arms. I can put my hand in God's, and feel that in this one instance He lifts me to the great duty of slaying my brother for my brother's good.

" In a few weeks I shall leave you, my friend. There is no need of haste for me. Others will go to-day, to-morrow. They will be needed. But our people do not understand the South. The struggle will not be the trifle they count on. Seventy years of merciless sin will not sink in a spoonful of vitriol. There is work before us, — hard, horrid work. The wondrous development of mechanical forces in the world, will alone preserve us from repeating the Germanic war of thirty years. Possibly we shall finish ours in five. If so, it will be the speediest on record. For, Charley, the South will fight, — will fight better than ourselves, in proportion to numbers. Will they not ? How was it with Spain three hundred years ago ? How was it with France when her cavaliers had their ten, twenty, or thirty duels before breakfast, and when one of her knights challenged the whole German nation to single combat ? Oh, yes ! the barbarism of the middle ages will fight; for it believes there is nothing fit for a man to do but to conquer and to domineer. The South is that barbarism. Not wholly so in its outward circumstances, but completely so in the central tone of mind from which all its actions proceed. No, there is one main difference. It has not the faith in God which inspired the Crusaders and their sons. Its only great faith is a glittering dream of conquest, — the conquest of the whole Western Continent.

"But, Charley, here is a letter from Stella. Read the song she sent me. And what do you think she asks me for? She wants me to write her out the philosophy of slavery, — the reason it has been in the world. I shall try to do it. (Perhaps she may never make me many requests.) Then I shall go to Boston myself. I want to see Stella, and have a fond word from her heart to help me along in the future tumult."

Charley Merlow was amazed at Earnest's hurried words, and at his intention of becoming a soldier. He knew that his friend had no taste for it, and that nothing but the feeling of duty could induce him to forsake his seclusion and his books, for the savagery of the camp. But he knew that dissuasion would be unavailing. He merely said: "We can't do without you. Think of it again. Don't decide so hastily."

Then Charley added a good-by, and walked sadly away.

"Not fit for any such thing!" he muttered. "Use him right up, and make a funeral for us. Plenty of others to go, — strong men, used to exertion. Ought to wait awhile at least. All wrong, all wrong!"

CHAPTER XXII.

ON the 25th Earnest wrote Stella the following letter : —

"Let it be, my dear friend, as you say. While the whole land is burning with activity, we will pause a moment and ask why.

"The immediate cause is evident. The South has honestly declared it, throwing down the glove for slavery, which it loves, and which it knows we at the North hate, daily more and more.

"But the North does not detest slavery as the South adores it. There are few John Browns among us, — men ready to fight and die for the absolute idea of freedom. In one sense, I should say we are not good enough for that. Then I should have to modify the assertion. Conscience is not conservative : yet I think it has largely entered into our forbearance and moderation.

"There is much to consider when we examine the North.

"For one thing, we fully appreciate the horrors of war. The South does not. Slavery never did. The system, in all parts of the world and throughout history, has always produced two classes of men, — soldiers and

serfs. The master, whose every whim has been gratified by slaves, will brook no contradiction, no restraint.
He is always practically a warrior. Oppose his will,
he draws his sword. To subdue and govern, or to find
' glory and a grave ' in the attempt, has ever been his
leading thought. His annals give no other account of
him, from Cheops to Beauregard. His conception of
manhood has always been to kill his opponent, if an
equal, and to crush his inferior into the menial of his
household or his land.

" No, the South has not dreaded war, but has desired it. I know the plea is ' to be let alone.' I think
a few Southern men, educated at the North, honestly
mean it, and would like peace on that condition. But
for years the one blissful vision of the South has been
conquest. The South expects to subdue us to its will.
It deems us too paltry to fight, and supposes it can beat
us if we should do so. Its most scheming men have
believed that we would eventually throw up every
principle for the sake of Union ; and now, seeing us
obstinate and enraged, it is glad of the chance to thrash
us into humiliation.

" Here is a mistake similar to that which a rough,
brutal man makes in judging a refined, serene man,
who dislikes contention, not from fear but from a sense
of its wrong. The rough man thinks his neighbor,
who will not fight with him, a coward. But surely
Socrates and Paul are no less brave than some roister-
ing Earl of Huntingdon turned into Robin Hood, or a
Captain Warner wearing on his coat, in silver letters,
the avowal that he is ' commander of a troop of robbers,
an enemy of God, without pity and without mercy.'

"The North is not timid. It dislikes war, because it sees there is a better arbiter of difficulties. It credits enlightenment, thinking that when men are truly enlightened they will wish to be just, to do right. The South cannot comprehend this conviction. Slavery inevitably believes that mildness and prudent industry are cowards. Feudal France thought that commercial Holland would not resist her, — thought so till the dikes were down and the land submerged. 'Nobility' supposed the early communes would not fight, until the conceit was knocked out of its head, the brains going at the same time.

"The civilization of the North is superior to the civilization of the South, as the world knows directly from experience, the leading nations having passed through slavery and sloth into freedom and industry, trying and proving both. The difference is solely an affair of growth.

"Here I come at once upon the matter of your request — the law — the cause in God's providence — of the system of slavery.

"How should I expect to enlighten *you*? I know, my friend, that you have been upon these universal grounds which now invite me. You have beheld the light above them which harmonizes all particulars, all incongruities, into one vision of the Creator's beneficence. Well, then, I shall recall and confirm to you that sublime view ; without which we are all children ; so that every toy of interest, of pleasure sets us spinning in its own little whirl.

"Let us begin as far back as we may, and speak the one commandment to every created thing : — 'Progress!' It is the key that unlocks all secrets. It is the password into all heavens.

"Was our globe once a mass of fiery ether, the first emanation of Deity that our science perceives? The step from this primary visible effect, back to God, we need not attempt to trace. But the fiery ether solidifies, becoming, in ages enough, the surface of a world. Now it is the barren extremity of matter, — a naked rock. From this point it ameliorates. There is the coral, the fish, the plant, the animal, and, when all is ready, man. Does this last production come up through the preceding ones, retaining their nature, dropping their forms? Is it their direct offspring? However this may be, it embodies all their qualities and powers, and carries them up to a wonderful height, — into the realm of intelligence, reflection, and modified self-direction. Behold a being who is the middle of the universe! God's spirit has been breathed into his soul; God's material forces have been thrown into his body and moulded to his shape. He will use everything above him, everything below. He will unfold more and more the wisdom of the skies, the knowledge of the earth, taking the result into himself and growing, — which growth through the spheres will be evermore his life.

"At first he is in a state of mental babyhood, — roaming the primitive wilds of the earth in unclad fierceness; strong in body, but merely instinctive; knowing just enough to sustain life and to extend it. Yet presently he will arrive at self-consciousness. He will ask himself: 'Who am I, in this strange world, without power to cause myself, and while I can do

17

much, am still limited on every side?' Asking the
question, he will draw the inference, 'There is something above me which governs and guides.' Then he
will look to the sun and moon as representatives of the
Power his thought has mirrored to him. He will
worship. He will say that not to worship is a crime.
After a while, he will commence to write a history of
himself, which will be called 'The Annals of all Races
and Nations.'

"At this juncture, my friend, he is well started in
life. Nor could we start him differently and speak the
truth. His mythologies all mean this; and you and I
have learned better than to read them by their coarser
sense.

"Now let us glance at Slavery as we read history.

"The system is very venerable, like polygamy and
cannibalism. We must make the broadest statement
for it in this respect. We may even assert a little
crustily, with Mr. Andrew Bell, that 'it is humiliating
to civilized man to know that, when authentic general
history first records the doings of his earliest progen-
itors, she speaks of his kind as being nearly all bond-
men if not absolute slaves.' The Mother of the
Nations said, — I know not how many thousand years
ago, — 'Some men came from the head of Brahma, to
think; some from his arms, to govern and fight; some
from his trunk, to produce and distribute the necessa-
ries of life; some from his feet, to dig and build, — to
bear the heavy burdens of the others.' The idea was
established, and became Hindoo Caste. By it the
lowest orders of society in India, the mass of men,
were slaves. They were such throughout Asia.
They were such in Egypt, in Greece, in Rome.

" Yes, slavery is venerable.   We must even say more for it.   In one of its chief phases it was once a bene-faction and a reform.

" Society, at the outset, was patriarchal.   The father of a family was the ruler over his wives, his sons, his dependants.   The family increased to a tribe.   A de-scendant of its head, or a strong usurper, was then its chief.   Men had two pursuits, — to fight for the ground on which they established themselves, and rudely to culti-vate it.   They were savages.   All men, as we have seen, look to some mysterious Power which creates and governs them.   A great spiritual intellect. pierces through all manifestations of that Power, and calls it Unity, Allah, God.   A cannibal believes it to be a more majestic cannibal than himself, with a bigger club and more ferocious appetites.   The Hebrews, just emerging from darkest bondage, and entering upon the track of rapine, regard it as a haughty and jealous God-at-arms, demanding the blood of men, women, and children, who worship some opposing military deity.   Hence the hot-headed, miscalculating, capricious Jehovah is their conception of the Creator of heaven and earth.   He demands the extermination of enemies, — the cutting them up root and branch, leaving none alive.   In this state, society is too barbarous for an extended and ma-ture system of slavery. · Women are servants or play-things ; the weak, who cannot fight, are the same. ·But veritable, historical slavery is yet to come, an im-provement.

" Now, the soldier kills his foe in battle, or offers him as a sacrifice to the favoring deity who is supposed to have aided in capturing him.   The bones, perhaps, are heaped up as a trophy. By no means must the worshipper spare an enemy to his God. But later, both mercy and selfishness conspire to the innovation. It seems rather harsh, even to a Hebrew savage, to murder a poor mortal after he is rendered totally defenceless. Why not make him a 'hewer of wood and a drawer of water'? It is done. The captive, formerly slain, is preserved as a slave. Yet afterward, if a battle go wrong, the conservative priest shall snuff 'infidelity' on all the winds. He shall declare that Jehovah has been disobeyed, Israel has been defiled by mercy to Canaan, and the retribution has appeared. So flinty and frivolous is mankind, in the red, dripping history of his childhood! Slavery is the result of war, and of the proud indolence of the warrior, governor, and priest.

"We pause here for an instant. Does God, the true Father of all races, ever permit a system to exist which is not best for the time and place, and for the people who are its builders? No. Let us revert to the Hindoo, with his doctrine of caste.

"We shall find a great truth at the foundation of it. We remember that, to the Hindoo, Brahma is the impersonation of God's creative faculty. Well, some men came from the head of Brahma, to think. These are the highest, — the Brahmins. Here is a declaration that the sage, the saint, is the salt of the earth. The maxims are identical. They mean that God has so constructed the universe that the religious genius is always the first gentleman and the greatest force in any realm.

"The second class are magistrates and warriors.

They come from the arms of Brahma, to govern and fight. But they are under the guidance of the Brahmins, whom they must consult and obey. Here is a recognition of the fact that the practical administrators of the State — those who mould the perceptions of genius into laws and customs — are next in importance to genius itself, — that Aaron must needs execute, while Moses designs.

"Then come the merchants, — the distributors, — from the trunk of Brahma; and last, the laborers, — the diggers and builders, — from his feet.

"Really there have always been these four classes of men in the world, perfectly distinct from each other. So far, caste only expresses a universal truth of human nature.

"But it was made permanent. One class must never rise into another. No member of a lower order must ever attempt to enter a higher, or to perform any of its functions. As one was born into the world, so must he go out of it.

"This part of the institution is a terrible, unmodified assertion of our maxim, 'Like begets like.' We may state its underlying truth thus: Some men are born with natural endowments superior to those of others; culture is necessary to eminence; eminence and culture should transmit superiority.

"These are rules of every one's mind and conduct. When, too, the sources of culture were very few, and were necessarily monopolized by the few; when it was literally impossible for one condition to ascend into another; when the masses were sunk in hopeless, stupid, willing ignorance and debasement, — caste merely

17 *

proclaimed a practical, undeniable fact. It was a necessity. It was a blessing, not a bane. But as soon as the sources of improvement multiplied, and it became the wish and the possibility for men indiscriminately to rise, the weighty millstone became a shackle about the neck of progress. Bitter and bloody has been the struggle to throw it off, — a struggle in which millions have yet found their employment, their hope, their gratification, and which has afforded to history nearly all its pages of heroism.

"In one form and another, caste has existed from the beginning, and to-day a remnant of it is about to fall in America, drenched in blood. Here, you say, it rests on color, and we term it American slavery. Is it a sin? — an absolute, unqualified sin?

"We must say *yes;* we must say *no;* we must add that there is no such thing as an absolute, unqualified sin.

"Why is it that we all have two eyes, while so few can see two things at once, or two sides of the same thing?

"Sin is a matter which is heaven to-day, hell tomorrow. The patriarch may think himself a man after God's own heart, yet be a polygamist and a slaveholder. While he does not know he commits a sin, he is no sinner. Refusing to grow, — this is sin. Clinging to the old, while seeing the new and knowing it to be better, — this is sin. Excessive conservatism is the only crime ever committed in the world. If I am a fool or a savage, who shall blame me for mumbling blasphemy or torturing my foe? But if by any means I can be taught to know better, and my conscience rebukes the former ignorance, dare I linger in the old way? Then I am Satan's own.

" ' An eye for an eye ; a tooth for a tooth ; burning
for burning : ' — this was once a law of God.   That is,
it was the best a barbarous people knew, and consequently their conception of God declared it.   It was
Jehovah's mandate.   Virtue and necessity obeyed it.
But when there was one came to look deeper, and to
say : ' Nay, love your enemies ; bless them that curse
you; do evermore as ye would be done by,' — and
when the hearts around him reiterated this command,
— the virtue which had obeyed the old law, if continued,
degenerated to a vice.

" There are a thousand illustrations.   But sin is
always the refusal to enact the perceptions of conscience, or the weakness which postpones the deed.

" Slavery was not a sin when the low condition of
the race rendered it conscientious, satisfactory, unavoidable.   In the nineteenth century, in North America,
with the New Testament in every house, and the Declaration of Independence acknowledged as truth, it is
the sin of sins, which has debauched and disgraced
thirty millions of Christians into such Atheism as ventured to jeer at any law higher or better than a barely
tolerable Constitution.

" Now the retribution is upon us.   It cannot but be
terrible.   We shall deserve to lose every life that will
be laid down.   God's law of universal justice is exact.
The pendulum has swung far into darkness.   Its return
will be just so much death.   Then there will be a better life.

" I have made the assertion of Progress.   *You*
would scarcely ask the proof.   You have known it.
But the argument is not complete without one more

word, — Experience. How do we know that we advance from the lower to the higher? That word gives the answer to men and nations. For the history of nations is only a reflection of man, — the shadow his presence throws upon time, — the outward image of his inward unfolding. Each soul lives, in greater or less degree, the annals of the world. The soul itself is barbarous or civilized, beauteous or unlovely, precisely in accordance with its growth, — its intellectual and moral growth. There is no enduring reward for it except its own enlargement. There is no real punishment save its own debasement.

"'There is no crime,' said Goethe, 'which I might not have committed.' Why this acknowledgment? Simply that he knew himself, and recognized in his impulses and ideas, from infancy to manhood, those things which, if he had possessed the means of executing every one of them at the moment of desire or temptation, would have paralleled the record of all misdeeds. Rousseau's "Confessions" are a most unreserved and detailed avowal of Goethe's admission. Here was a man of remarkable virtues in his time and place, who had yet broken about all the commandments, and might very easily have made no exception of any one.

"Early boyhood makes small scruple of coveting, lying, swearing, stealing, and the like. If I have never killed a person, it is not but I had a hearty will to do so, several times, when a boy, as I distinctly remember.

"An honest and fair lady once told me that 'every girl is at some period of her life a flirt.' Vanity is active, and craves the admiration of many, before love — a higher, later faculty — is satisfied with the affection of one. I might have told my friend in return, that every boy is at some period of his life a snob. I have never known a bright boy, well circumstanced, who did not think himself a natural lord, born to command and to be obeyed. · How many inferiors such a boy imagines are around him, and how gladly he would reduce them to the menials of his wants! The boy is a slave-holder. That is, he would be one if he could. Fortunately he cannot generally carry his views into practice ; so he is spared being a Hebrew patriarch or a mediæval baron. At seventeen, give him full power to express himself in action, he would be Themistocles or the Sultan of Turkey.

" Slavery and polygamy, always inseparable, are in every youth. I mean the spirit and will of those institutions are in undeveloped human nature. Restraints of circumstance may prevent them from taking shape in action. But there they are, in the boy.

" So much I have known for myself, and have seen in others. Why not make the statement, as any other truth ?

" But, my friend, let us think not too ill of our kind. You know the features of even the animals are in us, too plainly to be denied. Yet their rough forms are much suppressed when we take them on, and are overgrown by our superior structure and traits. So, the youth's outward action may be decorous and pure, the notions and desires of barbarian ancestors being overborne by the weight of present civilization, until he can grow, perhaps unsullied, to the summit of the loftiest thoughts and emotions that man has ever entertained.

" This constitutes the thinker, great and good, who

comprehends folly as well as wisdom; for he has passed through one state to the other. He knows, from experience, that love is better than passion, that justice is better than will, that kindness is better than hatred, that beneficence is better than oppression. He has found that life is growth. Not that it is the mere accumulation of culture and aids about a certain tone of mind, which may yet be selfish and low; but that it is the ascension of tones of mind themselves, each into a nobler and happier, until the sublime height is reached where the man desires to resign himself to wisdom, to justice, to love, — the height where his will blends with God's will, and where his only selfishness is in seeking welfare by subordinating all things to universal law, — the method and manner of the One Only Perfect.

" A friend of mine had arrived at an insight of this last ascension, though too often he stood at a distance, looking rather than doing. He was not always good, though always better than many others. Gross and common forms of sin were no longer a temptation to him. He preferred death to dishonor; poverty to mean wealth; insignificance to wrongfully-acquired popularity. He would be his own servant rather than secure his leisure or elevation at another's expense and degradation. He was true and just to man, true and tender to woman. He would not have held a slave to own a continent.

" But he had not always been so. He had been full of faults. He had wept for not a few sins. We know that man always errs and sins and weeps. My friend, by stumbling, had learned to walk with surer step; by sinning, he had been taught to rise above

many sins ; having hated, he knew how to forgive hatred ; by weeping, he had felt how to pity those who
wept. He was natural and human ; nothing more.
But many changes and many periods of history had
been incorporated in his experience. He knew how
events had occurred; for they had occurred to him.
He spoke from within, and with certainty ; for his mind
had been a picture of the world, with its lights and its
shades. The old and the new made the picture ; and
the new included the old. It was greater, nobler, happier ; so he knew it was better.

"If any one doubted his argument, as applied to
individuals or nations, he did not deem it worth his
while to dispute. He knew the doubter did not yet understand himself, — that his nature had not introduced
itself to his own observation and reflection.

"But my letter has become too long ; I will close it.
I have written only the matter of your request, and
of course the subject could be much amplified. But,
when writing or speaking to you, I feel as though you
had already uttered all that I declare.

"In a week or two, I trust I shall see you. I intend
spending a few days in Boston. Then I shall bid you
good-by for a long while. I am going South to phi-
losophize under brass-buttons and danglers. Yet how
can I help it? The cause is very sacred, though many
of the present motives connected with it are little and
heartless. At starting, I shall want your encouragement and a smile. They will be more valuable than
most things I shall carry with me. I think you will
not refuse them to me.

"Your friend,
"EARNEST ACTON."

CHAPTER XXIII.

TEN days passed, and Earnest was in Boston. It was not long, as will easily be inferred, before he presented himself to Stella. As he mounted the steps, and stood in front of the massive door of her residence, he could not but remember how empty and sombre the elegance of that stately mansion had been to its caged inmate; how gladly she would have exchanged it, and all its surroundings, for simple comfort, and one deep, fond, sympathetic heart.

His name was hardly announced when Stella met him, with an extended hand, a smile, and a slight blush.

"I am very glad to see you," she said, "and have felt for several hours as if you were near me, although I had received no intimation of your arrival in the city."

She conducted Earnest into a spacious drawing-room, and seated herself at his side. They conversed a few minutes, and then she said, —

"Now that you are here, my friend, you will stay with me a while, certainly. And we can do quite well, I presume, with no others to enliven our conversation. In this room we may be interrupted.

Some one may call. Let us sit awhile in my ' sacred
rooms,' as the domestics term the library and a room
I have used in connection with it for my music.
There we shall be undisturbed."

Earnest was quite willing to accept her invitation,
and to see that Stella did not shrink from him in the
least, but seemed to desire that no minute of their
interview should be wasted.

Again they were seated, side by side, now in the
library. It was a pleasant apartment, of medium size,
furnished plainly, yet with much grace and elegance.
Since Mr. Torson's death, Stella had renovated and
rearranged it in conformity with her own ease and
tastes. He had filled it with heavy and elaborate
furniture, which she had removed, and replaced by
less weighty and cumbrous articles. Each chair in the
room seemed to indicate, by its size and shape, that
its occupant could find in it a new and relieved position, without intermission of reading or meditation.
Everything was for use and comfort. Even the
pictures and ornaments seemed for suggestion. Consequently there was an air of luxury about the place
that no amount of mere costliness could have produced.

Earnest observed this at once.

" What a cosey, inviting sanctum you have, to be
sure," said he ; " but I should think it would almost
persuade one to laxity instead of application. Here,
I should count myself in the paradise of the peaceful,
I fear, and never work for improvement, as my friend
has done."

" And I could very well dispense with the place,"

18

replied Stella, " although now that I have it, I make
it as comfortable as possible, and then try to occupy
myself so that I forget all about it. I am better content here, and in the other room there, than elsewhere
in the house."

So saying, she rose and drew aside two large, magnificent curtains, and revealed an apartment in which
was a grand-piano, and looking down on it from every
side were the tuneful " Nine " in marble.

" Ah ! the home of the Muses," said Earnest.

" This, too," she continued, " I do not need. I
would gladly let it go for the gratification of simpler
feelings than it inspires. But, you know, perhaps,
that it will not let *me* go. So I am as thankful as
may be, and make the most of my surroundings."

" It would be almost a pity," Earnest rejoined, " to
decrease, in any way, their elegance and suggestiveness.
Yet I am aware they have not brought you complete
happiness. I suppose, however, you owe them a large
debt for that very reason."

" Certainly I do," said Stella, " and I try both to
acknowledge it frankly and to appreciate it. We are
all very much beholden to our misfortunes, as no one
has declared to me more clearly than yourself. In
some way we must all be mellowed to a certain indifference to mere circumstances, before we can be
permanently comfortable. We must be willing to
forego happiness before we can be happy. Everything
is liable to be taken from us but hope and trust. They
are worth all the rest, and I am thankful to whatever
has been a discipline forcing me to think, to feel, to
know.

"Your life has been very different from mine; yet, if I am not mistaken, we have unconsciously striven to reach the same goal, — a summit from which we could view the world intelligently, devoid of fear, of hate, of misgiving. Our tortuous paths to the height — the mere means of gaining it — are indifferent, now that they are in the distance behind us. To you, were they ambition? — want of wealth, want of station, want of fame? Were these the dreams and playthings that first drove you to the highway of truth and exertion? Well, the result, my dear friend, is generous, noble manhood.

"To me, also, there were dreams and toys. I dreamed of love, and I longed for admiration. But I wanted the best. Thus I too was in search of power, such as it was; thus I too was inspired to labor. Then, when disappointment and pain came to me, the labor itself had become my inspiration and my solace.

"I have won something; for it is something to see that I can win nothing more except by new labors and cares and duties, and to accept my lot as Providence imposes it upon me. Nor is this quite all. When I met you, I had so attuned the chords of my nature that it was in harmony with yours. May I say it? — I think I could comprehend and appreciate you; I am sure I could respect you. If one would choose friends, such sympathy is not the least of attainments."

These last words were calm. There was no tremor in Stella's voice; but that eye, — its soft, deep azure was unspeakably full. Earnest looked into it. His spirit and his will beckoned it to draw nearer.

" Your friends should be very happy," he said. " God grant they may never be unworthy of your choice."

And as he sat there by her side, his soul still said: ,Come, come, come ! Her eyes she could not take from that look, that imploration, that command. They were fixed, they were charmed, and now they saw the supplication alone. Come, come, come ! — and tears blinded the blue, and Stella was in a lover's arms, — a lover whom she loved. The arms folded her all about, and warm lips pressed their fervor upon hers.

" Speak to me ! " she cried. " Oh, it was cruel, — that behest which I could not disobey, — while yet I feared, and grew weak, and — Earnest, speak to me ! "

" Yes, my own, my darling, my beautiful queen ! — speak to you and say that your heart rests at last, where mine has throbbed to place it since almost the first moment I saw you ; where still I dared not place it, where still I did not mean to press it, as now I do ! For I meant to bow lowly, — to tell you I was a suppliant who asked merely to hope, — to think sometimes of love for some very distant day, if life should be spared, and happiness and duty could be yours, while you were mine.

" But our hearts have spared me several very gallant and very self-sacrificing speeches," he added, with a smile, " while you, the dearest of women, are here, here, bound to my soul !

" What have I done ! Well, I would not undo it. We were created to love each other ; were we not, my own ? Our fates were joined when we met, and it were better to die for them, if they ask it, than to live and forego this moment!"

Thus these two restrained, thoughtful young people had resigned themselves to their feelings, and, like the children that we all are at many an hour, they were absorbed and glad in the present. But they were "children of a larger growth." They knew their own hearts; they knew the hearts of others; and, as all emotions blended in the meeting of their lips, they only realized a rapture for which they had long seemed to be waiting. They did not tremble at love, nor shrink from loving. They were young, but they had learned much; and of the heart's wisdom they were not afraid.

The hour, the morning passed away. Still they were there together.

"How happy I am, and how secure!" said Stella, as she awoke at last to a thought of the future. "How much delight I find in these caresses, which we cannot hope shall last! You are to leave me in a few days. I cannot bid you stay; and perhaps you will never fold these arms about me again. But I know that you love me. I knew it before, my idol; but now you have told me so, with kisses and embraces. How could I ever see you turning fondly to another, feeling, as I do, that, for both our sakes, you should be mine, I should be yours! Now we may wait, we may mourn, we may suffer. You may be killed, and then I shall not stay long here alone. But what of that? Now we can die for love as well as for duty. We will think, we will pray, we will do

18 *

no wrong, my guide, my guardian, my only-loved. But our hearts are bound together.

"We will ask no promises; we need none. Neither of us can be faithless in a thought. God has given me what I have asked. Now, if he should take it away, I will bow, and bless him, and die.

"Surely I do not think that would be so hard a fate as many another. Better so than to live unloved. Better so than to live unloving. Far better so than to live for love to chill, for enthusiasm to burn out, for life to grow selfish and timid and empty. I am right, dear Earnest; am I not? Whatever may come, we will not regret this hour. I do not feel unworthy of it; for I would give all that you would have me give, for it and for you.

"My fortune seems a burden, weighing me, as it does, down, down, away from you. How quickly would I push it from me, if I could, to hear you speak one word, — call me that nearest, fondest name I long to hear as I look at you : — to be yours wholly, to us and to the world.

"But no, you need not speak. I know what you would say. We remain lovers. It is best for us, best for my poor old parents, best for my duty. Were it not so, I would not live apart from you one moment longer than you bade me. And, Earnest, you would not hold me from you long. Surely you would not.

"Let me dream. We could live, if my wealth should go. Hopefully we could live on little, and thankfully on more. Much, we should not need; for ourselves, not our circumstances, would be our care. Common vanities we have conquered; display would be beneath us ; and the opinions of the world regarding our estate, — we have seen their shallowness too fully to heed them. Something for a little home ; something for a friend who might come to it ; something for books and music ; then something for the poorer man or woman or child we should see : would this be so very hard to procure ? If one could not do it readily, two, I think, could ; finding their tastes cultivated and their improvement secured in the process.

" Earnest, I have often mourned over the incomplete life I lead. Nothing seems to me so grand as to elevate one's powers, whatever they may be, and to impart the result to others, for their happiness and benefit. How much time and labor, for instance, I have given to my music. Now perhaps you will smile, even against your better judgment, which will sustain me ; but I have often thought I should delight to instruct others in the knowledge and pleasure I have gained from that delicious source. And mind you, if anything very, very romantic, or sad, or strange, should occur to tempt me, I would turn public or private performer on my piano, and show that I had not possessed the advantages of wealth so long, without cultivating some taste or talent that could enable me to dispense with it."

" Hush, my darling, I pray you ! " said Earnest, the tears falling from his eyes. " Your dream is noble, and for you it is not at all impracticable. I will acknowledge no sentimentalism that would terrify me at the thought of congenial and worthy employment, for myself or for any other human being. But just now, the vision saddens me. I cannot bear to think of myself as committing you to the smallest inconvenience or discomfort. I should never have come here if I had not intended to fly directly away from you. I knew you loved me. You were to me the dearest object on earth. How could I avoid merely saying as much? It seemed as if I could even die better and more bravely afterward. And in that event you would not mourn me more than as though I had never allowed myself this precious interview.

"I could not look to the end. Yet I hoped that, in the rapid changes of present affairs, your fortune would soon cease to be in the way of the world's progress, and that you could do with it as your long consideration and deliberate judgment might choose. Perhaps I have too much confidence in myself. But I also have labored hard and a good while to unfold certain powers and attainments. Certainly, if I were unable to render you and yours comfortable, I could quickly decide on some things I would not do.

"But we will see. For three years I am vowed to the service of my country. What will happen meanwhile, we cannot tell. But I deprive you of nothing by loving you, and I increase my own happiness by adding to it one beautiful hope.

"There, — a kiss, my darling Stella, and let me go from you. We have been with each other a long time. This evening shall I come again?"

CHAPTER XXIV.

THAT evening, and every evening for the next ten days, those two fond hearts were together.

This was not all. Stella had suddenly taken a liking to her carriage. She must ride to Bunker Hill, to Cambridge, to Mount Auburn, to Dorchester, to Concord, — wherever there was aught that Earnest spoke of with pleasure or enthusiasm, — wherever there was aught that Stella thought he would esteem or admire. Anything that they might be together; everything that as few moments as possible might be spent apart, — this seemed her constant, almost her only thought.

"My dear Earnest," she said, "we can be with each other only a little while; then long, long months must drag heavily between us; or who knows what besides? I have always lived in the future, — always given the pleasure of to-day for the good of to-morrow. But now, during these days you are with me, I will exist for nothing else than for you and for them. They will pass away. Desolation may follow them. But I shall have known God's sweetest gift.

"Yet, Earnest, you will try to come back to me again, — will you not? You will never be reckless, —

never run into needless harm! I ask so much; I dare not ask more. For then you would no longer love me, and I should blush at seeing the image of my poor, weak self. I will never ask you to be unworthy. God help you to do all you ought. I bid you go where you should; so, if it be down under the red sod, my soul will not be unworthy to follow yours, but ' will wake, and remember, and understand.' But walk carefully, Earnest, — my Earnest now; — walk carefully, where prudence shall not be a crime. Think of me always when you can; yet I too must needs say, think of duty first."

He kissed her fair, clear brow; he kissed her warm, melting lips; he pressed her to his heart.

"I will do all you wish, Stella. Let us not paint the future. I too, say, let us live these few days in all their sunshine. How bright and hallowed they are!"

.   .   .   .

They would not stay always, — those ten bright, sunny days. They were a delicious revel for two full souls, — a banquet of love such as not every life affords, such as no life often spreads. The chill whisper that breathed of separation, stole among their joys to tip them with the keener zest. But at last the whisper was, "Now: the time has come."

They tore themselves away from each other, mournfully, tearfully, speechlessly. Yet the warm hands, which wrung out the farewell that their lips refused to utter, were joined in hope; and there was the prayer to God, such as is alone written in the blood of hearts that love, when they are cleft asunder, per haps for months or years,—perhaps for so long a season that earth cannot again join them.

Now they had parted. Almost it seemed to them as if there was no one left alive in the world. The dream had ended,—the dream in which all but their love was a blank. It had ended, it was broken. But they could wake to nought else.

Well, there would be time enough to wake, and duties enough to be done. Let them think yet a little of the heaven that was the dearest they had found.

CHAPTER XXV.

"STELLA, my dear, it seems to me you look very pale and very sad this morning. May your poor old father, who hasn't always done the best for you, but has yet always thought he loved you, ask why?"

So said Rufus Maign to his daughter, the morning after she and Earnest had parted.

The old gentleman had offered no comments on anything that Stella had done, or wished to do, since he came into her household. Not because he selfishly feared to offend her, but simply because he had come to think, at last, that she was not to be questioned and judged like others. Her seclusion from choice; her tenderness to the humblest of those around her; her constant application to her music, or to studies deeper than he cared to understand or investigate; her wonderful brilliancy at times, in the presence of such friends as she enjoyed to meet; and, withal, her solicitous care that he who had forced her to the one great sacrifice of her life, should have whatever could make him comfortable and happy; — all these things had latterly impressed Mr. Maign with his daughter as with no one else.

"Ah! mistaken man that I was!" he had more

than once soliloquized; " she was born under a loftier
star than ever shone over my old counting-room. I
didn't comprehend her. How I wish I could make
her amends! Perhaps I can yet."

And ambition rose again beneath those gray hairs;
and he toiled and schemed, settling old debts, and
freeing himself from their weighty trammels. Happily
they were not many now; and using a few thousands
of dollars as he knew how to use money, they were
soon cleared up. Once more he stood erect, owing
no man a cent, as he declared. But still the gray
head was busy, — crammed with money-articles and
market-reports. The old merchant was again on the
scent, and in a few years who could tell what might
happen to him? So he thought; so he said — to himself alone.

Now, for the first time since he came to her home,
her father asked a question which Stella could answer
by any commonplace, if she chose, but which she
knew expressed a desire to probe her heart. Yet the
tone was so kind, and the manner so considerate! The
man's old haughtiness and abruptness had all gone.

" Stella, my dear, it seems to me, you look very pale
and very sad this morning. May your poor old father,
who hasn't always done the best for you, but who has
yet always thought he loved you, ask why?"

Gently these words came to the sadness of which
they spoke.

Earnest had met Mr. Maign every day, — the
young man coming in and going out when he pleased,
riding with Stella, sitting hours with her in the " sacred rooms," till the servants stared with wonder at

19

such unusual proceedings. But not a word had been said on the subject, and Mr. Maign always smiled on both his daughter and her friend.

Yet who was he? It was indeed strange. .... A young man she had met while visiting Cora Clandon; a good-looking, well-bred, intelligent fellow. Well, Mr. Maign would wait. Stella knew her own affairs; he, or any one else, could well trust her. But now he asked the cause of that pale cheek, the melancholy brow, and the eyes which seemed to have been very tearful.

"Father, I will tell you. Why should I not? Mr. Acton, the young man who has been here during these last few days, I love; and I love him, knowing that perhaps I shall never see him again."

"And why not, my daughter?"

"He is going into the army: — a man who really has no more business there than I have: as gentle as a woman, — shrinking from the least harshness, — his mind having dwelt for years with the sages, the poets, the saints. He thinks it his duty to go, and for that he leaves a quiet seclusion of thought and study, which to him is a sort of earthly paradise, for the life of a soldier. And I know him. I know his will. That hand, which has so tenderly held mine, will be terrible to others, terrible to himself, if necessary, when it grasps a sword. He will laugh at danger, and spurn security. Duty — solemn, stern, unbending duty — will be all he thinks of. He is not like most of us. He means and welcomes death in the cause, if death needs to come. Such a man I have loved, and have seen him leave me. Yes, I am very sad."

And tears gushed from Stella's lids, and her head fell upon her hand.

Presently she looked up and continued.

"I have told you all. It was your due. It seemed strange to you, no doubt, that a man you had never before seen should be with me almost constantly. But we loved,—had done so in spite of ourselves. We were not to remain with each other. I knew there would be time enough to think, to consider everything, after he had gone:—perhaps a whole lifetime. So we filled the hour as it came."

"Who is he, Stella? Is he rich, or poor? No, no, my good girl; don't curl your lip so. I'm not going to deserve it. I know you think I've considered that question once too often, at least, already. So I have, dear; but this time, you mustn't blame me. You shall have no reason to do so. Let me come to the point, then, as soon as I can. Thanks to you, I've paid all my miserable debts that have been hanging over me, and I've made a little besides. In my judgment, there was never, since I was born, such a time to make money as now. In two years I mean to make twenty thousand dollars. I think I can do it. I couldn't understand such a girl as you. I did you wrong. But the old post-horse is good for something yet, in his own way. In two years, I say, I mean to have twenty thousand dollars. I've almost broken your heart; but I'll try hard to mend it. I want the money for you. If the young man should live to come back, you shall have it, or he shall have it, or we will do what you like with it. I couldn't buy you such a house as this, or the one we used to have. But

I know you now : you wouldn't care for it. I'd do
my best, and maybe make you happy. Then you
could leave these traps of Jabed's behind you, or let
them go to the secessionists and the dominies, if they
must. The will was a bad affair, a bad affair, — the
meanest of all, — curse the thing ! But we'll get the
better of it somehow. Yes we will, Stella, my dear
child, and you shall be content."

Stella was speechless with surprise. Such words
from such a father ! — a man who had always been
grasping, and worldly, and vain, — whose first thought
and foremost endeavor had been possession, accumulation. What had effected so vast a change ? Was it
the loss of his money ? Was it her imprisonment in
her own wealth ?

She had noticed that, since he first came to Boston,
he had been ceaselessly active, — busy in the morning,
thoughtful and engrossed in the evening. He gave
himself scarcely any relaxation, unless when it was her
hour for sitting with him and conversing, and sometimes smoothing his white hair. Then the restless,
knitted brow became unoccupied and sunny.

Had he observed her loneliness of heart, which had
nearly become an accepted part of her life ? — that
loneliness which her retirement, her music, her studies, had so often been evoked to solace and to cheer ?
She could not tell. She had striven to appear happy,
that he might not be reminded of his having impelled
her to be sorrowful. She had often really felt happy in
seeing him once more occupied and unbroken.

But he had made no allusion to former days, to her
husband, or to any alteration of his own views and pur-

poses, until now. Now she comprehended, in an instant, the meaning of that renewed energy, that intent, anxious, tireless look.

She was too deeply moved to speak ; but she went to her father, and putting her arms about his neck, kissed his forehead and his lips, then hurried out of the dining-hall to her own room.

The name of *father* had now a significance which it had not hitherto borne, — which she had longed, only, that it could bear.

19 *

CHAPTER XXVI.

WITHIN a week after leaving Stella, Lieutenant Earnest Acton was in the Volunteer Service of the United States.

When he first thought of entering that service, he had determined to do so as a soldier in the ranks. He felt himself without capacity to lead men to battle. But many others, possessing quite as meagre an acquaintance with the " tactics " as he, were stepping forward, ready to take high places. Young merchants, and clerks, and lawyers, competent enough, doubtless, in their several employments, appeared. to gauge their modesty and their yet undeveloped military skill, precisely by the best possible positions they could secure. It is certainly well for soldiers, as for other men, to have confidence in themselves, if they would succeed. But Earnest supposed that being a commander implied fulfilling the duties of such a person ; and although he strongly inclined to trust genius and native good sense more than mere drill and routine, he fancied that he ought to know something of these things, before aspiring to a trust which might easily involve a considerable number of precious lives.

" But bother your fancies," said Captain Norcum,

(222)

the friend in whose company Earnest had purposed
enlisting; "you shall go as one of my officers, if you
go with me. Your conscientious hesitation is all very
fine. But you have a head and a heart; and those are
things, I can tell you, that will be very much in demand. Come; I am considered quite proficient, as
holiday captains average; but you shall be my twin in
tactics before the month is over.

"Besides," added the jolly captain, laughing, "you
can resign, you know, and step into the ranks, any time
you please. You shall be my first lieutenant. Alf
Bowles will be second."

But Earnest declined.

"Well, then, Bowles shall be your superior. You
take the place I had intended for him."

"I will try it," said Earnest, and the matter was
settled.

As every newspaper teems with accounts of battles,
and with the details of camp and field life, it would be
almost uninteresting to follow Earnest through the particulars of his military experience.

From Ironton, his regiment was sent to Fortress
Monroe, where it remained while the battle of Bull
Run was fought and lost.

Earnest's first taste of warfare was at Bethel, — an
unfortunate and inglorious taste, he thought; and
especially bitter, as the following day he learned the
fate of Major Winthrop, the eager and devoted, whom
at first sight he had admired as a great-hearted, cultured
gentleman, and had loved as native to a more generous
and genial world than our poor eyes are accustomed to
behold.

The Major fell on Monday. The Saturday preceding, Earnest with fourteen of his men, was out on a scouting expedition between Hampton and Bethel, when suddenly a party of rebels, numbering twenty or more, and mounted, appeared on the road, swung round a brass howitzer, and let fly at the fifteen. Earnest ordered his men to the side of the road, where they were partly sheltered by woods; and by some loud shouting to imaginary reënforcements, and by a cool use of the muskets, he beat a safe retreat for his own party, having had the grim satisfaction of seeing two of the enemy fall from their horses, wounded or dead.

He supposed that, all things considered, he had done pretty well, and was not dissatisfied with the exploit. But presently he met Major Winthrop, who rode up and questioned him minutely about the skirmis.

He answered, stating the number of rebels and the number of his own men.

That dashing hero's eye glistened.

"Twenty rebs!" he exclaimed, "and you were fifteen! Why didn't you take their gun?"

This view of the case had not entered Earnest's mind; and the attempt would certainly have appeared somewhat rash. But he felt, instantly, that if Major Winthrop had been in command of the fourteen, the effort would have been made to capture the howitzer.

Perhaps it would have succeeded. Perhaps the hero would have fallen two days sooner than he did, — "the only brave man," as the rebels declared, that they saw among the Union soldiers, on the memorable day of his death.

But what was his own life to that great, magnanimous heart, that keen, thoughtful spirit? One of the few was he, who knew the magnitude of the struggle to which he had given himself, — knew the North, knew the South. Freedom for mankind he asked ; not long life for Theodore Winthrop, who was ready and willing to die that his country might live. To be early in heaven was for such as he !

On the 31st of May, 1862, Earnest was in the van of the Army of the Potomac. He was now Captain Acton. He had been in the service a few days more than a year, having passed through four battles and nine skirmishes without a scratch. Eleven days he had been in the hospital, and every other day on duty. He had not been home, nor had he asked to go. Sternly punctual, and ever ready at his post, he had waited upon duty or death, as that which he had come to do, that to be done. No wonder he was loved by his men ; no wonder he was trusted by all.

In another week he was to be a lieutenant-colonel. Captain, now Colonel, Norcum was in command of the regiment. By rank, the post of lieutenant-colonel belonged to Alfred Bowles. But his turn had come to be magnanimous. He was a good-hearted, faithful officer, yet slow, and wanting in address ; while the quick, cultivated mind of Earnest had enabled him to become " every inch a soldier ; " and his natural free and easy kindness, all of which he could express, had made him the pet of the rank and file. Besides, he had twice ventured his life to save that of another, and each time it was a private not belonging to his own company. In one of these instances, he carried off a wounded man in his arms, and with his pistol disabled two of the enemy who were trying to oppose him.

The example of personal valor, and his invariable touch of the cap to the humblest, were in themselves sufficient to make him the private's favorite. But beyond this, he had the name of strict temperance and unmistakable integrity. When, therefore, Major Bowles received friendly intimation that the lieutenant-colonelcy would shortly devolve on him, by the resignation of the incumbent, he frankly said, in his homely but noble way, that he knew of a better man; and if the boys all round would'nt object, he would hold his own, and see Captain Acton go over him.

The offer was hailed with applause, and a torrent of compliments soon rolled upon the honest Bowles from officers and men.

" It is very generous in you," said Colonel Norcum, " yet I think you'll never regret it. Between you and me, Acton is to-day better able to lead the entire army, than some others that you and I know of. He *means fight*, at least."

But the plans of Major Bowles were destined to be sadly frustrated in every way. In his self-sacrificing estimate, he had not taken into account that in a few days was to be fought, and lost, and won, the battle of Fair Oaks. On the 31st of May, and on the 1st of June, 1862, such was the work to be done.

The record of the battle is known. Heavily, and in force, the Confederates bore down from Richmond on General Casey's division, shattering, and forcing it back upon the larger body. Then came the fearful, the desperate struggle for recovery. Colonel Norcum's

regiment was to have its mettle thoroughly tested.
Gallantly it went into the fray, its gallant colonel at
the head. Another instant, and he was thrown speechless to the ground, his horse killed by a shell. The
lieutenant-colonel was sick, and absent from the field.
Major Bowles did his utmost, rushing to Colonel Norcum's post, and holding the regiment firmly up to its
task. But those terrible rebel sharp-shooters coveted
the life of so brave and upright a man. He, too, fell
from his horse, shot through the body. As he was
raised for an instant, he spoke the name of Captain
Acton, glanced at the line, and fell back dead.

The regiment began to waver. There was not an
instant to be lost. Earnest leaped upon his friend's
horse, which had not been harmed, and thundered
along the front.

"Boys!" he shouted, "will you see me die alone?
Come! Once more!" And away he dashed, straight
for the rebel columns.

With a mournful, dissonant yell, the "boys" followed him. They fought like a regiment of tigers over
their young. Yet they lost ground, foot by foot, inch
by inch. Only once they gained a few rods. Earnest
had shared, in part, the fate of his colonel and major,
having been violently dismounted, and shot in two
places, through the neck and the arm. Then the
regiment, especially the members of his own company,
seemed to stake everything on him. Without command, but with united impulse, the latter forced their
way to his body, supported by frantic squads along the
line. Fifteen Federal soldiers, seventeen Confederates,
lay dead and dying, immediately around him, on that

disputed piece of ground. But he was borne from it, at last, by those who would know nothing else, for the time, than to achieve their purpose, or to die.

He had done all that man could there do; and they had done for him all that mortal might can be inspired to do for one who loves and honors men.

.　.　.　.　.　.　.　.

On the 2d of June, removed from the late scene of conflict, Earnest was receiving what care and attention could be bestowed on him by the as yet dishonest and ill-regulated medical and commissary departments at F——. His wounds had been probed and dressed, and it was thought he would recover. Two telegrams had been sent homeward, one to his father, at Ironton, one to Stella, at Boston, stating that he was badly wounded, but doing well.

From the moment the news of the battle of Fair Oaks reached Stella, she had been exceedingly distressed, as if with a presentiment of terror and misfortune. Her determination was fixed. If word should come from Earnest that he was in danger, she would go to him herself, and provide for his wants. The word came. It was brought to her at the same time with a letter, the superscription of which she recognized as the handwriting of Cora Clandon. She read the dispatch, and threw the letter aside. She then wrote a short note to Earnest's father, informing him that within an hour she should be on the way to Washington, accompanied by her butler, — an old and trusty servant, — and should proceed immediately to F——, to take care of Captain Acton, and to supply him with every comfort and attention.

She called the man whom she intended to take with her, and, to the utter amazement of that worthy individual, which his rather dark mulatto face did not fail to show, asked him to have a carriage at the door in forty minutes, and be prepared to accompany her to the Army of the Potomac.

"Don't wait for explanations," she said. "You have lived with me five years, and know me. Please get ready at once."

"Yes, ma'am." And the old butler left her.

Stella went to her room, and in a quarter of an hour was draped in plain gray travelling apparel.

Late the next night she was at F——, and was inquiring for Earnest.

"Shall I tell him who waits to see him?" asked the person to whom she was addressing her questions.

"Yes, a sister, — the dearest he has on earth."

She was in no mood for formalities.

How surprising, and how welcome was her tired, anxious, sleepless face, to the wounded young lover, pale and haggard, lying there on his pallet!

"Ah! Stella, I can want nothing now!" he murmured, as he saw her; "but what a place for you!"

"Never mind that," she replied. "But you must be quiet. I shall stay with you."

Fortunate was the young soldier to receive such care as that which, during the next two weeks, was supplied by Stella. Carefully was every direction followed by a nurse who had so much to gain or lose. Tenderly were his parched lips moistened; tenderly his hot brow bathed. Gentle was the restraint which

20

soothed him to sleep, when his mind wandered away into the conflict again, and he shouted and begged to be followed to the death. Bravely she bore it, when one of the surgeons told her that, in his next lucid interval, if she had anything she was especially desirous of saying to him, it would be well to communicate it; for he feared that Captain Acton would live but a few hours longer. Tearfully at last, and only then, she sank away, completely overcome, when Earnest was pronounced not dead, but strangely better, and out of all danger. Then she slept a long, deep, heavy sleep, from which it appeared almost as difficult to waken her as it had been to recall her enfeebled lover from his decline toward the land of shadows.

But the burden had been lifted from her, her prayers had been answered, and her heart was filled with thankfulness and joy. ·

Five days still she lingered at F——, an angel of mercy in the abode of desolation. Not Earnest alone, but many another helpless sufferer, blessed her, and prayed that God would spare "the sweet lady's brother" to her who had a kind word and a helpful hand for every one she came near.

In fact, there were some special reasons for their benedictions. Soon after her arrival, she had ascertained that some of the pale skeleton-figures she saw — young men, many of whom had left good homes, to fight and die for their country — were here actually pinched with hunger, — put off with pitiful, undue allowances of food, that the blood-suckers of the commissariat might fatten their pockets upon these ghastly cheeks. What could she do? Nothing but send John, her dark butler, to the nearest place where provisions could be procured, hand him her purse, and order him to buy whatever was needed, without stint. In her flame of indignation and grief, she thought not of the consequence to herself, — thought not of the annual allowance for charity to which she was limited, — but only remembered that she had a plenty of money with her, and that servants of their country and their God were literally starving to death under her eye.

John employed the purse freely, and gave it back to her lighter by nearly six hundred dollars. He was honest to buy, and faithful to distribute; and was unaccustomed to question whatever he was told to do.

"Madam, my mistress, wished me to bring you this; and would you like some of this?"

Then tears would well up to the eyes of those rough men, their languid faces would brighten, and their voices grow very soft.

Later, the report was circulated that the mysterious lady who had come to attend Captain Acton, whether his sister or not, was very rich, — worth millions; that she was personally acquainted with the Secretary of War; that she would represent affairs to him as she had seen them here; and that somebody would be sure to suffer in consequence.

She allowed the report to pass for what it was worth, and instructed John not to lessen its value.

When, a few days afterward, a certain burly-faced quartermaster desired to be presented to her, she replied, loftily, that she should be very sorry to form the

acquaintance of so unscrupulous a man, and should not
only be reluctant to take his hand, but, if matters were
not mended, she should do what little she could to prevent that hand from repeating its recent niggardly acts.

Her words, her look, her bearing, were not to be
mistaken. She was evidently a lady, and had money.
The plethoric rascal of the commissariat was satisfied
on this point, and Stella had the happiness to see an
immediate change in the rations.

But for the accidental rumor of her wonderful influence with governmental functionaries, which some
imaginative youth had probably dreamed, she would
never have thought of attempting to displace a quartermaster of volunteers. On her return to Washington,
however, she did make the attempt, in person, stating
who she was and what she had witnessed. Her words
carried with them the weight of indignant truth,
which it almost choked her to utter; and the tears
which she could not suppress were perhaps eloquent.
At any rate, Earnest, who was yet unable to start for
home when she departed from F——, wrote to her that,
three days after she left him, the man of whom she had
complained had been ignominiously dismissed from the
service, and that the poor fellows she had fed from her
bounty were then fully impressed with the belief that
his " sister " was a " near relation of Mrs. Lincoln."

CHAPTER XXVII.

STELLA had been at home several days, when suddenly the recollection of Cora's unopened letter occurred to her. She had been pondering, with some mortification, her hasty benevolence to the soldiers at F——, which, if it should come to light, or should be honestly revealed by herself, as she believed it ought to be, might deprive her of her fortune.

The issue could easily be avoided. She could call the money she had spent, her father's; she could say that John had exceeded, in his purchases, the amount she had designed he should expend; she could replace the money in a hundred different ways. But had she, or had she not, really, though unthinkingly, broken one of the provisions of her husband's will? She acknowledged that she had.

What, then, was her pleasure and surprise, as she read Cora's long, chatty epistle.

"DEAR, DEAR STELLA : —

"I've lots to tell you, — lots to begin with, about yourself, and another sweet, charming dear, and Captain Bub. She — the lady sweet and charming — is

20*

a Southerner, or pretty nearly one, and Captain Bub
likes her. She is a relation of yours that you have
never seen and don't know ; and the whole matter
is romantic and curious enough for a novel.

"You remember, Captain Bub went to New Orleans with General Butler. Well, only a few days
after he arrived there, a young lady accosted him in
the street, and asked if he would be kind enough to
conduct her to the commanding general. She was very
genteel and modest, and didn't offer to. spit on him,
or pretend to be sick at the stomach when he touched
his cap. (Captain Bub is always *very* gentlemanly, if
he *is* my brother.) He told her he should be very
happy to conduct her to General Butler, but that the
general was engaged, and would probably not be able
to see her before the next day. At this she appeared ·
utterly dejected ; and she kept looking behind her, as
if she was afraid of something. He stood in front of
her, with his cap lifted from his head (I can see just ·
how graceful and handsome he looked), and, when the
pitiful tears fell from her eyes, he asked her if it
would be possible for one of General Butler's subordinate officers and one of his particular friends to be
of any immediate service to her ; at the same time
handing her his card, with the name of Captain Lawrence Ide Clandon on it.

"'I don't know,' she answered; 'but I think you
can if you will.' Then, looking straight into his face,
but blushing as she did so, she asked : 'Do I look
like an honest person ?' and, turning away, she wept
like a flood.

"'By Jove! you do!' exclaimed Captain Bub.

' It would be unsafe for a man to tell me you do
not.'

" ' Then can you see that I am protected — protected even from arrest as a thief, it may be — until
General Butler can see and hear me ? '

" Captain Bub looked at her with perfect astonishment. She bore every mark of being an amiable and
cultivated lady. Her conversation and manners both
indicated it. Moreover, she was very pretty, — not
quite so tall as you, and rather stouter, — with dark
hair, brown eyes, prominent but regular features, and
an unusually intelligent and sweet expression. Captain Bub was struck with her. · He pitied her, and
instinctively perceived that there couldn't be any cause
to charge her with crime.

" ' I think,' he said, ' that a word to General Butler
will procure me permission to keep you from all harm.
But the general will want to know your whole case in
twenty seconds. May I ask you some questions, so as
to speak intelligently to him ? He never admits anything on one's predilection or supposition, but dives
right for the facts.'

" Meanwhile, since Captain Bub had noticed her
frightened glances backward, they had naturally walked
towards General Butler's quarters.

" Clara — that is the young lady's name — Clara
Summers — appeared perplexed and abashed at the
further information thus demanded of her by a young
stranger-officer ; and she hesitated for a moment.
Then, looking up into his face, she inquired, ' Have
you a wife, or a dear sister ? '

" Captain Bub smiled, and said, ' I am not so

fortunate as to have a wife yet; but I have a very dear
sister, not far from your own age, as I should guess.'
(Of course he meant me, Stella. I'm glad that he
and I think so much of each other.)

" ' I'll tell you my story,' Clara said to him. ' But
it is shocking, and would be painful to relate even to
your sister, if she were my near friend. Think of
what she would have to do if in my place; and forgive me for telling you some such dreadful things as
I must refer to if you are to hear the truth.'

" Then she gave him an outline of her whole history.

" She was born in Virginia; but her parents came
from Boston. Her father's name was James Summers.
Her mother's maiden name was Julia Torson.

" You will see instantly that Clara is your husband's
niece, — the person who, if found, was to have his property, in case you shouldn't abide by the will. Isn't it
funny that she should turn up in this way, and now be
actually in the house of your best friend? — for she is
here with me.

" But I must go back to the story.

" When Clara's mother was a young lady, she was
a great favorite, it seems, with some old stick or other
in Boston, who was very rich, and whom her father
desired she should marry. But she couldn't be persuaded to do it. She had formed certain preferences
of her own, which were in the way of any such
arrangement. The affair ended by her marrying
Mr. Summers, — a young man whom she loved, — and
being forbidden ever afterwards to enter her father's
house.

" Her brother, who was several years older than
she, and who had already acquired some property,
sided with her father, called her a fool, and said she
had disgraced them both.

" It wasn't so very easy to see why; for Mr.
Summers was a young lawyer of considerable promise,
who soon moved with his wife to Virginia, becoming
successful, and even quite distinguished in his profession.

" But he had one proud fault. Having been snubbed
by his wife's father and brother, he was determined
to maintain her in style and affluence. He did so;
but spent his income, instead of saving it. He was
young, and his practice was constantly increasing. He
thought there would be time enough to accumulate
money when he desired.

" It was so for eleven years; when suddenly he
died.

" His wife had been more prudent than he. She
had persuaded him to buy a house, at one time when
he was able to make the investment; and when his
affairs were settled up, she found herself in possession
of this and some other property, which, being sold,
yielded her a few thousand dollars.

" She then came North, Clara being about ten years
old.

" On the way from Philadelphia to New York, Mrs.
Summers was sick, and was confined to her state-room
on the boat. Clara was permitted to run about in
the cabin, promising she would go but a certain distance from the door of the state-room. A number of
the passengers took a good deal of notice of her, and

as she was not timid, she was quite willing to receive their attentions and their sweetmeats. One gentleman seemed to take a special fancy to her; but finally, asking her name, and being told it was Clara Payson Summers, he let go her hand abruptly, and said not another word to her while she was on the boat. She thought it a strange incident at the time, but soon forgot it. A day or two afterwards, she happened to recall it, and spoke of it to her mother. Mrs. Summers inquired minutely about the gentleman's appearance.

"'He was pretty big,' Clara said, 'and had a scar on his forehead, the shape of a *y* upside down (λ), and a large ring on his little finger, with a white stone in it; and on the stone was a lady's head, which looked, mamma, a great deal like yours, when you have your hair put up in puffs. He told me it was a picture of his mother.'

"'So it was, Clara,' replied Mrs. Summers; 'and it was a picture of *my* mother too. That man, my daughter, was your uncle. But he hates me, and he will never love you.'

"Clara says she has never forgotten the sad, weary look with which her poor mother said this.

"You knew the man also, Stella; and you have known him still better, since. Do you suppose he relented a little, in after years, and that the image of Clara *would* haunt him? For you know you told me about the chance he gave her in his will; though he evidently didn't really believe it would avail her much.

"She never saw him again, and I presume he never took any pains to inquire after her.

"Mrs. Summers' object in coming North, was to give Clara a thorough education, and to fit her for a teacher, as she might some time have to rely wholly on her own exertions for support. She was placed at school; and, if my judgment is worth anything, she must have realized every expectation. My dear Stella, she is positively the smartest and sweetest girl I ever met, your own peerless self excepted. I don't wonder a bit that Captain Bub took a fancy to her.

"But how I ramble all around in the account of her!

"Clara and her mother lived at the North eight years, Mrs. Summers being an invalid most of the time.

"About the close of the eighth year she died. The money was nearly all spent, but Clara had as good an education as one of our best seminaries could afford her. Six months after her mother's death she was prevailed upon to go to South Carolina as a teacher in a gentleman's family there.

"Now comes the bitterest part of what poor, dear Clara had to tell Captain Bub.

"Colonel Rawlston, with whom she went to reside, was an elderly man, polite and pleasant, whose household was composed of three daughters and one son, the latter a young lad of ten years. Colonel Rawlston's wife had been dead a few months, and his eldest daughter supplied her mother's place as mistress of the mansion. Her education was presumed to be complete. Clara's duty was to instruct the two younger daughters in French and music, and the lad in whatever he could be persuaded to learn, except riding horses and shooting birds, — two accomplishments to which his mind was principally given. He immediately became attached,

however, to the ' Yankee lady,' as he termed Clara, and
an occasional lesson was coaxed out of him. He told
Clara that she wasn't at all the woman he had expected
to see when he heard she was coming. He thought
all the Yankee women had ' peaked noses, long, bony
arms, only a little thin hair on their heads, and couldn't
see without specs ; ' but that she was ' handsomer than
any of his sisters except Sallie, and a heap pleasanter.'

" This Sallie, the youngest daughter, was Clara's
favorite. She was, as young Ben had said, the prettiest
one of the three, as she was also the most amiable.
She was quiet and sad, and very unobtrusive. She
always dressed with remarkable plainness, and shunned,
instead of courting society. Her sisters generally treated her with kindness ; but appeared quite willing to
encourage her seclusive tastes and habits.

" You'll hardly believe why, Stella. Southern men
are strange beings. Colonel Rawlston, Clara says, was
an educated, agreeable man ; but Sallie, though *his*
daughter, was not his wife's child, but the child of a
quadroon woman, at one time his mistress and slave,
who was herself the daughter of a Southern senator.

" She didn't wish to live in the relation imposed upon
her by Colonel Rawlston, and her reluctance was well
known to his wife, who, like a Christian Northern
woman as she was, pitied the bondmaid instead of
hating her.

" Sallie was born, and her mother dying within a
year, Mrs. Rawlston insisted on adopting the little one
as her own child, which she finally did. When Sallie
was fourteen, she heard the circumstances of her birth
related by an old slave, and went directly to Mrs. Rawl-

ston, to know if it was possible they were true. The good woman told her they were; but called Sallie her own dear daughter, soothing and comforting her in every way she could.

" The dear girl's heart was broken. From that hour she was melancholy and timid, shunning nearly all acquaintances. But to Mrs. Rawlston she was more than a daughter, — she was truly a willing, a devoted slave. During the lady's long sickness (she died of consumption) Sallie was her constant attendant and untiring nurse. She saw her last faint smile, and received her last blessing.

" Clara had been but a short time in Colonel Rawlston's family, when Sallie informed her of these things, asking the young teacher if she could love and instruct her as well as if she were really Mrs. Rawlston's daughter. Her sisters, she said, had obeyed their mother's dying injunction to be kind to her; but they were proud, and, as her history was not a complete secret, how could they be fully reconciled to the relation she bore to them? Little Ben, she was sure, loved her fondly, and now, while he was a child, she found much happiness in his attachment. But her chief hope was that Clara would teach her all that she herself knew, so that in two or three years she could go North, live there, and take care of herself.

" O Stella! how I wish she could have done so, and could have come here to me! But worse than that was to befall the darling.

" When Clara had been with her a year and a half, — the scholar, as Clara asserts, being superior to the teacher, — and when they had vowed inseparable friendship at the North, where they intended going together, Colonel Rawlston died. His estate was found nearly insolvent, and the charge of the family devolved on Captain Raspar Rawlston, the eldest son, who had lived many years in New Orleans, and who seemed almost a stranger to his sisters and his young brother.

"He was a terrible man,—a dealer in cotton and slaves, who was very rich, but reckless and dissipated. (I believe that nasty rum puts out the last spark of a man's decency.)

"What do you think he did? He introduced the two sisters into the most aristocratic society of New Orleans, and claimed Sallie as his slave, that he had bought in settling up his father's estate. She was a ' nigger,' he said, ' but one that had been a favorite in the family.'

"Then he tried to make her his mistress, having, it was reported, three others already. He kept her away from his sisters and little Ben, threatened her, and persecuted her, until at last, in a fit of desperation, she snatched one of his own pistols, and spattered her brains in the wretch's face.

"A week or two previously she had insisted on giving Clara an elegant necklace, which she had worn, and with it a locket containing her likeness. Rawlston found it out. Not satisfied with what he had done, he soon attempted to repeat the experiment on Sallie's friend, the free, white Clara; and, as one of his loving bits of persuasion, swore he would have her arrested as a thief, if she made any disturbance. He actually abducted her from his residence, where she had remained with his sisters. But she escaped from him.

"'And now, sir,' said she to Captain Bub, as she finished the account, — which I, of course, have spun out so as to give you every particular, — 'and now, sir, I have found *you*, — a gentleman I am sure; and can thank God I am safe.'

"Perhaps, my dear Stella, you can imagine how Captain Bub bore the recital. I asked Clara. She said that he was perfectly dumb with astonishment. When she came to Sallie's death, his eyes fairly turned round in their sockets, and flashed with a green glow, like a cat's. He didn't speak a word for several minutes, and then his voice was calm and low. But she says she inwardly prayed that Captain Rawlston wouldn't permit himself to send for her that day, and almost as much for his own sake as for hers.

"She wasn't inquired for; but the next morning a file of soldiers proceeded to Captain Rawlston's house, to summon him, with his two sisters and little Ben, to appear at General Butler's head-quarters. It was a summons which didn't admit of hesitation or delay on the part of any one of them. They were there in a short time, and were questioned separately.

"Captain Rawlston was disposed to be haughty and imposing. He said it was quite likely he had accused a certain Miss Summers, or one passing under that name, — some Yankee woman of no account, — of stealing. It was also quite likely he might have threatened her for so doing. He was not aware, however, that such a matter had anything to do with the military government of New Orleans.

"'You have much to learn, sir,' replied General

Butler. 'Do you know the whereabouts of a young person named Sallie Rawlston?'

" ' A certain girl Sallie, whom I suppose you mean, was my nigger. She was foolish enough to blow her head off some days since. If you want her, you'll have to look for her in h——.'

" ' Take care of this brute!' ordered General Butler. ' I shall want him again.'

" The sisters were each examined. They were lady-like, and both seemed surprised, though pleased, to see Clara. They hesitated, evidently not knowing for what they were there, or what they were expected to say. They testified wonderingly to Clara's attainments, integrity, and gentleness.

" Then little Ben was brought in. He appeared slightly intimidated at first, probably having heard terrible stories about the Yankee soldiers. But the sight of Clara reassured him. He ran to her, and, putting his arms around her neck, kissed her, and wanted to know if anybody had dared to keep his dear Clara Summers there against her will.

" No, she said, she had come there of her own accord.

" ' My son,' asked General Butler, ' would your dear Clara Summers steal anything? — say this chain and the locket.'

" The child stamped his foot, and burst into tears.

" ' Are you her friend, or not?' he asked.

" ' Yes, my little man, I am her friend,' the general answered, with a smile.

" ' Well, then,' cried Ben, ' if you'll lend me those pistols of yours, I'll fight with any man that says Clara

Summers would steal. I'm little, sir, but I can shoot like the devil. My sister Sallie, my dearest pet sister, gave those things to Miss Summers, and I saw her do it. Will you let me take the pistols?'

" ' Perhaps I will let you take the pistols some time, my little friend; but no one here believes Miss Summers would steal, any more than you do. Your brother thought so; but he has made a mistake.'

" ' My brother thought so? He's a fool. He's mean, he is. He made Sallie go away from us; and she's dead, sir.'

" Such was little Ben's testimony; and, as you may suppose, it was satisfactory.

" Ben was sent out, and Captain Rawlston brought back.

" He was found guilty of using vile, slanderous, and threatening language to Clara Summers; of an assault upon her, and attempted abduction.

" ' I have seen and questioned your sisters and little brother,' said General Butler. ' I respect them highly They alone save you from Fort Jackson. You will pay within an hour, into the hands of Captain Clandon here, five thousand dollars, as a partial compensation to Miss Summers for your insults.'

" Such was the substance of General Butler's decision.

" ' I'll do no such thing!' shouted Captain Rawlston : ' I'll be d—— first.'

" ' Just as you please, then,' was the general's grim reply. ' Captain Clandon, you will please fill an order to have this man hanged to-morrow at sunrise. Lieutenant, what comes next?'

21*

" Rawlston was thunderstruck. Here was a Union general to be obeyed by the 'chivalry' of New Orleans. Or, if not, the chivalry must swing for it.

" 'I'll pay the money,' growled the culprit; 'but such usurpation I never heard of.'

" 'Probably not, sir. Captain Clandon, he proposes to pay the money. It must be in gold. You will accompany him, take a man or two with you, and, when the proper amount is in your keeping, discharge the fellow. Should he attempt to escape, remember that you are reputed to carry the surest pistol, next to mine, in the Department of the Gulf. I doubt he has a soul; but let that at least be the only part of him that shall elude you.'

" The money was paid. It was given to Clara, and as soon as convenient she came North. Captain Bub insisted on having her come right here. He acknowledges, in his letters, that he likes her very much, and wants me to see how much I can think of her. I shall have no trouble in being very fond of her. She seems sweeter and more pleasant every day. She's stylish too as a princess, though as plain in her tastes as yourself.

" I've told her all about you. Captain Bub informed her that he knew her uncle's widow, — 'a young woman,' he said, ' to be sought and respected as much as any lady in the United States.' That was starting Clara with a fair impression, — wasn't it? — and I've put on all the finishing touches. I wish you could meet her right away: only then, with you two together, I should have to sit demurely in a corner and play with my thumbs.

" But I must stop writing, or you'll never get through my letter in the world. I'll let the rest I had to say go till the next time ; or still better, till you come and see me again.

" Can't you do it right away ? Yes, do. Make Clara and me a visit. We'll have good times. You and Clara can talk up the past, present, and future, interspersed with great men and women ; and when I can't reach your sublime heights, Charley Merlow and I will perhaps try to entertain each other in such poor way as the like can.

" Do come, Stella, and I'll tell you when Charley and I are going to be married. We've been lovers an age. 'Twont be possible to wait much longer.

" Good-by.

" As ever,

" YOUR CORA."

CHAPTER XXVIII

STELLA dropped the letter, and, after sitting immovable and wrapped in meditation for several minutes, she hastened to her piano, and the beautiful song, "We may be happy yet," rang through the house, with every shade of force and expression, from the simple melody played with the utmost thoughtful tenderness, to the storm of frantic hilarity in which the air itself was almost covered up and lost in the exuberant wildness of variation. Then she stepped to her writing-table and penned a note to Cora, stating that she should be at Ironton the next evening.

Stella had confidence in her judgment of persons. She wished to see Clara Summers at once, and satisfy herself regarding the mind and heart of one on whom her happiness now so much depended. For she had determined that if Clara should prove to be all that Cora had depicted, she should very soon be placed in possession of the greater part of that estate by which Stella herself had been so hampered and circumscribed.

Yet now, more than ever, she desired the means of her own comfortable independence. She remembered, of course, the object for which her father was indefatigably laboring. He had already done even better than

(248)

he anticipated. He was making money very rapidly, and she knew it was for her. But the most of it was constantly invested. As her father's operations had become larger, he had grown to be more and more the venturesome old merchant, seeming bent on making good all his former losses. He was vigilant and shrewd. Still, it was possible that his plans might again miscarry. Then Stella would need something of her own, for him and for her. Earnest had been so badly disabled by his wounds, and, still worse, by the fall from his horse, simultaneously received, that, although he would not probably be maimed, he might never again be able to resume his duties as a soldier; and his surgeons had told him that, for many months at best, he could not completely recover his strength. Him above all else, Stella could not but include in her desires and calculations.

She had always felt that in strict justice she was entitled to a part of her husband's property, — sufficient to support her comfortably. If he had awarded her so much unconditionally, leaving her mind and body free, she would have been perfectly satisfied. Had she known of such a niece as Clara, she would have begged to have her handsomely endowed, as she would have done for all others having natural claims on the estate. She appreciated the value of money, having no sentimental abomination of it, but only of vanities, frivolities, and abuses so generally attaching themselves to it. She knew that it gave, in special, the best of all the world's good gifts to a superior mind, — the leisure for cultivation and for self-satisfying action. One mode of such action might easily be to aid hundreds of fellow-beings, — a matter, certainly, which Stella, if any one, could comprehend.

Would it be proper, then, for her to be the recipient of a small part of this fortune which she had about decided to turn immediately over to Clara? Such a person as Clara must be, would not fail in generous appreciation of a transfer, which one word spoken by her uncle's widow could prevent in any case. No, surely not. And she would wish that Stella should still derive some benefit from what she had in so large a degree possessed. Stella thought of her old father, and of her stricken young lover, and said this would be right: she should have some little of Mr. Torson's large wealth. Clara would surely make her the offer.

Stella was not mistaken. Clara Summers was as represented, — generous, enthusiastic, noble, and highly intellectual. Having been thrown upon her own resources, she was self-dependent; and, with the most feminine delicacy of perception, she had a masculine business tact. Stella perceived at once that her new-found niece was an impersonation of the most lovely features of the present, and a mirror of the future; that her mind dwelt in the realm of ideas; her soul revolved, one with the stars, in the orbit of obedience, law, duty. There was no mistaking that frank, unreserved manner, those eager, unstudied words. What she looked and said, that she felt and meant. And her glances were reflections of the heavens, and her sayings were not those of the selfish or the common. For Stella they were easy to interpret. In three hours she knew Clara well, and loved her fervently. In three days, she trusted her thus: —

Her arms were about the daughter of Virginia, and they sat together.

"Clara, dear," she said, " I want you to take your uncle's fortune. You have heard how it has grieved me, perhaps."

" Yes ; and what will you do then ? "·

" What would you have me do ? "

" Take three quarters of it, or what more you say, directly back, at my hands, and then love me as your niece and your friend. Will you do that ? "

" No, my Clara, not wholly. I will love you in any way you please. But I do not feel as though much of that fortune belongs to me. Your uncle did not want to trust me with it. He said so. He did not know, of course, that he had a niece who could use it more effectually than myself; and that too in ways I might like to employ it. But that was his own affair. He ran the risk. I regard it as his own responsibility. Yet I have a theory in the matter. I think that when he, a rich man, contemplated leaving me as his widow, it was my right to have a comfortable provision to use unfettered. I would have been content with two or three times my yearly income, as the entire amount, if he had wished. He gave me, instead, the use of the whole estate, but bound me to it like a slave. You shall have the money, — the whole of it. I will then take, if you say so, as a gift of your love, twenty-five or thirty thousand dollars. I think I have a rightful claim to so much."

" Well, you *are* a scrupulous soul," exclaimed Clara, with a smile and a tighter clasp of the arms. " But why, in the name of sense and sensibility, are you not

as much entitled to ten times the amount you specify
as to that little end of the fortune ? You were his wife.
I was only his niece. My parents displeased him. You
lived with him, faithful and trusted ; and all the more
to be treated handsomely, as you did so without loving
him. It is evident that he only gave me a chance in
the will because he knew nothing about me; and he
probably doubted my ever reaping any benefit from it.
I shall employ the money as much against his bygone
wishes as you would do. I shall take that course, devoid the smallest twinge of conscience. I am clear on
the subject. To me, it is plainly my duty to disregard
the inclinations of my sometime uncle. It is only a
trifle of indirection to put the whole estate on me. No,
positively, my good aunty, my dear Stella, your terms
are ' out of the question,' as the merchants say. You
are altogether ' too hard on me.' But I am sure it is
impossible for us to quarrel seriously about money. We
already know each other too well for that. Let me tell
you, however, what you may do. You may transfer
every cent to me as soon as you please. Then, what
I can induce you and yours to accept, by the power of
tongue and quill, I suppose will be my affair."

She kissed Stella as she finished speaking. The ca-
ress was returned, and Stella said that she must content
herself, she supposed, with being persuaded.

CHAPTER XXIX.

ON the 7th of July, the "Ironton Evening Chronicle" announced that Captain Earnest Acton had arrived in town, still suffering severely from his wounds received at the battle of Fair Oaks.

"We are sorry to say," continued the article, "that it is feared this gallant officer will not be able to resume his place in the field. It was supposed at first, as our readers will remember, that his wounds were fatal. In his almost superhuman effort to hold our heroic boys up to their task, after it seemed a hopeless one, Captain Acton's person was necessarily exposed with utter indifference. The result is fresh in all minds.

"He has partly recovered from his bullet-wounds, and it is thought he will fully recover from them. But in falling from his horse, he received injuries which will probably affect his spine, rendering him weak for many months, if not permanently preventing him from again serving his country in battle.

"We sincerely regret to learn the fact. He was soon to have held a higher position in the army, and would have filled it with signal ability.

"It is a loss which the service can ill afford, to be deprived of those who, in addition to bravery and address, have a thorough understanding of the present momentous contest in all its bearings, and who feel that no sacrifice can be too great, in securing for a continent impartial freedom and enduring justice. Captain Acton was one of these. As he fought at Fair Oaks against all odds, so we hope, against all opinions, that he will yet live to fight again."

The day after the above mention of Earnest's return home, he was not a little surprised by the following letter.

"AT CORA CLANDON'S.

"DEAR SIR : —

"I do not know that you have yet heard of any such person as myself. Permit me, then, to introduce you to Miss Clara Summers, the niece of the late J. Z. Torson, Esq., and, much better, the friend, as well as niece, of his lovely and accomplished widow.

"During the last few days I have been placed in possession of my deceased uncle's entire property. While living, that gentleman did not see fit to own me as his relative ; and at his death, did not know, I suppose, — at least was not at all certain, — that I was in existence. Still, he saw fit to make in his will a provision through which my dear Aunt Stella has turned over to me his fortune. On so doing, she expressed herself willing to take back, as a gift from me, the very modest, or rather, under the circumstances, the very pitiful allowance of twenty-five thousand dollars. We could not agree upon that sum. She has, it seems to me, by every principle of equity, a much better right to three quarters of the whole estate, than L have to keep for myself the remaining quarter.

" However, she cannot be brought to my terms. She says that she became my uncle's wife against her judgment, and very reluctantly. She took no thought of his money ; and, as he did not want her to have it, she thinks that, out of self-respect, she ought to take no more than will support her comfortably and pleasantly. I cannot look at the matter in any such light. I have therefore insisted on putting into her hands twice the sum she proposed (fifty thousand dollars), and, by my utmost powers of persuasion, have at last prevailed upon her to retain that amount.

" Now I want to ask a favor of you. It is, that you will receive the like sum, and make what disposition of it you choose. Then I shall beg of Stella's father that he will do the same.

" My uncle has, living, two or three distant relatives, — poor and common, but worthy people, — whom he did not recognize in any way, as I can learn, but who have, I think, some natural claim to a small part of his property. I intend they shall have moderate bequests at once, just as though they had been remembered in the will.

" There will be left, as I compute, something over a hundred and fifty thousand dollars for my share. If you and her father should agree to my proposals, my dear aunt, my sweet friend Stella, will have, directly and indirectly, about that amount also, — the estate being divided not far from equally between us.

" It appears to me that *my* self-respect is at stake, as well as hers. She should have had the unfettered use of the estate. It was a gross insult and injustice to so noble a woman to deprive her of it. I, the distant, unknown niece, might have had, by right, a small provision, — as much, or rather more, than Stella first proposed to accept from me. And then I should have been much richer than I ever expected to be. Yet, simply because I can do so, I have now figured for myself one hundred and fifty thousand dollars, to half of which, at least, Stella has a better right than I. Is it fair to insist on my being still more avaricious?

"Furthermore, if my uncle were now alive, holding his former views, he would be as much averse to seeing me in possession of his riches, as any other person whatever. For the most of his opinions I have no respect, and for his prejudices I don't care a fig. I shall employ the bulk of his wealth directly against his selfish and obsolescent notions. The system of slavery, for instance, which he inclined to propitiate, if not to foster, I hate heartily, knowing it thoroughly. His property shall aid in supplying materials for its destruction. My religion, too, is practical, — a thing to be used for the welfare of God's children *here* as well as hereafter. What my uncle termed New England 'infidelity,' — that intense purification of ritualism, and a purification whose exponents have been some of the greatest religious souls living or dead, — I do not fear as he did, knowing more about it, probably, than he had the inducement to comprehend. I would lend it my dollars much more readily than for theological propagation at Timbuctoo. For all these considerations, my mediocre uncle's superior and magnanimous wife might just as well have his fortune as might his wilful and headstrong niece.

"But I have another reason for mentioning my own

tendencies. Sensitive people recoil from gifts; and if you are not persuaded that you should accept my offer as a right due Stella, I want to prevail on you to take it as a present due yourself. You would not consent to an aimless donation; probably not to one of mere good-feeling: — you must understand the giver; the giver must understand you. Now, if I can give from sufficiently exalted grounds, perhaps you will grant me the pleasure of acceptance. I have listened with deep interest to much I have heard very discriminating friends say regarding you; I am acquainted with many of your actions, as well as your thoughts. You have been occupied with the gravest questions and interests which affect the human kind. I can easily perceive — it was never plainer than now — what vast influence for good, a generous mind, powerful, cultivated, and independent, can exert in the world. You would commend me, if I saw fit to tender a considerable present to a beneficent institution. Yet I know several Americans, each one of whom is a greater benefit to the country than any hundred such institutions that could be picked out. Pardon me for offering you the sincere compliment of thinking that you have begun life in a way to become such a man.

" Believing so, I shall be very grateful, I assure you, if permitted a contribution to the more ordinary materials of your advancement and usefulness. What I shall expect in return, yet have no need to ask, is, that the zeal of the scholar for the true and the right will equal that of the former soldier, who now, it is said, can be a soldier no more.

" Hoping that I may have, at the proper time, the

22 *

honor of being your niece, I content myself now with being

" Your friend,
" CLARA SUMMERS.

" To Capt. EARNEST ACTON."

Clara's letter was enclosed to Stella, and sent to Boston, whither the two had gone some days before, Clara having returned alone. Mr. Gebard, a conscientious and able young lawyer, had accompanied them to Boston. Their purpose had been to enter at once upon the transaction which Clara's letter now referred to as complete.

Stella had acknowledged her infraction of the will, and nothing could be done but to execute the provision in favor of Clara Summers. So Clara became an heiress.

The parties representing the pro-slavery interest in the will had materially changed their views since the inauguration of rebellion, and said that they should now be heartily ashamed to lend their efforts in even the remotest manner to oppose the cause of freedom. They were democrats of the Butler persuasion.

The theological interest was at first disposed to stand out, especially as it had just entertained hopes of coming into its share of the property, through Snorton Ruffat, the peculating quartermaster of F——, who, after being dismissed the service of his much-abused country, had come to Boston, and, seeing Stella in the street, had made inquiries by which he learned something of her history, and obtained a clew to the tenor of the will. He was immediately eager for retaliation, offering to prove that Stella had no further claim upon the Torson estate. The regenerated hunkers were cool to him; the agents of theology hailed his statement with gladness. But at this juncture Clara Summers stepped in, Mr. Gebard's keen eyes twinkled humorously, and the necessary documents were in his pocket. Distinguished counsel on both sides declared the case to be clear, all argument to be futile. Discomfited theology therefore concluded to be peaceable, — its invariable course in all history, when it has been able to take no other.

The business settled, as far as Clara's presence was necessary, she returned to Ironton, Stella promising to follow her soon, and to complete the visit, never too long, which she had intended for Cora.

" And where we can be conveniently near our dear friend Captain Acton, my delectable auntie," suggested the smiling Clara.

But, as we have seen, the " delectable auntie " had not yet come.

So Clara's letter was sent to her. Earnest would not conclude anything in her behalf without consulting her, and he asked her judgment concerning his own acceptance of so large a gift, provided she should not wish him to take it, having her welfare in view.

Stella replied: " Do as you like, my dear Earnest — as you think right and best. I trust your judgment more than my own. Perhaps my feelings were morbid regarding my apportionment. But I never craved a very large fortune, and I came almost to *hate* Mr. Torson's money.

" Now it is Clara's. She certainly has a right to dispose of it as she chooses.

" One thing I will say of her. She is regal in mind and heart. She is not to be judged by others. She can be injured neither by granting nor by submitting to favors.

" Pardon me, my love, a bit of pleasantry. Clara is the only person I have met, whom I would do the honor to be jealous of, if you knew how to be capricious. She is a pearl of great price."

. . . .

Earnest soon had an interview with Clara, and, after conversing with her an hour or two, he concluded to take from her fifty thousand dollars, which she bestowed with as simple satisfaction as that with which a generous child shares an orange with a pet companion.

Yet this superb young woman had, on one or two occasions, been in actual need of a few dollars. She had labored for her daily bread, and was already meditating upon the manner of investing her remaining capital, so as to make it pay every fair and honest cent. She was prudent, and of Yankee stock. Only she knew the meaning of a sacred trust.

CHAPTER XXX.

STELLA soon fulfilled her promise, coming back to Ironton to complete a visit of uncertain duration.

Clara remained there for the present, and to Cora's inexpressible, yet constantly declared satisfaction, the three friends were together under one roof, — all happy in the commodious mansion of Richard Clandon.

Cora wrote to her brother, "Captain Bub," all the circumstances of the young teacher's sudden transmutation to a lady of fortune; and deputed him, in Clara's name, to hunt up little Ben, and assure him that his friend Clara Summers remembered him with much affection, and would hold for him at the North five thousand dollars, — the money his brother had been obliged to pay her, — which the boy should have, with interest, whenever he should need it.

"Tell him, too, that if he is ever in trouble, he must come to Clara; and she will try to be a sister, almost as good to him as his poor Sallie.

"And now, sir," she continued, "you may as well be assured that Miss Summers will be, in this place, a person of innumerable attractions, acknowledged by several more than innumerable adorers. So look sharp, absent soldier. If you don't want her for my sister-in-law, what in the world shall I do with a brother of such sorry taste? If you do, — well, that's all: but time is precious where rubies are scarce. Get a furlough, my tall brother; get a furlough, and come to pay us your respects."

Captain Clandon replied that he should do so as soon as he could without personal discredit or injury to the service.

"In respect to Miss Summers," he wrote, "I shall defer, in my taste, to no one, not even to the crazy and bantering Sissy Cora herself. When I think of Miss Summers, I almost wish, momentarily, that I were one of the 'peace party' with you at home. Yet I suspect a man must be worthy of his country to win *her*.

"Seriously, dear Cora, the lady has left a deep impression on me. I think of her very often. If the beaux multiply to my harm, say to her that when the celestials are raffled for, I must positively have one chance in the chief prize. Then I will do my best, and abide my luck quietly, like a decent, practical fellow."

Cora was certainly proud of the fine, soldierly Captain Lawrence Ide Clandon, whose lofty figure and almost imperious bearing appeared in ridiculous contrast with her diminutive appellation of "Captain Bub." How could she help reading to Clara a brief extract from his letter!

"What shall I tell him?" she asked.

Clara smiled and blushed.

"Tell him the celestial raffle shall not come off while he is deprived of a chance."

Here were indications of more lovers for the future.

But Earnest and Stella, Charley Merlow and Cora, were soon to be established in another category. They were to move out of the world of " young people," all migrating together. The day was set. It was to be early in September.

By close care and constant attention to his ailments, Earnest had regained his health much more rapidly than was at first deemed possible. He was still rather weak, — so was easily fatigued ; but otherwise he appeared nearly as well as ever.

The marriage ceremony was very simple, — the immediate relatives and a few warmly attached friends being present at Mr. Clandon's, where the two young couples were joined in wedlock till death should sever the solemn tie. Weighty forms and profuse display were needless, that to them the hour and the lesson should be impressive. They had read the meaning of that blessed sacrament, in life and in their own souls. Thoughtfully yet gladly and trustingly it was to be received ; sacredly it was to be regarded and preserved. Years ago, in his boyhood, Earnest in particular had questioned the rite, as he had done with many another, — demanding its central import to him, to the world, to God. He had scrutinized its historical phases ; he had worked upon the problem of its moral aims.

Like all other of the world's chief institutions, he had found it established, first in human nature, then in customs and laws.

In the earliest ages, when the mind of childhood, with its restless and wilful strivings, was the motor and guide of mature men — their wishes having almost no limitation save the boundaries of their mere strength to do, — intellectual, reflective morality not yet evolved, — marriage was, as Earnest had found, the conjunction of tyrant and his toy or slave. The equality of woman's nature with man's was not perceived; for only the roughest properties of man's nature were held in esteem. Virtue was physical courage and force. Beauty was a sweet bauble, to occupy one's leisure; to be tossed aside or changed at one's pleasure. But the race grew out of childhood. In Greece, it became a sprightly, enthusiastic, sensitive youth. Man's attachment to woman was then purer. Spiritual values and refinements could be considered. The Grecian could love; and mere passion was no longer paramount. Civilization thus began the disuse of polygamy. Out of civilization at last came a soul loving enough to bestow Christianity upon the nations; and this was to complete the amelioration.

Earnest had but to look into his own experience for a reflex of the entire transition, except that his sentiments, through these changes, had not, as in history, been unfolded into multifarious actions.

Marriage, then, was to him, as its forms declared, an indissoluble bond, holding him to the pure, radiant woman there at his side, until her mild, happy eyes could look no more into his, or until his own should lie cold, rayless, and closed. "Love, cherish, and protect;" — this he would do, and would impart to her what wisdom and worth might be given him, that lasting benefit might flow upon her; and he would receive the promptings of her tenderness, her perceptive goodness and truth, that enduring profit should flow to him. "Love, honor, and obey;" — this *she* would do ; for to both there should be no standard of will or whim. The true, the right, which are that heaven the soul exists to seek, should claim the allegiance of each, and to this she and he would gladly bow.

Thankful for every good thought, for every noble deed of his life ; grateful to Heaven for every crystal of purity garnered, and for every temptation repelled ; glad that he was in some sort worthy, yet very humble that his worth was less than he or the angels might wish, — Earnest took the hand of her who was the chosen of his heart. Charley Merlow and Cora stood at their side. The few questions were asked, the few responses were given, and the friends were husbands and wives.

23

CHAPTER XXXI.

AMERICAN events of the year succeeding Earnest's marriage were to be momentous in their effect upon the ages, and prominent in the history of man. But amidst them Earnest was to be an observer, not what is commonly considered a doer. Cheerful and happy, capable of regular and continuous mental exertion, it was still much as the physicians had predicted : — he did not recover his full bodily vigor and endurance. Among half-invalid civilians he passed as sound. Old Doctor Wisely, and many another friend, bade him look well to his health if he wished to stay long with them.

His sword had been thrown aside. Now, however, he grasped the pen. He wielded it often, sometimes assured that error was weaker for the stroke, — that man was stronger in faith, higher in freedom.

Thus he gave the soul's mite of charity, as best he could, to the needy, while his open hand never withheld the more material offering with which God's rich are favored, not vulgarly, for themselves alone.

But, toward the close of the year 1863, Earnest determined upon visiting New Orleans. His chief motive was to see for himself the condition of the many poor beings, suddenly emerged from slavery to freedom, who were in that vicinity and at Port Royal, and to look into, or at least glance at, the noble efforts which had been made in their behalf by humane men and women of the North. He thought that perhaps he too might lend his hand, his brain, or, if nothing more, his purse, to the cause.

Not men now — not any one class of men, but man — all men, he regarded as his kin. There were threads of relation, he observed, however subtile, between him and the highest of these, — between him and the lowest also. He ignored none. But he perceived that of all classes in the land, the slaves and the freedmen most required, and best deserved, the philanthropic attentions of the intellectual, the wealthy, and the benignant. They were the most helpless, and had been brought to their impoverishment by the selfishness and sin of American citizens. It was for American citizens, then, to try, even at the eleventh hour, to afford them what incomplete reparation might be possible.

And above all, Earnest saw plainly that until the Negro should be recognized as a man, with all the natural rights and privileges of any and every man, the White would himself be petty, tyrannical, lazy and snobbish, — far enough from the likeness of God, in which he supposed himself created, — a sorry child, indeed, needing costly and severe instruction, some portion of which he was already receiving, from the sabre, the rifle, the cannon. Whatever then might contribute to the manhood of the Black, would contribute in quite as large degree to the manhood of the White; and

Earnest had traversed the centuries and the soul too carefully to be unaware that the White's manhood required enlargement much more than his pocket, however astonishing the fact might appear to him.

The riots of the preceding summer, induced by those not without a certain kind of intelligence, though consummated by the most ignorant of the vile, showed that in both the hyena and the jackal were to be tamed and overgrown, and that thousands of Americans were like the diseased and bloated German in the play, who was cured of his malady by having a large number of fools cut out of him. Education, employment, encouragement to martial valor, — anything that would aid the Black to assert his equal humanity, — would cut one fool of prejudice or distrust out of the White; and for the good of all, such surgery was unmistakably the achievement of the age. ·

It is probable, too, that those truculent demonstrations of July made Earnest, as many others, actually prefer, in most respects, the loyal, unoffending Negro, to the Celtic or Saxon savage, who ground him into bloody dust. Even the pictorial newspapers represented the rioter as uglier in face, uglier in form, worse smelling, and in every way lower and more beastly, than Sambo was ever depicted in the palmiest days of Pierce or Buchanan. The persecutor or persecuted — which would the sane, not to say the cultivated, deem superior ?

Indignation is sometimes a powerful auxiliary to benevolence. Possibly it was a spur to Earnest's action, when he decided to proceed South, and throw all the energy and means he could spare into a single channel.

For his health was not yet secure, and although Doctor Wisely said that the mere change would not be detrimental, he declared that his friend would be sure to excite and overwork himself, " into the box, into the box ! "

But go the young man would, and his wife, with their friend Clara Summers, accompanied him.

Clara enjoyed participating in all good works. Perhaps, also, she enjoyed the prospect of meeting Colonel Lawrence Ide Clandon ; — for " Captain Bub " now wore that title, with the corresponding insignia on coat and cap ; and he was still stationed at New Orleans, where the party were to proceed at first, stopping at Port Royal on their return. Three months after Cora had advised her brother to " get a furlough," he had procured it, and had spent a few weeks at home. It was not long before numerous young ladies began to whisper to each other, that Captain Clandon and Clara Summers were " engaged." It was probably true in this instance, though it is not infallibly so in all instances, as we know, when young ladies whisper the like.

But Earnest's plans were to be suddenly frustrated. The day after his arrival in New Orleans, while in the street with Stella and Cora, proceeding toward Colonel Clandon's quarters, they were met by a person in uniform, who appeared slightly intoxicated, and whom Stella immediately recognized as her old enemy, Ruffat, the discharged quartermaster. He also recognized her as well as Earnest, and was unable to contain his rage.

" Ah ! you damned Miss Virtuous ! " he exclaimed

23 *

with a sneer, as he brushed past, " so you've got your *brother* cured, — have you ? "

Earnest's first impulse was to knock him down.   But as his face flushed, and his arm rose, Stella besought him to take no notice of an affront from a drunken man ; or, at any rate, to do nothing more than report it to Colonel Clandon.

They passed on, and in a few minutes were in their friend's apartments.   On mentioning the insult to him, and the causes of it, his eye glittered and his lips whitened ; but in a tone even lower and calmer than usual, he inquired the man's name.   Stella gave it, and Earnest said he wore a lieutenant's cap.

" He could not have entered the service again under his old name, however," said Colonel Clandon.   " He has changed it.   Describe him, if you please."

To describe him was easy : —

" A coarse, gross person, with a repulsive scar from the left cheek-bone down toward the mouth."

" I know him," said the colonel ; and, stepping out of the room, he ordered that a guard be detailed to arrest Lieutenant Murkin, acting in the commissary department, and that the prisoner be brought forthwith to him.

It appears that the man was connected with the brigade of which Colonel Clandon was then acting as commander.

About ten minutes elapsed before his order was obeyed.   Meanwhile he conversed cordially with Earnest and Stella, and with a tone of unmistakable pride and tenderness, as he spoke to Clara Summers.

Lieutenant Murkin was brought in, and the guard

was ordered to leave the apartment, but to remain just outside the door, in the street. The culprit seemed to read his fate at a glance, and to feel that humiliation and renewed dismissal from the army would be meted out to him, if nothing worse. He glared on the party with maudlin yet desperate fury, and, before a single question was put to him, he suddenly drew a pistol and aimed it at Stella. Earnest as suddenly stepped in front of her. The pistol was discharged, and the ball entered his chest near the shoulder. He staggered and fell, and for an instant he alone was heeded. Colonel Clandon caught him, and laid him carefully on the floor, perceiving at once that, however badly he might be injured, he was not killed.

Murkin sprang to the door and rushed out. His colonel, whose lip was perfectly livid, but whose movements were fearfully calm, followed him. The guard had raised their muskets to fire, as Colonel Clandon reached the door. He ordered them not to do so. Then, as he drew a rather small single-barrelled pistol from his pocket, he muttered, — "No musket-shots: sure work for the fellow this time!"

That unerring weapon, — not the second in the Department of the Gulf, as General Butler had once intimated, but the first, the surest, — was levelled and fired.

"Sergeant," he ordered, "have the body removed: he is dead: you will find him shot through the brain."

He then sent for the two best surgeons of the brigade, and, composed and grim, he returned to Earnest.

As he reëntered the room Clara looked up into his face, then turned away with terror. Her lover's ex-

pression, at that moment, she never forgot. The
trained officer bred to kill; the flaming volcano hide-
ously self-controlled; the gladiator with deliberate
death in his gaze, — had broken through those refined,
handsome features; and, as he replaced the pistol in
his pocket, she read the fate of the man who had ventured to insult, and had then attempted to shoot, a
soldier's guest and a lady.

The look flitted away. Bending over Earnest, and
looking at the wound, he said, "It is serious, but not
mortal. He will live."

Stella and Cora were reässured; and, under his in-
flexible, imperturbable will, were quiet and helpful,
like children.

The surgeons came; Earnest was removed to another
apartment; his wound was dressed; and once more
Stella's soothing and vigilant attentions as a nurse,
were exerted to prolong that dear life.

He recovered very slowly. The shock had been too
great for one whose constitution was already shattered.
Tedious weeks passed before he gained sufficient
strength to walk, or even to stand. Finally it was
thought that he could return North with safety; and, as
he was impatient to go, Colonel Clandon secured the
party every comfort that could be afforded them for the
voyage, and they started for New York.

The passage was long and stormy, and when they
reached that city, Earnest was obliged to wait there
several days. He was too weak to continue his journey immediately to Ironton.

"Once in our snug home, which you have arranged
so cosily, my Stella, and I feel as though I should
scarcely leave it many times again."

Such was his first intimation, — which was spoken with a quiet smile, — that he looked forward to what Stella and Clara had both begun to dread, in spite of their hopes, although neither would own it to the other by as much as a look.

Stella perceived his meaning instantly.

"O Earnest!" she murmured, and sank to the floor.

She had borne up with cheerfulness, even humor, until that moment. But she had come to place such implicit reliance on what her husband said, that now, when he spoke thus to her, she felt as though even this matter were settled ; that she must give him up ; that before long he would die.

Fair, loving young wife, — it was well, perhaps, to prepare her for the stroke. Yet how could she bear it? It seemed as though her own life would ebb immediately away, if his were taken from her.

CHAPTER XXXII.

EARNEST was not mistaken. He had but a short time to live. From this last infliction by the bullet, with the attendant debility, he never recovered, although he lingered several weeks, between life and death, after he reached home.

To him it was not dreadful to die. In his early youth, it will be remembered, life, not its termination, had appeared terrible ; and more than once, in his doubt, his misanthropy, his antagonism with the world's ideas and endeavors, he had longed to flee anywhere away from the hated scene. So trivial, so selfish, so mean it all seemed, that why should he stay where there was nothing, and yet worse than nothing, for one like him ? Bitterly he had asked himself the question ; then, from regard to others, and from sheer scorn of all possible events, he had still maundered and groped along, tempted, but not quite enticed, by every dark rolling stream, until at last the sunlight of truth and faith broke through upon his soul, and he felt as jubilant in his independence of persons and circumstances, as he had felt disconsolate before their secret was read and their tendency revealed. The sphinx answered, the riddle solved, the heavens opened, — what was there now to fear ?

(274)

" It is pleasant to die if there be gods ; it is sad to live if there be none."

" True, Marcus Antoninus," Earnest could declare ; " and I have beheld the gods : it is beautiful to live, it is beautiful to die. Sad ? There is nothing sad, but living to hatred, and littleness, and folly."

Whatever the sermons teach, the bed of death is not' commonly a spectacle of terror to the departing soul. Sorrowful it may often be to leave its familiar surroundings ; unspeakably pained it may be to sever from other loved souls whom it could aid and succor in this hard circle of fleshly phantoms, where none may be left to protect when it is withdrawn. But for itself it does not usually tremble, if left to its own thoughts, and to its God.

Every one views himself as no one else can regard him. He sees where his ignorance submerged him in sin, — where circumstances bore down upon him with a pressure, overwhelming at the moment, if -not at a later moment when he might have been stronger to resist. He would do better now, he feels ; but could not do better then. Somewhere there will be help for him, — somewhere, pardon. Such is doubtless the view and the hope of the very worst : else would he crave dissolution, annihilation, the sooner the better, by his own hand. For the universe is a poisoned dagger to the breaker of its laws, and stabs the criminal, of its own accord, at every turn.

Even the most vile and wretched often die with complacency, with gladness : for is not hope literally their all ? William Mumford the gambler, like John Brown the religious enthusiast, is hanged perfectly composed.

But a faith, little or great — anything that is trusted, — makes death a festival. Relying upon it, the Hindoo will pitch himself into the mouth of the nearest crocodile, and the Christian will sing hymns at the stake while his tongue shrivels in his throat, and the throat is crisping into cinders. If Voltaire the sceptic will meet death calmly and courteously, much as he would greet a polite Frenchman, what affright has it to the searching insight of Socrates, or the all-believing, all-pitying love of Jesus?

It had been Earnest Acton's fortune to live his short but crowded life, which was now about to breathe itself away, in a period when old forms of faith had been broken up, while many materialistic, and practically atheistical minds yet clung to the creeds and rituals for respectability or greed; while many other minds — the little and common — honestly worshipped in the old ways, unquestioning because unthinking; and while a few other minds, — active, conscientious, and aspiring, but without intuitive perception sufficient to melt forms and doctrines into their historical meaning and essence, — after struggling a while with doubts that *would* arise, looked upon all matters as doubtful, and then, unreconciled with their thoughts, but needing some faith, accepted the one of the most accessible evangelical church, and debarred the intellect from further questioning.

These three classes composed the conventional religionists, — a large body, excluding and misapprehending the loftiest intelligence and deepest piety of the time, and hesitant to accept the noblest works; but still helpful to themselves, and beneficent to the country, especially during the last two or three years, by magnificent undertakings of patriotism, charity, and practical Christian mercy.

Outside their circle, beyond it and above it, lived and labored in America some of the mightiest religious spirits that ever existed in the world. They were called infidel, yet they were most faithful ; they were called destroyers, yet they were constructors. They were confounded with the deists of the eighteenth century. But what were Voltaire and Hume and Gibbon? Strong men, it is true, and superior in a moral as every other sense to the majority of their contemporaries. But they were of this world: they lived in material facts. Seeing the rubbish which littered Church and State, they kicked it out of the way, doing noisy and disagreeable, but worthy service.

They were so impatient, however, of the rubbish, that they spurned spiritual truths which it concealed.

They caused every good intellect to doubt ; but this was all ; they helped it no farther.

The nineteenth century completed their task, thanking them for all their negative demonstrations, but reconciling these with the presence of God in the human soul, and with the exalted mission of the Christian Religion.

Through the thick darkness Germany first saw the new sun, while yet it has shone most brightly upon that favored granite where the Pilgrim landed solely that he might worship his God ; and, when it lighted Theodore Parker into the world, it made even the *piety* of ecclesiasticism appear as inferior as its mental capacity.

24

The number of minds that had completely and satisfactorily wrought out within themselves this transition, was comparatively very small. Earnest had followed them, had understood them, was one of them.

Then there was a large class in the process of that transmutation which he had undergone. They were rationalists, doubters, and sneerers, of all shades and degrees. The most of them were honest, well-meaning, and instinctively favorable to each noble movement for the freedom and elevation of mankind. Uncertain of man's relation to God, they yet held to man's just relation to his fellow-beings.

Earnest had known a few men, like his father, so natural and unconstrained in an artificial epoch, that they had walked along untouched by dogmas and mystifications, believing in God, believing in goodness, and asking no more. They were too healthy to catch the prevailing theological epidemics, and so had never been troubled with the affliction or the cure.

Through such a period of spiritual convulsion, with the changes it brought upon institutions and customs, Earnest Acton had journeyed to an overlooking, inclusive faith, and now the journey was to end.

To leave Stella, while they were both so young, and had just begun their glad dependence on each other, — this was the keenest sorrow, though less for him than for the dear one to be left behind. Heavy-hearted she would be, heavy-eyed and dreary.

But the world would still be around her; and her duty would ever be before her. If there would be few to bless her as he had done, there would be many whom she could bless, — poor souls who would much need that her kind, chastened heart should find rest for itself in being busy for them.

And was not the love of two hearts, each for the other, but a delightful initiatory symbol of a love that both were to feel for universal beauty, and truth, and goodness ?

Bright vision of earthly fondness — such was, after all, its enduring splendor ! The one great, happy lover of all history — was it not that most divine man of Calvary, who could sweetly, willingly embrace death itself, in his love for the fair, the true, the infinitely beautiful ?

To such love the soul of man and woman must rise before it can be free, before it can know the meaning of heaven. The end of life is to reach such a love; the beginning of joy is nothing else than this.

Upon such high ground Earnest consoled her who was worthy of such consolation, and would not forget it in his absence. It is all the living can offer to the living! It is enough to offer. It is all the dying can offer to the living ! Let them heed it ; for they too are in the presence of death, and to triumph is to know that death is easy to those who love so much that they cannot fear.

During one of the last days of Earnest's life he was visited by a friend, Mr. Welby, a conscientious and devoted young clergyman of the Methodist church. They had known each other several years, and, though very different in all respects, a warm personal regard existed between them.

" Well, my friend," asked Mr. Welby, " how do you feel to-day ? "

" As though I should last it out, and perhaps two or three days after it," Earnest replied, cheerfully ; " but I shall leave you pretty soon. Any day, almost any hour, may take me now."

The good, sensitive clergyman saw that here was the same friend he had so many times met in health, high-hearted, firm and trusting to the last. No need of discussion, — no place for it here. Mr. Welby had felt, at first, as if he ought to say some word to that dying man whom he loved, — some word even yet for his soul. But that soul was so calm, so content, so ready for the coming change, that he saw it rested on immovable convictions, and must be left to its God alone. He forbore all remarks, therefore, that might excite Earnest, but, before leaving him, asked if he might pray for one who was very dear to him, — one who was himself aware that perhaps they might never see each other again in life.

" Certainly, my dear friend," said Earnest ; " let us repeat together the Lord's prayer. You remember the old Grecian, Pythagoras, taught that we should not plead with God for particular favors, because we are perpetually ignorant of what God always knows to be best for us. We are to trust his plans, not beg for the fulfilment of our own. I have often felt this inculcation ; and some prayers I have heard would have choked me in the utterance. Yet we constantly aspire, in our feelings, to be something better than we are ; and the aspiration for good may surely come to our lips. And thanksgiving for God's bounty and his goodness must be felt and expressed, wherever his presence is truly in the heart. That beautiful prayer which Jesus addressed to his Father in heaven, hallowing his name ; asking that the divine will be done on earth ;

that our simple daily needs be supplied to us; that our sins may be forgiven, and that we may forgive the sins of others; that we may not be tempted, yet when tempted may be delivered from the evil: — that prayer has long seemed to me to include all that man may say to God, or ask of him, — all that a trusting soul can present to the Author of its being and blessings."

Earnest spoke with fervor. His eye brightened and his cheek flushed. The friend made no reply, but knelt at his bedside, and together they repeated those tender, touching, solemn words.

Mr. Welby then rose and took Earnest's hand.

"Good-by," he said: "I am very glad I came to see you. I hope we shall meet again."

"Yes, we *shall* meet again," answered Earnest, "and where there are better gifts than we know."

. With strange yet far from unpleasant feelings, the clergyman departed.

The next two days Earnest sank rapidly. The third morning the sun rose bright and warm, and though, during the night, a January snow-storm had covered the ground with pure white, the day was brilliant and beautiful.

When he had found himself unable to leave his room, our friend had requested Stella to have a bed put up for him in the little library, so that he might hear her play on her piano, in the adjoining room. Her music was never more welcome to him than now; and besides, he wished to impress her as far as possible with his own realization that his descent to the tomb was but a triumphal march beyond it. Could she only

24*

mount the car with him! When he thought of this, he sighed, for the moment, and longed to look back.

Stella would not leave him night or day. At first she shrank from her piano, almost frightened at its tone; but it was such a pleasure for him to hear it that she overcame her reluctance, and even gleaned some small comfort for herself as she played.

On this resplendent winter morning, after a fevered, restless night, Earnest sank into a quiet slumber of an hour or two, and then awoke.

"Stella, my dear," he murmured, "will you play me, 'Who Treads the Path of Duty'?"

She went to the piano, and the music of that grand, impressive, yet joyous song of Mozart's floated through the rooms. He thanked her with a fond smile, as she returned to him; and drawing her face down to his, he kissed her lips and her brow.

"Stella, you have been a dear, good wife, — all my soul asked. And even now you are worthy not to despair. Without this last sweetness and trusting greatness, I should not be quite satisfied. We are not dependent on so poor a stay as persons and circumstances. God bless you. God *will* bless you."

Earnest spoke clearly and unbrokenly, but with great effort of will; and when he had finished, he sank away exhausted. In a few minutes he looked up once more, still with a smile.

"My father, — poor old man, — love him, Stella, while he stays; he has done a great deal for me. Let Charley Merlow have my cane; and if Clara and Cora would like any little keepsakes, you select something for each. Give Jerry Kay a hundred dollars."

Saying this, Earnest dropped back on his pillow, closing his eyes. Presently his father, accompanied by Charley Merlow, with Clara and Cora, entered the room. Alger Acton had been in the house during the night, and toward morning had lain down for a little rest. It was early; but Charley and the other friends had called to inquire after Earnest, just as Stella left him for an instant, to tell his father that he was dying. They all followed Stella to the library without a word.

Earnest saw them as they stood around his bed, and his eyelids moved with an expression of salutation. His lips parted as if he was about to speak; but he only smiled, and, first placing his hand over his heart, he raised it slightly, and pointed upward. He then extended it to Stella, and held the other out to his father. It seemed as if he could still talk to them, if he should try, but that he had no more to say, and was quietly observing this last strange transition. He did not struggle, and he appeared to feel but little pain. But in half an hour, as the sunlight, which he would not have excluded, fell upon the spot where he lay, his features had turned to marble whiteness: they were rigid and cold.

Earnest Acton had entered upon a higher life. But there were sobs and tears; and muffled voices mourned him as dead.

LAST CHAPTER.

ANOTHER year has gone since Earnest died. Its months have not passed unfraught with changes in the world; they have not passed without some changes amidst the group which made up the attractions and repulsions of Earnest's life.

Let us glance at some of the group.

His friend Clara Summers, although she is still simply Clara to her immediate circle of companions, is called by society Mrs. Clandon, while the punctilious speak of her as Mrs. General Clandon. Her husband is one of the most efficient and trusted among the younger officers of the regular army.

To Charley Merlow and Cora nothing, save the absence of Earnest and the quiet, uncomplaining grief of Stella, has yet appeared to dim their joys. A baby-boy, Earnest Acton Merlow, has been given them to love.

It would be painful, very painful, for Charley to leave his wife and child; but as the war has continued, and he has felt that he might be called on to bear his part of the heavy burden, he has learned something of the soldier's duties; and both he and Cora look forward to a day when possibly he can no longer

(284)

remain beside her and regard his duty; when she can no longer bid him linger at home. They look at their infant, and perceive that what the father shall leave undone, the child must do; that peace cannot bless the nation till barbarism and its warriors are crushed. Shall one generation fail in the effort? — then it will be for the next generation to succeed. God has meted the task to the century, and they know that it cannot shirk the stint.

Rufus Maign is no longer in business. At the time of Earnest's death the veteran merchant had nearly retrieved his fortune. Stella had more wealth than she needed; and why should he strive and labor still? To comfort his daughter now, and to aid her in benevolent undertakings, would be enough, he thought, for a man over sixty. Father, mother, and daughter are again together, and together they are busy, — busy for many others than themselves.

Jerry Kay, the strange old Irishman, has followed Earnest into a higher life. On earth he was deprived of advantages; he was devoid of culture; he was deemed ignorant and common and low. He swept the streets, and went on errands about the markets. But the uses and manners of that other world are not as our customs and distinctions. Who shall tell what the old man is doing? Was he faithful and honest below? We may be sure, then, that the gods have missions for him now.

And Stella, — is she content? can she be happy? Not wholly content, not quite happy, as you commonly mean it; nor does she need to be so. She is very calm and placid, very sweet and kind. Her spirit dwells in

a high, pure atmosphere, and though she has been selected to bear much sorrow, she is not deprived of all
joys.

During those winter days, after Earnest had gone, it
seemed doubtful that she would long tarry to mourn
him. She was so prostrated with anxiety and fatigue,
that only through a prolonged sickness, she found renewed health and strength. Her soul was clouded with
grief, and her eyes were often wet with tears. So much
she gave to nature, and could not help giving. But she
knew there was brightness beyond the clouds, and that
not even to her was life for weeping. So when the
sunny spring days came, she placed flowers on the
spot where Earnest seemed to have been laid ; then
turning with a serene smile and a generous hand to the
needy and the lowly, she felt that his spirit descended,
and was close beside her.

She does not complain. She hopes, she loves, and is
loved by many. She has learned to renounce selfishness, that to unselfishness all things may be awarded.
She blesses God, and lives in the world to do his will
as best she can, until it shall be his will that she remain no longer. Then she will die as Earnest died,
still with thanksgiving on her gentle lips.

She sat, a few evenings since, alone, as she thought,
in the twilight. She sang; and her fingers flitted once
more along the key-board of her piano. I listened in
the distance, sacredly, but caught these words : —

> " I have laid my dead on my country's altar !
>   God gave me to moan : —
>   To moan with a broken wail, to falter,
>   And to feel alone, alone !

" But that dearest life — oh, yes, it was needed!
   God gives me to bear.
 It was Freedom's call that was heard and heeded:
   And now he is there — up there!

" The great and good of the ages are round him:
   He would not be here.
 Yet fondly he looks on the love that bound him,
   And is near me, very near!

" Sometimes in my dreams he will grandly murmur,
   And point me a goal.
' Droop not, dear one,' he says: ' be firmer;
   Come up to the height of the soul.'.

" I am well, O friend that wast with me, in wooing
   The heavens with trust.
 I have learned there is little of life but in doing
   One Will: it is gentle and just."

www.ingramcontent.com/pod-product-compliance
Lightning Source LLC
Chambersburg PA
CBHW030622030726
47497CB00006B/1598